KILLER WITH ICE EYES

KILLER WITH ICE EYES

J L HILL

Published By

RockHill Publishing LLC

PO Box 62523

Virginia Beach, VA 23466-2523

www.rockhillpublishing.com

For Mom,
the most loving and selfless person I know.

Learn to do right; seek justice. Defend the oppressed. Take up the cause of the fatherless; plead the case of the widow. "Come now, let us settle the matter," says the Lord. "Though your sins are like scarlet, they shall be as white as snow; though they are red as crimson, they shall be like wool."
Isaiah 1:17-18 NIV

Thank you to:

Cover Model - Armani Whittiker

Cover Design - Neyra Gomez

Editor - Athina Paris

CONTENTS

1

THE BALL BUSTER

Corine peeks through a crack in the mud brick wall of her cell. She can hear the voices of men nearby; they are coming from the other side of the compound. She turns to the girls in the cell across from her, "they are coming back. Who do you see?"

"I see the tall one, the fat one, and the boy," whispers Talgi. "Corine, I am scared. They are coming for us this time." She clutches her dirty blazer tight around her neck. The other girls, ten in all, huddle around her. Talgi is the oldest of the Sudanese captives.

"Don't worry," Corine says calmly, "they are coming for me. Again." She ties the strip of dress she tore from the hem around her waist, knowing it will not stop what is about to happen. Her blue dress is nothing but a rag now, Derreon Gila ripped it down the front the first night he raped her, right after she kneed him in the groin.

She rubs her cheek; the swelling is almost gone. This is the third time this week he's coming for her. But this time is different, the big one, as the girl calls him, and Derreon's brother, the young boy, is with him. And they, are coming in the morning.

The door to the mud-brick shanty swings open with a thud. The girls in the cell on the other side of the room scream, and cower in the corner. Derreon loves scaring the young ones. He bangs on the bars with the inch-thick rebar he carries as a club, eliciting cries from the frightened girls. The jail is a hastily built square of foot-thick mud and straw walls. The roof consists of planks of wood held in place by the hard, dry sidewalls. The bars of the two cells run from floor to ceiling and wall to wall. There are no windows, no light within when the door is closed.

"Don't let that black gorilla scare you, girls," Corine yells as she grabs the bars of her cell. "He can't touch you. You are worth money to his boss if you are unharmed. If he hurts you, I'm sure his master will shove that iron bar up his ass."

Derreon spins around and grabs Corine by the throat before she can retreat. "But you are not worth anything to anyone, little French whore. You are mine to do with as I wish." He pushes her back with enough force to send her to the ground. He pulls a key from his pocket, unlocks the cell, and stands menacingly in the doorway.

Corine pulls her dress close around her as she scoots away from him.

He laughs and says, "I am tired of your little cunt. You no longer amuse me. Today, my little brother will become a real soldier. Katuma, get over here!"

The young boy, skinny and frail, stands in the shadow of his older brother, his eyes glassy with fear. He trembles as Derreon grabs him by the arm and flings him into the cell. He stumbles to the side as he tries to avoid tripping over the woman on the floor.

"What are you waiting for? She is nothing. A worthless piece of meat, Allah has placed her here for our amusement."

"He's just a boy, who should be outside kicking a ball around with his friends. Not toting a gun and committing these crimes you are forcing on him. You believe in God; He will punish you both for this."

The fat man laughs, "Maybe the boy does not like whores. Maybe he wants one of his own, closer to his own age. Or maybe we should take him to the other adobe where you are holding the bo—"

Derreon's rebar keeps him from finishing his sentence and sends blood flying from his mouth. The crack of bone reverberates in the ten-foot-cube hovel. The fat man's head rattles the bars of the girls' cage. "See what I tell you. You dishonor me and yourself. This fool insults your manhood. It is time for you to become a man and a soldier in this army!"

Disgusted with his brother's lack of action, Derreon grabs Corine by an ankle and flips her over. He rips his pants open and pins her head to the floor with his massive paw. With one arm around her waist, he hauls her up to him and shoves his stiffening penis into her. He humps her furiously for a couple of minutes before dropping her to the floor again. He rips her dress from her body and wipes himself off. Then he throws the garment in his brother's face. "See, that is all there is to it. Just a piece of meat."

He grabs his dick, shakes it at the other girls, laughs, and pulls his pants up. As he walks out of the cell and passes the fat man still unconscious on the floor between the two cells, he kicks him in the groin. He looks back at his brother who is covering the naked Corine sitting with her knees to her chest. "Careful, little brother, she's a kicker. Lock her cell. And when this Mutha Fucka wakes up, take him outside and shoot him. No, shoot him here. Show these girls you are at least that much of a man."

Katuma locks the cell and leaves the shanty. He returns a few moments later with a pistol in hand. His head's down while he fires one shot into the back of the fat man's head. The head bounces once. Katuma leaves, slamming the door without making eye contact with any of the captives.

THE SOUNDS of engines arriving at the camp fill the air. Corine peeks through the crack in her wall and sees a white man exiting the first truck. She studies his looks, the way he walks, his camo outfit. White-haired and plump, he sports a neat white beard; looks about fifty, or a little older. He is not a fighter but perhaps a businessman, who has come to buy the girls.

The camp is one long road, less than a mile in the southern part where the desert landscape has given way to green vegetation. It is hidden from the air by camouflage nettings and paint. Trees and tall grasses surround it and hide what activities take place on the ground. Training and drilling of the boys go on all day on the road under a blazing sun.

Talgi asks, "what is going on out there?" It is the first time anyone has spoken since Derreon raped Corine and Katuma killed the other soldier. Two other boy soldiers pulled the man's body out an hour ago.

"I'm not sure," Corine answers, while cupping her hands to make it easier to see through the narrow crack. In the two weeks since they were kidnapped, she hasn't been able to widen the hole by much. She pokes at a spot between the bricks that has dried uneven with her wet fingers. She instructs the girls to do the same in their cells. They find spots in all four walls and create lookouts. Without any utensils they can't fashion much more than peepholes—they eat their food with their hands and the tin plates are too big to use. But she can still get a fairly good view across the compound because it's always dark inside the jail.

"Are they here for us?"

"No. I don't think so." Corine sees about a dozen men; Whites and Africans exit the second truck. They unload crates from the last truck. "It looks like these guys are making a delivery. I promise, I won't let them take you."

"Corine, you can't stop them," Talgi says. "They take the boys for soldiers, and we are to make wives for them. Or worse, we will be sold as prostitutes. The LRA raided my cousin's village two years ago, I never heard from her again."

"That's not going to happen to you." Corine puts up her hand to end the conversation.

"What?"

"It's Commander Raska Diambu."

A fearful squeal comes from the other cell.

Corine again waves her hand over her head for silence. The white man in the pressed camouflage and the commander in his beige dress uniform are just out of earshot. She is trying to read their lips.

THE COMMANDER POINTS to one of the last boxes unloaded from the truck. An African soldier quickly pries it open. The commander uses both hands to pull a long black tub from the crate. He swings the strap over his shoulder and aims it at Corine's hut.

"This is the best rocket launcher on the black market. American made, reloadable, light weight, and with an advanced targeting system. The range is a mile. Fire and go," brags Otto Boone.

"Yes, it is as you say, a fine weapon. And the guns?"

"AK47s, as you requested. You are going to raise Hell in the capital with these weapons, Commander."

Commander Diambu tosses the rocket launcher to the soldier who opened the crate, "Derreon, why don't you bring out one of the girls for Mr. Boone? A bonus for you."

"Thanks," Otto says with a smile. "But it will be very hard for me to take her where I'm heading next. You know, a lot of questions."

"What about a nice French woman?" asks Derreon. "We can have her cleaned up in a few minutes."

Otto looks towards the hutment at the other end of the road and thinks for a moment, "let's just stick to the original deal. I'll take the diamonds and we will be on our way. There is no problem with the payment agreed upon, is there?"

"Of course not," concedes the commander, his thick black beard hiding a scowl from the rebuttal. This arms dealer suggesting he might not pay would have cost him his life if he did not need more high-grade munitions. "The offer was just a sign of our gratitude to you for undertaking such a dangerous and, shall I say, unpopular transaction."

"These affairs are always dangerous," Otto agrees, "whether they sit well with the popular opinions of the world or not. I for one, do not get involved in the political or social situations of my customers. It complicates matters unnecessarily."

Derreon hands Otto a briefcase. After a quick look inside the two men shake hands. The commander returns to his headquarters and Otto Boone climbs back into his truck and leaves.

⚊ ⟍⟋ ⟋

CORINE STEPS away from the wall, she has seen what she came for; the commander is in the camp. What she doesn't know is for how long. She sits on the floor and starts clicking her teeth together.

The girls don't know what she's doing, but it is odd behavior.

She looks up at the girls, goes back to her crack in the wall, and watches for a while longer. Then she turns back to them, "we are getting out of here very soon. I need you girls to gather together over there." She points to the corner of the cell behind the entrance to the room where one of the shafts of light streams in between the boards in the roof. The front wall of the jail is the thickest and the two corners offer the greatest protection. "When the shooting starts, stay low and keep silent."

"Who's coming to rescue us? And how can you know this? You are a UN teacher."

"Actually, Talgi, I'm not with the United Nations," Corine sees no trouble in sharing her secret now. "I work with a group of soldiers hired by your government to track down Commander Diambu. He has fallen out of favor with his supporters and he is in the camp now. I just sent a message to my troops; they will be here in a few minutes. My men are a couple of miles from here hiding in the forest."

Talgi comes to the bars, looking horrified and angry, "are you saying you could have freed us at any time and yet you did nothing? You let those men…"

"I had to. I had to wait for the commander to show up," she is unapologetic, "I get Diambu, and the kidnappings stop. We can break the LRA in this part of the Sudan."

"You put your life in danger… I guess that is your real job. But what about our lives? Do you not care what happens to us?"

"Of course, I care," Corine leaves the corner of her cell and goes to the bars. "At the first sign of danger to you, or any of you girls, I would have called in my strike force. I was never going to let them take you out of this camp, not for any reason. Now, quickly, take cover, there is going to be a lot of shooting."

Just as the words leave Corine's lips gunfire and yelling starts. It sounds close and she knows it's return fire from the LRA soldiers. Her men start the assault with snipers, firing with suppressors from the tree line. She used the transmitter imbedded in her molars to relay the location of the commander's headquarters and her own. His is the only building made of true bricks. Although, she figures in the two weeks she's been held captive, her troops must have scouted out the camp.

A loud explosion, quickly followed by a second, means they blew up the two trucks in front of the headquarters. Something heavy loudly impacts the wall of her cell. A cloud of dust and small bits of the ceiling cave in. The girls scream and cry. She wants to tell them to remain calm, that cries will draw the attention of the LRA soldiers, who might decide to execute them, over letting them be freed. But there is no time.

The gun battle gets louder and closer. Her men are moving in on the camp. Corine feels sorry for the young boys who are undoubtably being killed. She watched drills in the mornings and again at night, calculating about ninety percent of the soldiers, if one could call them that, were boys less than fifteen years old. She counted about a dozen men in the camp and a hundred boys. Like the girls in the cell across from her, the LRA has exhausted the older boys and girls in this war and is now gathering the pre-teens and teenagers. The Sudanese government is desperate to stop the recruitment and building of kid armies.

That was when she got the call. The Sudanese army is reluctant to go after Diambu and others like him themselves; it means killing children, their children. There was no way around it. Also, they had backed these militias for years. The solution was to secretly hire mercenaries to hunt down the commanders of the children armies and do what was necessary.

Corine took the assignment for personal reasons and gave orders not to kill the children. Her men use nonlethal rubber bullets against the kids. The snipers and the A Team—A for assault not the popular TV show of a decade ago, although they often play the theme song during a battle on a boom box—fire live rounds at the adult LRA members. There was no requirement to capture Diambu or his commandoes alive. The Sudanese government would in fact welcome a confirmed kill over a trial and hanging. Less to explain.

She thinks it ironic, hunting down men who do the same thing they do back in the States. They recruit kids, twelve years old, some younger, to be in the gangs. The only difference is that in the States the gangs fight each other, not the government.

There are run-ins with the police, naturally, but they aren't waging a full-scale war against the United States. Not outwardly, at least.

As suddenly as it started, it is over. Deathly silence takes hold of the camp. The girls sob nervously in the corner of their cell. Corine looks up to see beams of sunlight crisscrossing the shanty in the dust-filled air. When she stands up a few spots of sunlight dot her chest. The thick mud walls did little to stop the bullets that someone took the time to spray the shanty with. The door swings open, and the full brightness of the sun lights up the room. Dust particles, millions of them, twinkle in the shaft of light.

"Maria, you in here?" A thick, deep man's voice enters the house.

"Yeah, don't shoot! We are alone," Corine, whose true identity is Maria Delitanni, informs him.

"Jesus! You look like shit."

"Thank you, Barry. You always know how to make a girl feel special," Maria says, holding her tattered dress as closed as possible. "Can you have someone bring me some fatigues? And stop gawking, there are no mirrors in here. I can't look that bad, or that good either."

Maria comes out of the shanty dressed in camo. The girls stay close to her, their eyes squinting and darting around at the soldiers, afraid of them but relieved they are there. There are small groups of boys sitting on the ground around the camp, hands on their heads, heads down. They have been warned not to look up, not to move.

Maria approaches Barry Thomas, "I want these girls taken back to their village before nightfall. What about the boys?"

"The government is sending transportation for all of them. But it is going to be a little different for the boys. Those they can reunite with their family will go home. But they are all going to a… debriefing center first. It may be a while before they can go home. Those who still have homes."

"When I was their age, I would have been sitting with them," Maria confesses. "The only difference is I won the wars I fought."

SHE ALLOWS herself to slip through time and space back to her gang headquarters in the South Bronx a half dozen years ago. Four boys were brought before her in their training room. It was a hollowed-out apartment, no interior walls to provide cover or get in the way of a fight. The four, two ten-years-old, one who was twelve, and the last a thirteen-year-old were involved in that day's gang fight.

"I watched today's action from a rooftop," Maria informed them.

One of the ten-years-old started to speak and received a hard blow to the stomach with a stickball bat. Delivered without warning by the 22-year-old lieutenant everyone called Mouse.

She continued, "You four did not fight, you cowered behind your brothers. I know you were afraid. Fear is a powerful thing, it can stop you from doing what is expected, what you gave your word you would do. You promised to fight for your colors. You promised to protect these colors. Your brothers fought today for your colors."

Maria threw four, foot-long lengths of chain in front of the boys. "You will overcome your fear, here and now. When you were jumped into this gang you learned pain was fleeting and to be shared with your brothers. Now, you must learn fear is to be defeated. Defeat your fears and take your place with your brothers. Give into those fears, we have no place for losers in our ranks."

The ten-year-old, still on his knees, grabbed a chain first and swung it at the boy standing beside him. It wrapped around the twelve-year-old's ankle, and he yanked him off his feet. The others dived for the chains and started slashing at one another. The twelve-year-old finally got hold of the last chain, wrapped it around his hand and began punching his opponent with it. The fight lasted five minutes until each boy was bloody, then Maria gave the signal for the older gang members in the room to separate them.

The entire gang convened behind the gang's headquarters, a five-story brick building.

Mouse stood next to Maria in front of the line of gangbangers and asked. "Are you sure we should do this?"

"Are you getting soft? Is this not the life we chose? We run together, we hang together, we die for the colors we wear."

"But he gave his best."

"That's the problem," Maria said, "he gave his best and was bested by a ten-year-old half his size. Lessons are only learned when the consequences are real." She waved her hand and an object appeared over the edge of the roof.

It fell so quickly they could not hear the scream until a moment before the ground silenced it. The splat of the thirteen-year-old boy sprayed a cloud of blood across the gang. Maria and the gang turned and walked away, leaving the three combatants to dispose of their fallen comrade. Their final lesson of the night.

"Fumu, come here!" Maria waves a gun-toting young African soldier over.

He is big and stocky, his six-foot frame dwarfing Maria's five-four body, one of his biceps thicker than both her legs put together, his face menacing in green camouflage paint.

"Girls, stay with Fumu Akombi, he will get you back to your families. He's from Niger and I've known him for years." She says then leaves with Barry.

The soldier flashes the girls a big smile.

Maria and Barry head for the headquarters, "Tell me you took that bastard alive."

"Shot himself in the head when we surrounded his headquarters. But we got a couple of his friends. A big black African, tough motherfucker; when he ran out of bullets, tried to fight his way out. Took half a dozen guys to take him down. Hey, there is a shitload of weapons in that building over there. Looks like they just got dropped off. Some high-grade American stuff. Why didn't you call us in when the weapons were being delivered? We could have nailed the arms dealer too."

Maria shoots him a look of disgust. "Really? Is that what you think? You could have gotten a two for one here?"

Barry stops abruptly, "It is what we in the US government call a target of opportunity. We would like to know how he got his hands on some of our top equipment. And keep him from getting more."

"You can pick him up on the road," Maria resumes walking towards the headquarter. She passes a row of four metal cargo containers painted in camo colors; where they housed the boy soldiers. Bullet holes line the top of the sides, three or four lines to provide air and let out some of the heat. At night she had watched the boys get locked inside to prevent them from escaping. She looks in one, the floor is covered in dirty mats and sacks of dried leaves. It must have been an oven in there, even at night. The boys were as much prisoners as were the girls.

Barry is still holding his position. "Oh, you think so. Anyway, I sent a squad after him, but they only found his truck. He ditched it two miles down the road and took to the woods. He's in the wind now."

"Well, if you had shown up while his men and he were still here, it would have been a much different fight. It wouldn't have been boys and rubber bullets. It would have been men and lead. I'm not subjecting my guys to that. The commander was the target, we got him, that's what counts. Now, let's go see my friends."

MARIA SEES Derreon and Katuma are hanging by their wrists a foot off the floor from a beam in the ceiling. She passes between them and pulls on the rope tied to the bars in the window. Derreon is lifted another foot higher before she lets go and he drops. The handcuffs dig painfully into his wrists. She spins him around and stops him with his rebar she took from the desk behind him. "I told you God was going to punish you. I guess I should have also told you, I am your God!"

Derreon spits in her face.

She lets it run down her cheek then cracks the rebar across his knee. "Oh, we are going to have some fun now." She drops the rebar on the dirt floor where a large amount of blood has soaked in. "You should have been smart and followed your commander to Hell."

"I guess you know this guy?" Barry asks.

"He had the pleasure. And the other one is his brother. Why isn't he with the other boys?"

"Wouldn't leave the big guy's side," said one of the men standing guard, "said he wanted to die like a man."

"Ah, the old run together, literally hangs together," says Maria to Derreon. "You know, if you weren't a piece of shit for a brother, you would have helped your kid brother get out of here." She turns to Katuma, "I don't know what bullshit he's been feeding you, but this is not going to make you a man, in fact, it is going to be quite the opposite. And this is definitely not the way to heaven. But suit yourself." She swivels back to Derreon with a wicked smile. "Well, Barry, this piece of meat hanging here probably knows all there is to know about your arms dealer. And I'd like to know who he is and who he works for. Somebody, give me my helping hand."

The same guard snickers and hands her a black velvet sack.

Maria rubs the bag gently on her right cheek, the side that didn't get spit on then slowly slides her hand into the bag. "Know what I have in this bag? Don't guess, let me tell you; something I picked up in a castle in Spain. It's very old, but just as effective as the day it was created. They used it during the Inquisition. I call it, The Ball Buster!" She rips the bag off and holds up her hand encased in a shining silver gauntlet with short spikes on the knuckles.

She has made some improvements since she got it. The finger rings have steel threads running inside from the metal plate of the palm, over the tips, and anchored at each spike on the back hand plate. She is able to articulate each finger and ball a very tight fist. She added an air bladder between the outer leather glove that holds the steel in place and the silk inner lining for extra comfort. The gauntlet looks benign and cartoonish on her thin, malnourished arm. She nods at Katuma, and the guard, who gave her the bag, pulls the rope, raising Katuma another two feet off the ground. Just high enough for her to deliver a solid uppercut to the genitals.

Katuma screams. The guard lets him drop. Katuma's one wrist snaps and he screams again. The guard has performed this ritual before. Katuma's camo pants are quickly turning red, his legs flailing and kicking in all directions.

Maria rips his pants down to expose the young man's

shredded penis and scrotum. His testicles hang down from his body. "That's why I call it the ball buster. Now, Derreon, I'm going to tenderize this piece of meat here while you think of that gentleman's name. Let me know when I can stop, OK?"

Maria throws blow after blow into the young man's chest, abdomen, and ribs as he twirls around like a punching bag. Wherever her steel-spiked glove lands blood spurts and occasionally, the sound of a bone cracking is heard.

After a few minutes Katuma hangs lifeless. His chest completely collapsed. His abdomen swollen with blood.

Maria rears back and takes one final swing. Her fist imbeds into his guts which explode a sea of blood that flows up her arm to the elbow. "Really, you let your baby brother literally get the crap beat out of him and you have nothing to say?" She shakes the blood from her hand in Derreon's face. "Talk about your strong, silent types."

"Have you thought maybe he doesn't know the guy?"

"Barry, he's the number two guy in this place, nothing goes on that he doesn't know about. Hey, who's got the camera? I want to make sure we send his mother a nice family portrait. Let the folks back home know how well he took care of his little brother." Maria pulls a sketch from her pocket and holds it up to Derreon's face. "Hey, tough guy, you know this man? Has he ever been here? Perhaps with your gun dealing friend?" She rips the clothes from Derreon's body.

Barry throws up his hands and walks out of the room.

Maria watches him go then waves her bloody hand upwards a couple of times. The guard obliges and raises Derreon a few feet higher. She wildly throws overhand punches, concentrating on his groin.

He bites his lips until blood runs down his chin.

The guard can no longer hold Derreon's weight and drops him back down.

In a blind rage, Maria punches the man until he hangs like a bloody piece of meat. She walks out of the office and unstraps the glove.

Barry looks at her with sadness in his eyes, "Satisfied?"

Red streaks line her dark golden, tanned face. Pieces of flesh are tangled in her curly black hair which has worked itself out of the ponytail she wore earlier and is now shimmering from blood and sweat like a halo in the late afternoon sun. "No. But it will have to do."

2

SHADOWS OF THE PAST

Barry sits with MoJo in his lounge in South Palms Estate on his private Mediterranean Island. He downs a scotch and quickly pours another. Then he drinks that one straight down, only a slight grimace betraying the burning sensation in his throat.

"Something on your mind?" Morris asks as he sips his scotch. He holds his glass up to the sunlight coming through the twenty feet tall bay window. He peers through the golden liquid at Barry and says in a fortuneteller's voice, "I see troubled waters in your future. You are perhaps unhappy with your assignment. You wish the government assigned you to another task."

"No. Not at all," Barry shifts to avoid direct eye contact with Morris. His muscular chest fills out the black T-shirt, and the clean shave and close-cropped black hair gives him the look of a young man just out of bootcamp. But the three lines across his forehead and the beginning of luggage beneath his eyes carries the signs of a man approaching forty. "You are helping the USA in areas where it's best we stay out of. I'm okay with that. It's not like we haven't worked with mercenaries before."

Morris strokes his beard, tugging on the grayish streak in the middle. He gets up and walks to the bar, retrieves the decanter of twenty-year-old scotch and refills Barry's glass. "Well, then what is it? Because you are drinking my best liquor like water. When you drink for pleasure, you can never drink too much. But when you are trying to drown your sorrows, there is never enough in the bottle. There is only pleasure and sorrow when it comes to drinking. So, which is it?"

"It's Maria," Barry says definitively.

"You really haven't answered the question."

Barry takes a shorter sip and waits for Morris to sit back down. "Why did you let her go on the mission? You had to know there was a better than good chance she was going to be taken. She could have been killed."

"Ah, so it is pleasure that drives you to drink." Morris' face twists into a sadistic smile. He enjoys toying with the CIA agent. Watching his stone-cold face hold back his true emotions.

"What?"

"You find pleasure in my daughter, but feel sorrow she can be hurt," Morris puts a fatherly tone to the statement. "Totally understandable. But not to worry, I raised her to be tougher than most. She can handle herself in a rough situation. Besides, this plan was mostly her idea, and you did agree to go along with it. So, what changed?"

Barry finishes his drink and studies Morris for a moment. He can't tell if he really wants to know what happened in Sudan, if he already knows the details, or if he basically doesn't care. "I agreed to the plan because I thought she would signal us the first day she arrived at the camp. If the Commander was there, we'd take the camp, if not, we pull her out by nightfall. Not let her spend two weeks in captivity. She was out of control. She went—"

"Hello, Daddy. Barry."

"Well, speak of the devil." Morris stands and holds out a hand.

Maria crosses the room and hugs her father. She does a pirouette to show off her new lavender and verdant silk dress. "Do you like it? It feels good to be out of fatigues. Are you two discussing the success of the mission? I just got off the phone with the Sudanese Foreign Minister, a Mister hard to pronounce name, the money has been deposited and he is very happy."

"Barry was just giving me his critique of… how should I say this… your performance. Go ahead, Barry, continue."

"Yes, Barry, what do you think of my performance?" Maria's voice is sharp. She didn't speak to him on the flight back, spent the two days after the mission drinking with her mercs, especially Fumu, and avoiding him. Fumu told her when the girls reached their village most of it had been destroyed, burned down, but their families were okay. "And please don't hold anything back. I can take it."

"I'm sure you can," he replied, flexing his muscles and puffing up his chest under the black cotton T-shirt. He got up and poured her a drink. "As I was saying, you went berserk out there. Very unprofessional the way you beat those two men to death. Well, one man and a boy. I'm sure they did some horrible things to you there, but this was your plan. And for the record, Morris, I was against it. And for what it's worth, that is exactly why I was against it. Letting yourself get taken prisoner, and as I warned, subjected to all kind of torture… It was not a good plan."

"How else were you going to get someone into the camp? You think you could have been taken prisoner?" Maria shoots her head back downing the scotch. "You wouldn't even have left the village alive."

"She got you there," Morris joked, "they would have made you for a government man instantly. You have that look." Morris enjoys toying with Barry Thomas. He doesn't want an agent within his ranks. But the government, the CIA undoubtably, insisted on it as part of their oversight with their armament contracts. He lets Barry in on other aspects of the business to find out what the government knows. He also knows that one can learn as much from the questions asked as the answers given by your rivals.

"You were supposed to contact us the first day…"

"For what? Diambu wasn't there."

"And the plan was if he wasn't there, we get you out. And move on to the next camp," Barry stares her down. "You showed bad judgement. And your lack of control…"

"He wasn't in camp the first week," Maria says emotionless, "and you would leave those girls behind to face whatever was coming to them. Then they would have known I was a spy; the next squad would have killed me on the spot. However, he did show up to make that arms deal, and we got him."

"What you did was crazy," Barry shouts. "And you let the arms dealer slip through our fingers. If you had signaled us sooner, we could have cut off his escape. Maybe ambushed them in the bush before taking down the camp. That's how you run a professional op."

"I may have gotten a little rough," she yells back, "but they deserved no better. This isn't like an ordinary war. These people are animals, and we should exterminate them like the vermin they are. It is what we are paid to do. If you can't handle it, Mr. Special Forces, stay home and out of my way."

"She did go to extremes in Sudan, but that is not necessarily a bad thing," Morris interjects, "When details of those people's deaths get out, and I will make sure it does, other warlords will not be so willing to take children. What is the axiom? An ounce of prevention is worth a pound of the cure." Morris goes to refill his drink and pats his daughter's knee as he passes her sitting at the bar. "Do you know why I like drinking in this room?" He asks, slipping away from the argument to look out at the Aegean Sea.

"Is it the foot-thick bulletproof glass?" Barry seethes, knowing he's losing the argument. Naturally, father and daughter would team up against him.

"Yeah, that's part of it," muses Morris, "it's because I can see the world real clear from here. I can see my enemies coming from a ways off. Gives me a real sense of peace knowing who my enemies are and where they are coming from."

Barry isn't sure what Morris means, or to whom it is directed, but he knows he isn't going to win a battle on two fronts. He will have to come back later and talk to Morris alone. Maria is obsessed with finding that sergeant of hers. He was briefed on her history by the Agency and so far, she is living up to her reputation. On the missions he has been part of, she was reckless, ruthless, and murderous beyond reason. He gives Morris one last piece of advice before moving on, "your enemies might know what to expect from her and not give her the chance to do it next time."

MARIA POURS herself another drink and stands next to her father at the window. The medieval castle dominates the tiny island. Morris did a little modernization to the structure to make it a comfortable living place, but as castles go, it is impregnable except from an airstrike. He has anti-aircraft brigades on two of the turrets. There are a few people, mostly generational inhabitants, who aren't in the BSA.

"What is that man's problem?"

"I don't think he objects to you playing rough with the boys," Morris puts his arm around her shoulder. "I think he objects to you not playing with him."

"EEYOO! He's a government man. I don't know why you allow him to hang around. He can't be trusted."

"That sounds like your Uncle Nicky speaking." He turns her

head slightly and lightly pokes the bruise under her eye. "The lavender in your dress almost makes that look good. He does care about you."

"Well, at least you put him in his place."

Morris laughs, "Honey, I was speaking to you."

"What? Me? What did I do?"

"I was trying to tell you not to be looking for your enemies so hard that you can't see them coming. Remember, if you let people know you are looking for him, he will start looking for you. Don't become an easy target."

Maria drops her head. "That arms dealer had the types of weapons Warren would have been able to get his hands on. US rocket launchers, the new ones. I should have called in our guys sooner. He got away; it was my fault."

"Doesn't really prove it was him," Morris lifts her chin, "I can get hold of them too. And he didn't get away. I had a second team bird-dogging yours. We have eyes on him."

Maria leaves the huge hall with a bounce in her step. She wonders why her father didn't tell her about the other team. But she knows him well enough to know he wasn't leaving her safety to some government man. She may be a trained killer, but she is still his daughter, and he probably felt he needed to protect her. She wonders what would have happened if she sent the SOS signal. Undoubtedly, he would have leveled the camp to get her out.

The arms business is by far the most dangerous of all the illegal ventures they are involved in. And it was the introduction into this life at age twelve that made her Warren's and the government's target. It was also her first job a couple of years later, thanks to her Uncle Nicky.

SHE WAS in New York for a couple of months when a black caddy pulled up outside the building she was hanging out at. She sat on the stoop in a short fur jacket, jeans, and sneakers. She was surrounded by ten boys, some younger, some older than her by a few years.

The window rolled down, "Maria, your uncle would like to have a few words with you."

The boys formed a line in front of her.

She parted them with her two hands, "it's okay, guys, I know him." She walked over to the driver, "Hi, Rocky, what does he want to talk to me about?"

"Like he would tell me." Rocky rolled his eyes and smiled. He was eighteen, merely three years older than her. His boyish demeanor amused her the few times she had met him. "He said drive here, pick you up, and bring you out to the island." Then in a mock harsh voice he grumbled, "no detours."

She laughed, "Can I bring some of the boys with me? They would get a kick out of seeing the mansion."

"What? You trying to get me killed? I thought you liked me."

Maria turned back to the guys who had fanned out in front of the building. Two of the twenty-years-old were nervously fidgeting with the guns in their pockets. "Relax, guys. I told you I know him, he's family." Maria opened the back door and waited a couple of seconds to show there was no one else inside. Then she climbed in and rolled down the window, "I'll be back tonight. Maybe I'll bring back a nice present from my uncle."

Rocky put on the radio and headed for the highway. It was an hour's drive from the South Bronx and its burned-out buildings to the green lawns of Long Island. It would have been longer if he didn't drive like he was fleeing a crime scene. He was dodging cars left and right all the way there.

Maria walked in the front door and went directly to the office in the back. It had been years since she was last in the house. She stood at the window looking at the garden when Nicky walked in.

"Do you miss the old place?"

"A little, I guess," Maria turned and ran to hug him. "You haven't changed anything."

"Why mess with perfection," Nicky said and held her at arm's length. "Now, This! This right here is perfection." He pulled her back in for another hug.

"OK, what did I do? What do you want?"

"You haven't done nothing. Can't I just want to see my only niece? You come back to the city and not a word, not a hello, Uncle. How are you doing?"

"Come on," Maria laughed, "I know you are not the sentimental type."

"I am when it comes to you."

"Did Morris tell you to keep an eye on me?"

"Of course not. Why would he? He has enough eyes in the city, not even a shadow would pass unnoticed."

Maria couldn't tell if he was being truthful. Nicky and Morris were the same in that respect, she never could tell if they were lying or telling the truth. The only difference was that with Nicky she assumed he was lying. He always had a scheme working. Morris was the opposite, he said what he meant.

"I just want to run something by you," Nicky walked over to his desk and sat down. Maria was about to sit in the plush chair by the window, but he stopped her. "No, not there. Come sit at the desk, I have an opportunity to discuss with you."

Maria sat down and he laid out the details. In two weeks, during Christmas break, Rocky would drive her to Norfolk, Virginia. She would pick up a suitcase filled with books and take the train back to New York.

"Hold on," she interrupted, "you want me to be a drug mule? Uncle Nicky…"

"No! Not transporting drugs," Nicky protested. "I would

never put you in that position. The books will hold guns... pistols. I consider you more as a courier than a mule. It's really safe. No one checks baggage on the train." He gets up and walks around to sit next to her. "You know gun running is the cornerstone of my empire. It is how your father and I got started."

"Then Morris is okay with this?"

"Well, let's keep this between the two of us for now. I just need you to make a trip now and another during spring break. Forty guns each time, I'll pay you two hundred dollars each time."

"You're kidding me, right?"

"What?"

"That's five dollars a gun," Maria frowned, "guns on the street go for at least one hundred, maybe two if they are good quality. Five hundred a trip, Uncle Nicky, that's fair!"

"Your dad taught you too good."

MAIA BOARDED the train in Newport News, Virginia at 6:00 am dressed in a green and white school outfit. The suitcase was too heavy for her to lift, so a porter placed the black rolling luggage at the front of the car for oversized baggage and asked what she is carrying.

Maria replied, "Books. The nuns don't want the devil sneaking in while we are away for Jesus' birthday. So, lots of homework, lots of books."

She rode to Washington, DC. where they switched out crews and she waited to see if there was anyone left onboard. There were a couple of people who remained, and she got off with her suitcase. She went into a restroom where she turned her skirt inside out and it was now an orange and blue checkerboard pattern. She did the same to her blazer. She pulled the black covering off the suitcase, revealing a bright pink exterior and left the restroom.

Five minutes before her train arrived, a girl her age and size went into that same restroom wearing the exact same outfit as she had on. She waited a few minutes then switched to Maria's green and white outfit and pulled the pink covering from her baggage. She boarded the train Maria was on, taking up the vacated seat. Maria boarded a few cars behind her.

Except for the near panic attack she had, as she assured Nicky she would experience in the restroom, the trip went fine.

Nicky told her in his office, "I am sure you have been in a public bathroom since you were twelve."

She said sure.

"Then this will be no different. In fact, this will help you get over your anxiety."

But it was different, maybe the illegality of what she was doing wreaked havoc on her mind. She could not get the taste of chloroform out of her mouth, or the feeling she was about to be grabbed from behind again.

After her spring break trip, Maria arranged for another girl to make the runs. She worked out a deal with Nicky to make a monthly run using girls she supplied. She tried to bump up her cut, but Nicky held fast, saying, "you will be making six times the money, so pay the girls what you want out of your end. Pick your runners carefully, because if they lose a shipment, you will have to pay the eight thousand dollars."

Nicky was proud of the way she handled the business. He told Morris she took to it naturally and was a leader from the start. Morris contacted his gun manufacturer in North Carolina and told him to step up production. By the next year they were using the trains to move guns from the south to five major cities in the north. All the couriers were Maria's school girls. She cut the number of couriers on a run to one girl, who just did a quick change of clothes at the layover stations. Also, there was no need to change the color of the luggage, she kept them in basic colors, indistinguishable from other people's bags.

———〜〜—

BARRY WAS BACK at the bar in the Window Room, as he called it. It was late in the evening and he was waiting for Morris, knowing he'd be there soon. Morris was not a creature of habit, but he did like to watch the night sky. And Barry knew for the last two years, this was where he watched it from.

"Am I going to need to send for more scotch?"

"I'm just having a short one this time," Barry replied. "Don't you have a cask or something down in the dungeons?"

"No, I keep drunk CIA agents in the dungeons," Morris laughed. "Look, I know why you are here. Yes, she can go a bit overboard. I guess she gets that from me. I'm sure you have been briefed about New York, Washington, the whole situation. But as long as we are getting the job done, and might I add, Washington is getting their weapons. You know, staying ahead of the Ruskies. They don't care."

"But I do," Barry insisted. He steeled himself with the remainder of the scotch in his glass. "It's not just that she is putting her life at risk, and mine, and the team's. She is doing it for insane reasons. She is chasing a ghost and it's going to catch up to her one day. She's going to dig herself into a hole we can't get her out of."

Morris poured a drink and took a seat in his favorite chair. He stared out the window for a good while before continuing the conversation. "Ghosts aren't real. They can't hurt you. But I have real enemies. And so does Maria. And for the record, she was a soldier in the gang when she was fifteen. She asked to join, and I facilitated it. She trained hard for years, and when I said she could handle herself, I meant better than you. If she gets herself into a situation she can't handle, you will be of little use to her anyway."

Barry stood in front of Morris, this was the conversation he wanted to have earlier, "I know what you are really afraid of. You are afraid that without Sgt. Warren, your personal boogieman, she's going to leave you. I see the hate in those cool blue eyes. I know you see it too. I'm not sure if you know who that hate is directed at... So, you keep her looking for someone you killed years ago. Hell, man, you blew up half of Washington D.C. to do it."

Morris laughed, "I heard it was a gas leak. You know... bad pipes." He rose out of his chair in one smooth movement and was face-to-face with Barry. "You know the only way to know if someone is truly dead..." he put two fingers to the side of Barry's temple. "You look them in the eyes and put a bullet in their head. Now, I actually came in here to watch the senate hearings on terrorism. I'm testifying."

He clicked the remote and the panel behind the bar slid open. The television went on and the Senate was in sessions. The committee chairman was asking his question. The camera then focused on Morris for his answer.

"You bugged Congress?"

"No, you idiot! This is C-Span."

"So, this is live. How are you able to watch it over here?"

"You do know how television works, right? They broadcast, I have a satellite receiver," Morris chided, knowing the real meaning behind Barry's question. "Now shut the fuck up! I need to hear this." He turned up the volume.

"Terrorism is on the rise around the world. Suicide bombers, militia groups here and elsewhere, are finding it easier to plan and carry out attacks," said TV Morris. "The war you are used to fighting is not going to be the war you will be fighting. A handful of dedicated people willing to die for a cause is nearly impossible to stop," Morris and TV Morris said in unison.

"Instead of a large army, you are going to need to station small rapid response teams, like SWAT teams all around the world. People in places that will not be big targets but can unleash devastating firepower quickly."

"Are you suggesting we scrap our bases overseas, for what…" the chairman asked.

Morris put on a headset, "Not scrap them. Downsize and spread them out." TV Morris repeats his response.

"Why not just appear before the Senate yourself?" Barry enquired.

"Yeah, that's not going to happen. If you want, take the bottle with you. I must watch and make sure this guy sticks to the script and doesn't screw up anything. So, if you please, shut up."

TV Morris hesitated before answering the next question, "the best use of government forces, and dollars, would be in operating high altitude bombers from airfields around the world. But instead of dropping bombs, they launch guided missiles at selected targets."

"Guided by whom?" asked the congressman.

"By an operator here in the United States," Morris said and a moment later the words came from the television. "We can have assets on the ground, either our own or trusted allies, pick out targets. We can then remove them with surgical precision. We strike small sites with greater effectiveness."

"It sounds rather inhumane."

"Does to me too," adds Barry.

Morris gave Barry a stern look, "there is nothing humane about war but this is the fight we will be having in the future. Our enemies are not going to line up thousands of men and send them charging across a battlefield. And even if they do, it will be far better to take out their headquarters than to cut down countless numbers of troops."

TV Morris echoes his sentiments with the same conviction. Barry left and Morris continued, "it is cost effective in a number of ways. The cost in equipment, the cost in human lives, our troops as well as theirs, the cost in collateral damage. This is the war of the future, and I am bringing it to you today."

"And what happens when this technology falls into our enemies' hands?"

"Most of the technology will be here, State side. Or on our planes. What tech is in the missiles will be destroyed in the strike. Like it or not, big war is going to be downsized. You are going to need to redefine your armed forces, first to identify your enemy, then to snuff them out quickly. And my company can help you do just that."

TV Morris was done. The closed-door hearing, which was not broadcasted publicly, was wrapped up with a few superfluous speeches by senators. Morris clicked the remote and disabled the hack into the senate chamber.

Morris sat staring out the window at the night sky. The hearing had gone well. He didn't mind dealing with the government as a whole, it was having to work with individuals, either persons or agencies, that he distrusted. They wanted his knowledge and technology and were willing to overlook New York and Washington, and some wanted it bad enough to have caused what happened in those places. His life was a double-edged sword, and he could never forget it. He started for another drink then sat back down. He needed to be clear-headed for the moment.

Barry was right, Maria was becoming more aggressive in her pursuit of Warren, impulsive to the point of recklessness. Without a body, or any other evidence to prove Warren's death, her past haunted her. He trusted Representative Webber had given him the correct time and place to strike Warren, the damage caused by the missile verified that. Webber was too much of a coward to have lied. But somebody else, Senator Carter for one, could have tipped him off. And he didn't really know who Warren worked for. So, he created a ghost.

Perhaps, Maria working with Barry Thomas was causing her to become unhinged. She had become more dangerous over the last year. He laughed out loud when he thought about the glove. It was a dingy, tarnished, old relic falling apart when she found it in that crypt. The whole castle had been about to come down around them, but she saw it and had to get it, crawling over bones between crumbling slabs to reach it. A week later, she had restored it, and proudly showed it off as the most valuable treasure she had. He had no idea what she had in mind to do with it.

When he heard her tell the tale of beating the two guys to death in Sudan, saw the glee in her eyes as she relived the moment, her standing there with the glove on, mimicking her actions… At least she said she disinfected the gauntlet, taking great care of her favorite weapon. He did teach her to always clean her gun after each use, keeping it battle ready; she treated it the same. The way she held it up, flexed her fingers in it, he knew she had gone over the edge.

There will be no more missions with Barry. No missions at all for a while. But she isn't going to like that, he thought.

Morris looked at his watch, it wasn't that late in London. He picked up the phone and dialed. "Hey, I need you here… Now, that's when." He hung up. He would wait until tomorrow night, maybe a day or so later to ground her. He saw his reflection laughing at him in the window.

I know she hates it when I ground her. But it is for her own good, and safety. She is not a kid anymore, she'll get over it. Yeah, I know, she is not going to take it well at all.

He decided it was finally time for that drink, and he needed to come up with a catchy name for his new proposal for the government.

Something with a good acronym. The military loves their

acronyms. Something like STRIKER, Sky Threat Reconnaissance and Interceptor Kinetic Energy Rocket, or Worldwide High-Altitude Missile, WHAM. That's it, I'll give the assignment to Maria. That will take her mind off Warren for a while.

THE JET TOUCHED down on the airfield predawn. It dropped off one passenger and left immediately afterwards. The blacked-out Mercedes arrived at the south gate a few minutes later. Morris was on hand to lower the drawbridge as the car rolled slowly and quietly into the castle's grounds. It turned left and proceeded to the underground garages. The dozen men on duty never saw the driver; it didn't matter, everything that happened on the South Palms Estate Island was strictly on a need-to-know basis. If Morris opened the gate, that was all they needed to know, and no mention of the visitor would ever be discussed.

LEMURES

Terrapin Station was what MoJo called his castle. He told Maria he named it after the Grateful Dead album because it was as far from the one-room log cabin on the cover as it could be. It was built of iron-red granite from Brazil during the Roman Inquisition of the sixteenth century. Its black and gray veins running through the deep blood red stone had given the castle its original name, Sacratissimum Cor Iesu, the Most Sacred Heart of Jesus.

It was not as elaborate as other castles of the era, but it was fiery brilliant at both sunrise and sunset. It served its purpose of frightening people brought there into renouncing their Protestant ways. Two towers of six stories at the northwest and southeast corners anchored the west and east wings. Each was four stories and ran north to south ending in two-story high walls. The walls had a gatehouse and drawbridge in the middle that crossed a moat that was still filled with water four centuries later. The moat disappeared under each of the towers and showed up on the other side. In between the walls, towers, and buildings was a lush green field.

The castle had as few as six rooms on some floors and twice

as many on others. The ground floor of the north tower had ten, each separated by steel airlock doors. The west side of the castle was the business side and was doubly fortified. The eastern side was the residential wing where the keep was situated, and the south tower rose from its foundation. Undoubtedly it was as fortified, but it didn't show. Gunners had permanent positions along the parapets and at various crenels and merlons. And teams of men patrolled the grounds, which were augmented by electronic surveillances. Terrapin Station was virtually impregnable, except from the air, which was why Morris had installed in the north tower an air defense missile system he developed with the Israelis.

Maria enters her father's office on the ground floor of the north tower. She is dressed in fatigues with a sidearm slung low around her waist. She has regained some of the weight lost from her ordeal in the Sudan.

Morris gives her a second look from behind his desk, "Is there something you are not telling me? Are we under siege?"

She laughs, "no." Her face turns to stone as she becomes serious. "I am heading for the range, I need to get some practice in, but first I want to talk to you."

Morris doesn't like the sound of her voice, or the look in her eyes. He is slow to respond. "What do you need to practice for, we don't have another mission."

"That's what I want to talk to you about. I want to take a team and go after Gavril Avakian, the Armenian."

"Absolutely… not going to happen!"

Maria never heard that tone in his voice before, it waivered. She rushes forward and slams both hands on the desk. It is like a crack of lightning shaking the room. The tempest begins to brew. She stares at her father with ice eyes. "The arms dealer is probably the link to Sgt. Warren. I can go get him and make him talk."

"I'm sure you can," Morris says calmly, "but there are two

problems with that idea. First, he is back in Armenia. And second, if you are successful, and he gives up your Sergeant, then Warren will just cut and run."

"We can pull off a covert operation," Maria demands. She made up her mind before coming to see him, and like her father, once she had a plan nothing was going to change it. She wasn't there for her father's approval. She had picked out her team, informed them of her plan, which was long on details and short on goals to accomplish. "It will be a lightning attack! Myself, and three others on the A team making the extraction. Four others on the B team to suppress interference and clean up afterwards. He's not even in a fortified location."

"I know, we have eyes on him." Morris thinks for a minute. "If Warren reaches out to him, or he contacts Warren, then we have him. Just hold on for a while and let's see what develops." Morris drops his head, avoiding her accusing glare.

"I'm tired of waiting! That's what you did before, and got Akilina killed. I'm going after him now." She turns and starts to storm out of the office.

Morris gets to his feet and yells, "Stop right there." Then walks over to her. "These are my men. I give the orders around here. You need to calm down and think."

"Think about what, how you let him get away?" Maria breathes like she ran a marathon. Her face is flushed with anger, yet her eyes are still, and cold stares at him.

"That was my mistake," Morris admits hesitantly. "I went for the overkill. It was like trying to kill a fly with a shotgun." Then he takes a moment before continuing, as if weighing his next words before uttering them softly, "but this is what you don't realize, he's not going to show himself, not as long as I am alive. Warren is more afraid of me than he is of you."

Barry walks down the hall of the East Wing. It has been a couple of days since he was here last, maybe Morris will be in a better, more agreeable mood. His bosses at Langley are very interested in how their Javelin missiles ended up in the Sudan. They want him to press Morris for more information on Raska Diambu, how one of the most ruthless men on the planet could get his hands on the newest high-tech battlefield weapons without much money. The US Army only deployed them a year ago and there are a dozen of them floating around Africa.

The Agency knows Morris has more at stake in Africa than he's letting on and Barry figures he pulled the strings that got the government to hire his mercenaries to track down Diambu. He's also sure Morris didn't do it for the money. As the saying goes, Morris holds his cards close to the vest, but he seemed to know where the LRA was going to strike next and got Maria in there a month ahead of them. Langley was sure the operation was to get the weapons even though they slipped through his fingers.

With the Commander out of the picture, Morris seems to be scaling back operations in the Sudan. The Agency had him there because Morris is a big-time weapons manufacturer and by default, an arms dealer. But is he taking out the competition? Trying to become the only dealer in the region, or is he trying to install his own government? The Sudanese gave him a port on the Red Sea, and access to the countries of Central Africa, many of them unstable. With the right amount of influence and pressure he could rule a large swath of Africa from the shadows. Barry hopes that if he plays his cards right, he can find out what Morris' true objectives are in Africa.

He stops by a window near the end of the hall in the residential section of the castle. He can see through the window of Morris' office across the courtyard. "Damn," he mutters, "what is she doing now? Are they planning another operation?" He backs away from the window and continues to watch at a football field's distance. It becomes apparent the two are arguing, but too far for him to read their lips. *She is a piece of work. Serves him right.*

The intel on Morris and Maria is considerable. After the episode in New York, he moved her to the Greek Isles and home-schooled her with private tutors until she went to universities in Spain and France. Of course, under assumed names, so it was hard to track what she had done there. But they got good information from the tutors. Her home life was chaotic and until a couple of days ago, no one knew of her involvement in the gangs. It was assumed he kept her out of that life, considering what she had been through. Barry re-evaluates everything he thought about her, and Morris.

Morris lives with three women, Maria's mother, Elizabeth, who is retreating from life; the Russian hooker turned movie star, Yana; and a Venezuelan, but not much is known about her. What did become clear from the interrogations and investigations is that Morris trained his daughter to be a killer. Along with reading, writing, and arithmetic; there was small arms and sniper training, hand-to-hand combat against men, and a host of bomb making and disarming classes. For what or why he was training her wasn't clear to any of the tutors they talked to, but some called it, "father/daughter time."

One of her teachers quit abruptly when she was trying to finish assembling an explosive device in his English class that started smoking. She jumped up and ran from the room. He wisely followed her, managing to get a couple of feet down the hall when the bomb went off. It left a hole in the building where the classroom used to be. That was when Morris bought this island and castle, at the insistence of the Greek government.

The reports said she was often at odds with him, mostly over the death of her nanny. She had fits of rage where he had to physically subdue her. One tutor said he knocked her out one afternoon, breaking her nose when she was fifteen. She had gone crazy at his insistence she accompany her mother on a shopping trip to the continent.

"Why? I'm not her bodyguard. Send one of your men, or don't you trust them not to stick their dicks in her like they do me."

"Why do you say such nonsense?" Morris shook his head sadly. "My men wouldn't touch either one of you. First, each man on the team has proved their loyalty many times over. And second, they know I will not hesitate to kill anyone who puts a hand on you or your mother."

"Even if I tell them to?" she screamed, "I tell 'em… FUCK ME, FUCK ME, FUCK ME. LIKE YOU DO MY MOTHER!"

Morris threw a jab so fast she never saw it coming. Her nose flattened and turned purple. Blood ran down her cheek and pooled on the floor beneath her head. He watched her spasm on the floor for a few moments before scooping her up and taking her down the hall to the infirmary.

Another said she stabbed him during a combat exercise. They always practiced with real knives as it made one aware of what not to do. Over time, she had become very quick and slippery, and did not like to lose. He disarmed her, but she had another one, a jailhouse shiv taped to her back. As he released her, she pulled it and stabbed him in the stomach. Not once, but several times. She stood over him laughing as blood streamed from his body, laying him up for weeks. And with all that, by all reports, everyone said, "She is Daddy's Little Princess."

But no matter how unstable her teachers said she was, all agreed they were in no danger. Well, not directly, her anger and vitriol were always directed at him. To everyone else she was as gentle as a kitten. However, none of them ever crossed her.

The shouting was inaudible across the courtyard. The thick, double-pane bulletproof glass in all the windows made eaves-dropping impossible. Morris had spent a fortune fortifying the castle against attacks and spying. But what Barry was witnessing was the buildup to an epic battle. He had seen Maria blow up over things big and small. She was a ticking timebomb. They were at each other's throats, face-to-face, and screaming nonstop.

___ ___

"YOU CAN BLAME me all you want for Akilina's death, but it was me who put her in your life! And she didn't take the job because she found you so cute and adorable. It was either your house or a whorehouse."

That cut deep into Maria's psyche.

Morris wants to inflict as much pain on her as she does on him. Every time they argue it always ends in the same place. And it isn't just her who blames him. "For ten years, Yana looks at me as if I put a gun to Akilina's head and pulled the trigger. I did everything I could to keep you safe!"

"Like what? Abandoning me for four years? Letting me believe, and Elizabeth believe… all of us thinking you were dead. Well, guess what DAAAD? You did a fucking lousy job of keeping me safe. You might as well have put a bullet in Akilina's brain. It was because of you she suffered the way she did. You could have got us out of there on day one. You could have made a deal, but YOU chose not to."

Morris looks lost; his eyes searching the room for something to say that will end this battle, "Oh yeah, well, you are alive today, aren't you? And unharmed. If I didn't do what I did ten years ago, you wouldn't be. You think if I had just talked to Warren… Maybe met him in a dark alley somewhere in Queens, he would have let you and Akilina walk out of that warehouse." He lets his voice drop, takes a deep breath, and sighs, "he would have killed me and then the both of you afterward."

"Why? Because that's what you would have done. Kill your enemies at all costs, right dad? What is it you always say, 'tie up your loose ends before they come back to hang you.'"' Maria is sweating, her long curly hair matted to her face. Strands carving her countenance like a jigsaw puzzle, her face flushed and red. Her eyes fixed on her father's face. Transformed and possessed, she says, "maybe he should have killed you!"

"What did you say?" His voice climbs again.

"Maybe he should have killed you. Then I'd be free to go after him like I want. I'd get revenge for you, that would make you happy. After all, you don't really care that he killed the only person I truly loved. The only person who really cared about me."

"Oh, my Little Girl…"

Her eyes glaze over at the words, she hates him immensely when he calls her that.

"You're not hearing me. He would have killed Akilina and you. I couldn't… I would never let that happen. Don't worry, you will have your revenge. The Sudan was a good trap, and you did well in springing it. But do you really think I'm not trying to find Warren? I have three bullets he gave me in Colombia, and I intend to return them. We will find him. He can't stay hidden forever."

"Yeah, but it's like you said," Maria is cold and calm now, her words leaving her lips in a whisper, "he won't come out of hiding as long as you are alive."

Morris looks at her unblinking eyes. He reaches up and with his right hand sweeps wisps of hair from her face. His left hand shoots out for her right wrist. But he trained her well, too well.

Maria steps back, draws her sidearm, and tilts it up. She fires, causing her father to stumble backwards. She extends her arm and fires again. The second bullet from the Taurus .45 pistol hits him just below his left eye, shattering his face. He hits the floor, half his head landing on his desk across the room. Maria holsters her weapon and closes the door to the office. She steps over her father and takes a seat in the blood-splattered chair behind the desk.

⸺ ᴎᴧᴦ

Barry's mouth drops open. He can't believe what he just witnessed, but doesn't doubt that it just happened. He watches Maria for a few minutes as she sits motionless at Morris' desk, her face and clothes speckled with blood. After what seems like an eternity she starts to go through the drawers. He can't imagine what she's looking for, or what led to this outcome.

A few minutes go by, then Maria picks up the phone and presses one of the buttons. Before she hangs up Morris' men are running down the hall to his office. They burst into the room and come to a dead stop; four, big, burly men are stunned by what they see. She stands and starts giving them orders. Two more men arrive with a body bag for their ex-boss. Two of the original four men leave to carry out whatever orders their new boss has just issued.

The king is dead, long live the Queen. Barry has been around criminals and their organizations long enough to know there will be no reprisals for Maria's actions. Whatever she told those men she called in, it is a done deal. Fumu was among the first group that arrived. It makes sense; he would protect her if the others thought to take revenge for their boss.

From what he gathers about Morris' gang on the island, more than half were recruited by Maria. Morris trained them, fed them, paid them, but it is Maria who leads them. She is the one going on missions with them. In any army, you are most loyal to your battle buddies. This is what her time in New York taught her, those with whom you spilt blood would never spill yours.

Another team arrives to clean the office, Maria stays and keeps an eye on everything. It's about an hour later when Barry hears the commotion from his room. He had left the hallways a

41

few minutes after the shooting, not wanting anyone to know what he had seen. The women became frantic as Fumu broke the news of Morris' death.

No one came to inform him. It was late the next evening when Maria saw him at the bar. "So, we are taking his body back to New York for burial."

"Are you inviting me to attend," Barry stated and continued sipping his drink.

"I'll give you a ride back to the States," Maria offers offhand, "but you need not show up at the funeral. You know, given who you work for and all."

"Don't worry about it. I'm sure I'll be busy for the next couple of days filing reports. The news travels real fast in certain circles as I am sure you know. So, what now? Did they take a vote? Or were you just crowned?"

Maria chuckles lightly at his questions. She knows he already has the answers. "This is not a democracy. No vote. It's not a monarchy either, so no crown. It's just business as usual."

"Hey, for what it's worth, I did like your father." Barry drains his glass and heads for the door.

"I did too," Maria whispers as he passes.

"Don't worry about me," he stops and looks into her eyes. They are emotionless. "I've got my own way of getting back. This is family time, and I don't want to intrude." As he walks down the center hall of the North Tower to the elevator at the back, he knows he has to work fast, certain his welcome expired when Morris did. Maria's offer of a ride back means he has a little time, a day or two at the most. It also means she isn't planning on killing him, although he can't really count on that.

Langley is going to want answers and he has none to give. The one answer he has will not satisfy but it is the closest to the truth as he sees it, *when you're a psychopath and you raise a psychopath, crazy shit happens.*

He keeps an ear open but there is no talk about Morris. No

one says a word about how he died or why. It's like it didn't even happen. Morris was there and then he was not. Not even the women, after their initial outburst, say anything. Barry is good at making himself invisible to glean information but there is nothing. It is like living in a void. He thinks about how Maria looked and acted the past two days. *Maybe she is in shock. Or denial. Or she is a cold-blooded killer. Daddy's Little Princess.*

4

A SORT OF HOMECOMING

Bulletproof Morris MoJo Johnson was flown back to New York on his private jet accompanied by Elizabeth Delitanni, Maria Delitanni, Yana, and Gisella Montilla, all dressed in black. A motorcade left JFK airport and drove through the five boroughs, giving Morris one last look around before arriving at St. Athanasius, the little church in the South Bronx. The old iron bell in the octagon tower above the Narthex sounded three times to announce his arrival.

The neighborhood had changed a lot since he hunted these streets. Many of the old five-story red brick tenements, which were ravished by neglect and arsonists, were replaced by pastel, sandy-brown, co-ops apartments three and four stories high. Single family houses dotted the streets, suggesting a peaceful lifestyle, a far cry from the war-torn days of his youth. Some of the gangs still roamed these streets, but less noticeably against the façade of respectability. The nightly gun battles which plagued these streets and given the neighborhood its notorious nickname, Fort Apache, had subsided.

The old gray and black stones of the church were the last vestige of the world of Warlord of the Flaming Stars. It stood alone on a street, once a refuge for sinners and the saintly, and rumored to be the lair of the infamous Angel of Death. An apparition who exacted the highest payment from those who crossed him. How often did he nail an opponent to those wrought iron gates before the priest could rescue his prey? How many times was Morris forced to seek asylum behind those same gates? Now, he passed through the gates of Heavenly Hell, as he called them, for the last time.

As the pall bearers carried his black casket in, photographers snapped pictures of the small group of mourners who turned out. The FBI agents were there to get pictures of Nicky Rocci and his associates. Some were getting pictures of the license plates of the cars. An old, white Ford Mustang pulled in behind the last black limousine.

Sam Black got out. Long and lanky with thin white hair draped below his ears, he stepped with authority. He walked up to the agent in charge, flashed his badge, gave his name, and although he had been retired for more than a decade, the agent snapped to attention. "You are not going to find any new faces in this crowd. Morris didn't make a lot of friends or keep many enemies alive. You and your men can pack it up early."

The agent didn't question him, he waved his hand above his head in a wide circular motion and the six agents started heading to their cars.

Sam walked over to the limo and waited for the door to open. "Senator, I am not at all surprised to see you here."

Senator James Harris said, "He was a good friend. We played stickball on these same streets many years ago. So sorry to see him come home this way." The senator was still a big man with broad shoulder at age fifty. He held out a large hand and an elderly lady draped in black took it and stepped out. She reached up and touched James' face then strode strongly up the white marble steps of the church. Each black high heel clicking loudly in the well-worn rut in the center of the steps. The church had stood before she was a child and attended mass here. Built when the neighborhood was comprised of Italian immigrants. Then it became the worship house of the Irish, and later was taken over by African Americans. Now, it was the spiritual home of Puerto Ricans.

There were fewer than twenty people in the pews, and less had signed the memorial book at the entrance. The four women who made up Morris' immediate family signed. Three more women who arrived with Nicky, known as the Russian Dolls, signed. As did Nicky. A couple of Morris' old gang-banging friends, retired from the life, signed. The elderly lady who arrived with the senator started to write, "Alice", then crossed it out. It had been so long since she used her real name, she wrote in a big flamboyant script, "Christina Johnson." And next to that she wrote, "Mother."

Morris' mother sat a few pews from the door and a good distance from the closed coffin. She looked over the dark drab interior, not much had changed in the place where her son was baptized and had his first lessons on right and wrong. Admittedly, not all the lessons took hold. The Nave floor was a Breccia marble of gold, tan, brown, and red with perfectly round black and gray bubbles that appeared to be trapped in the stone. The pews were deep mahogany, polished to a high shine. Eight massive white Carrara marble columns held up the vaulted ceiling, four down each aisle. Brass candle holders ringed each column seven feet above the floor, four candelabras held subdued yellow electric flames. Beyond the Nave, the floor was covered with a bright red carpet and on that was the altar of the same Carrara marble. And what church would be complete without stained glass windows depicting Jesus' last days.

Sam took a seat at the back of the church with the Senator. He whispered, "do you know what happened?"

"Details are sketchy. I heard it was an accident. I heard it wasn't," James admitted quietly, mindful of Morris' mother sitting a few rows in front of them. "Either way it wouldn't surprise me."

"It does me," Sam murmured. "I didn't think anyone could get the drop on Morris. He was wound tighter than a cheap watch. And I know he had eyes everywhere. But I guess time runs out for us all."

Father Benny began the services with the usual Catholic prayers, going on for about fifteen minutes. When he asked if anyone had anything they'd like to say, the church was as quiet as it was empty. There was one reef of white roses with a banner reading, "Loving Father 1957 – 1997."

Finally, Sam stood up. "Oh Hell, I guess I'll say something."

All heads turned to the back as he walked to the front of the church.

His plain black suit looked like something a man on a government pension would wear. He stopped in front of the coffin and knocked on it three times. "Hey, you really in there?" he chuckled lightly. "I only ask that because I'm sure you know MoJo, he once told me I could… should call him that. He said it was what all his friends called him. He was pointing a gun at me at the time, so I figured I'd better make friends with him quick. MoJo died more times than anyone I've known. This is maybe the third funeral of his I've attended. Like all of you, this is the one I never wanted to attend. Morris and I ended up on opposite ends of the gun a couple of times, but I was never afraid."

"If he really knew MoJo well, he would have been," Nicky muttered to his Consigliere, Joseph Castor, who nodded in agreement.

"My father told me when I was a boy, 'You never have to fear an honest man.' MoJo was an honest man. He never lied to himself, didn't lie to you, he told you what he was all about, and what he planned to do. I am sure it was that honesty that got people to follow him. Through the gates of Hell and out… Now, I'm not going to lie to you, I tried to put him in jail, damn hard. I believed if anyone deserved to go to jail, it was Morris. And one time, when I was holding the gun on him, he agreed."

Sam remembered the day as clearly as if it had happened yesterday. After Tom Green's atrocious execution in the Bayou, he made it his business to track Morris down for the murder. He caught up with him in a bar in Honduras, a place his badge held no authority. At the time, he thought the payouts and Agency pressure finally yielded results, but as the years went by, Sam knew Morris arranged the meeting. They sat at a little table; Sam holding his gun under it pointed at Morris' gut. He told him to leave quietly. Morris told him if he pulled the trigger, both would die there. Morris advised him to go back into retirement and let him know that Tom Green had paid for his hand in Maria's abduction.

"But MoJo… he knew, he was never going to prison. He was too good to go to prison. Too honest to let himself slip into a situation that would lead him there. Here to the last good, honest man I know. I can tell by this gathering here today; this will be the last funeral for Morris MoJo Johnson I will ever attend."

THEY BURIED Morris with his friends from the Bronx, right next to his love, Maria Marino. Nicky finally worked up the nerve to say something before they laid him to rest.

Unashamed, he wiped away a tear and cleared his throat, "He has loved her for a lifetime, so I know he is finally happy he is with her again. Not here in this cold earth, but wherever he and his witchy woman conjured up." Then he told everyone at the secret grave site to meet back at the Sons of Italy bar.

Nicky, James, and Russell Mills, Morris' second-in-command of the street gangs, were at the end of the bar. Nicky told his wife, Rosalina, to pour one red wine, three whiskeys, and a Stoli vodka. She had seen many wakes for dead mobsters;

the red wine was for Morris. The three whiskeys for the men's goodbye toast, but the vodka, that she wasn't sure. That was something new. Morris drank Stolichnaya most of the time so why would Nicky ask for two drinks? It didn't take long for her to find out.

Nicky raised his whiskey and the others followed, "Morris, may you be in Hell three days before the Devil knows your name."

James was next, "Ashes to ashes and dust to dust, here's to the one thing you can't fuck up."

Then Russell, "Friends will come, and friends will go, but a true friend will only leave you when he's six feet in a hole."

They threw down their shots. Nicky took the shot of Stoli and swiftly slammed the glass upside down on the bar. Not a drop escaped from the glass. At the end of the night, he would take the glass of wine and throw it against the wall, Morris' final sendoff. The shot of Stoli would remain on the bar for as long as it would stand. Nicky would make it clear that anyone who moved the glass would die on the spot.

MARIA SITS ALONE in the corner at the back of the bar, staring off into space.

"I don't see much of him in you. Not on the surface, but I see a lot of her in you."

Maria doesn't look up; her voice is ghostly quiet. "Who are you?"

"Excuse me. I didn't quite hear you over the music. Jimi Hendrix's "Hear My Train a Comin'". That's one of my son's favorites." The woman sits across from her. "I'm your grand-mother, Christina. I know this is a terrible way to meet, but…"

"You really expect me to believe that you are my grandmother?" Maria leans forward in a menacing manner. "My father told me his mother and father were dead."

"Well, his father is. Died working in the transit tunnels when Morris was five. His brother was killed in a gang fight when he was ten. But I'm very much alive."

"Yeah, so you know a little something about him," Maria's voice is stronger. Her eyes narrow and lock in on the woman across from her. "Doesn't mean you're his mother. Or makes you my granny, old lady."

"Now, I see him in you," she replies, unafraid. "You have his anger. And probably his stubbornness. Let me explain. When the others were killed in the poolhall, Morris had me go into hiding. He was afraid the Mafia would come after me, you know, to get to him."

"Those things happened years ago…"

"Really? You can sit there and say that?" Christina knew she sounded disparaging, her eyes glistening with tears she had fought to keep inside all day. She needed to stay strong and push through this moment. "I'm sorry. I have no right to criticize you. And this is going to sound a little crazy, but I have never been that far away from you."

A long silence fills the space between them. Maria is unsure what to do or say. This woman was stalking her? How? And for what reason? Finally, she asks, "so, why are you here now?"

"Well, he's gone. No reason to keep hiding, is there?" Christina sees the doubt in Maria's face. But she has come this far, might as well go all the way. She has nothing to lose anyway, "You are all the family I have left. When you lived in Aruba, I moved there too. Lived on the nearby island of Naxos while you stayed on Syros. I lost track of you for a while, but I found you again when you went to school in Spain."

Christina watches intently for some sign of acceptance in Maria's face. She isn't sure what she had hoped to gain when she first approached her, but now she wants to reach out and hug her like a long-lost child. As she thinks it, she knows it's insane, an impossible outcome, but that is what she needs now.

Instead, she gets a cold, cruel rebuke, "You have been around me my entire life and only now come with this ridiculous story? And I guess my father never knew you were around. I find that hard to believe. He knew every fly on every leaf that was within a mile of him. How did he not know you were around?"

Now, Christina feels this was a mistake. Perhaps she should have waited a few days to approach her only grandchild. Maybe gotten one of Morris' friends to make the introduction. This young girl is full of pain, and she may not have another opportunity, knowing Maria will sink back into the underworld. A world that will be out of reach to her. "I think my son always knew I was near but kept his distance to keep me safe. I kept mine to be able to see you from time to time. I was in the background when you were on shopping trips, or on holidays. I thought about introducing myself when you were in Spain. But there was always an element of danger in that."

"So, what do you want?" asks Maria flippantly. "There is still a great deal of danger here. Just take a look around you, we are in a mob bar with gangsters and killers. My father's friends are my friends, and his enemies have become my adversaries. If you think his troubles went into the grave with him, you are sadly mistaken."

NICKY HAS BEEN WATCHING the two women at the table the whole time. He can't see the older woman's face, but from the look on Maria's she isn't winning any popularity contests there. He needs to talk to her about the business, but that can wait for another day. He is sure she has a good handle on things. Morris groomed her well, and he probably left things behind to put her on the right path. Besides, he is Uncle Nicky, she will come to him.

She always turned to him when she was in trouble, and he was there for her without question or regard for the danger. He is her Godfather in life and business. She is going to need him now. And he needs her. But not today, she has things she needs to deal with first.

CHRISTINA STANDS UP TO LEAVE, "Don't think I don't know what my son was into, I've known quite a few of these men since they were boys. I'm not afraid of any of them, never was. And I'm not afraid of any one not here to remember my son. I didn't keep my distance because I was afraid for my life, I did it because I was afraid for Morris'. Like I said, that's all behind us now, so you don't have to go through this life alone."

"We have suites at the Dorian on Central Park," Maria finally relents, "you can come if you like. But it's your funeral."

NICKY WATCHES the woman walk out of the bar. Instant recognition strikes as he finally sees her face. He says to James, "Are you going to take her home?"

"I came in her ride. But not to worry, I'll call for a car soon."

"Senator, you are slipping," Nicky jests, "what would your constituents think? You, leaving a place of such ill-repute."

Senator James laughs, "Who said I was going to call a car from this den of thieves? But if anyone should ask, Morris was an upstanding businessman and a patriot, who deserves the respect of this nation. He helped me rebuild his neighborhood, with ample and favorable contributions from your construction companies. And you, well, they've never been able to pin anything on you."

"And they never will. Morris was a great business partner, the best any man could hope for. He was smart, and ruthless, both qualities needed in today's world." Nicky downs another drink. The night is young, the music is playing, and there are stories to be told. He picks up the wine glass and holds it up high.

The bar slowly quietens down. Everyone is soon watching him.

"Jesus refused the drink of the vine until he came back in his purified Self. In three days, maybe a bit longer, God willing, Morris will be drinking better wine than this!" He throws the glass across the bar.

It smashes against the back wall. Everybody cheers, the music resumes, and the drinking continues in earnest.

Nicky grabs a bottle of Jack from behind the bar and turns it up. He intends to drown his pain, even if it takes all night.

Rosalia is at a table with the Russian Dolls. The glass of wine flew dangerously close to them before smashing on the wall. Shards of glass sparkle around them. She shakes her head and holds Yana's hand, "he often told me he wanted to go before Morris. Tonight, is going to be a hard one for him. For us all."

The four women turn up their bottles of Stolichnaya.

Elizabeth Delitanni sits by herself at the other end of the bar. She can see her daughter out of the corner of her eye; misery consumes Maria. Elizabeth never thought she would feel this way, euphoria is washing over her like waves on the beach. Each one bigger, more intense, more satisfying. For the first time in decades, she is happy. Not happy that Morris is dead. There is a little dark spot in her mind at the thought of that. Happy… no, overjoyed, that she is finally free. She smiles in the mirror behind the bar at the thought that at long last she is free of Maria. Her tormentor has released her from the prison she birthed.

With Morris reunited with his true love, she has broken the curse put on her for stealing Morris and causing Maria Marino's death. Her daughter, conceived as penance for her passions, has brought death into her house from that first night Morris returned to murder her father. She feels the lashes her father laid upon her body for that sin so many years ago, however, tonight, they do not sting anymore. The thirty-three burning cuts in her skin have finally healed. Each night she felt their fiery torment anew. Never again, she tells herself. She hears the gunshot once again as distant thunder, not heralding the coming storm, but the clearing of the clouds around her.

Maria's birth was a moment of guilt that her mother never let her forget. Even as she coughed up blood in her final moments, her mother pointed the accusing finger at her daughter, as if to say, "See what horror you have brought into this world."

The blood in her eyes as she drew her last breath painted Elizabeth as the reason for her family's ruination. It was a burden she could not escape, not while she lay with Morris. Now, the Hell he created claimed him. No one told her so, but without doubt, his undoing was using her in his cruel plan. She loved him, but all of her life, she knew he never felt the same. So, for that one night, when she let a murderer inside her, she has paid a deadly and dire cost. The bill issued by Maria Marino from beyond the grave, finally paid in full.

5

NEW BUSINESS

The Dorian is an eighty-four-floor modern high-rise on Central Park, east side. It is home to bankers, brokers, businessmen, and a wide assortment of politician, and naturally, heads of states. Built in the art deco style of the Empire State Building it has a multi-level façade. Morris had the spire removed at a great cost so he could add a private heliport on the roof. He also had to buy the top five floors as insurance. The lower two of those floors served to reinforce the structure and housed the offices of the Bright Skies Agency. The upper three floors were the family's living quarters.

Christina arrived at The Dorian at 10 A.M. and was greeted by Henri, the Doorman, as he held open the door, "Good morning, Mrs. Johnson."

"You know who I am?"

"Yes, Madame," he replied with a slight French accent, "you are expected. Victor, at the front desk will get you checked in. I hope you enjoy your stay with us." He offered his hand in the direction of a small wooden desk in the tiny lobby.

Victor immediately rose and stepped from behind the concierge desk with a broad smile. He beamed a gracious welcome, "hello, Mrs. Johnson. I am Victor Beechum, and will take care of all your needs. We will get you checked into security first and then have some of the boys take your luggage up."

"Checked into security?"

"Yes, Mum," his British background slipped out. He slid open a panel in the desktop to reveal a small scanner. "Just place your right hand on the glass and look straight ahead." The bar of green light went across the glass and back. "Okay, please place your left hand on the glass and if you can turn your head to the right." The scanner captured her left handprint. Then he said, "one more thing, if you will be so good to turn to the left for your last profile picture."

"Profile picture?"

"Yes, Mum," he smiled and turned slightly to the wall behind him, "there is a camera behind the black panel in the wall. Your fingerprints and facial image will allow you to access the elevators and take you to the penthouse on the eighty-second floor. You do not need a key here. Now, about your luggage, is there a car waiting out front?"

"A car? Luggage? No, I didn't bring anything. I'm not sure if I am staying that long." Christina looked around, "are those the elevators over there?"

"No, Mum. Those are for our less illustrious guess. Princes, presidents, and kings," he smiled widely, "your elevator is right behind you. There is always one car waiting to take you up and one car waiting to bring you down. But, Mum, I was informed that you were coming to live with us."

"Really, informed by whom?"

"By Miss Maria," he was surprised but not more than Christina by his answer. "Perhaps, I misunderstood her instructions. She said you were to have unlimited access to the private entrance, that you would be moving in."

"Well, I guess I am." She smiled a little embarrassed by the whole situation. After the reaction she got from Maria at the bar, she was sure this was going to be a curtesy brushoff. But here she was getting the keys to the castle. "Where is this elevator?"

"Just stand in front of the mural of The Flight of the Valkyries behind you, one of them will open up."

Christina turned and stared at six Viking women spear-warriors scantily dressed in golden armor riding various horses out of a gray and stormy sky covering twelve feet of the lobby wall.

Victor offered, "Just step forward."

"Yes, I will. Just admiring the artwork." She took a step closer and the first Valkyrie on a brown horse on the left slid back a few inches and then to the left. She sucked in a surprised breath as the red and gold velvet interior of the car invited her in.

Just before Christina disappeared behind the closing door Victor said, "call down to me when you are ready, and I'll have someone go and retrieve your things. Or if you like, I can have a few of the Misses' clothiers come up."

CHRISTINA STEPPED out of the back door of the elevator into a small atrium. She ran her hand along the hibiscus and orchids that lined the walls. A waterfall reached up three floors to a glass dome. The door at the end of the room opened as she approached. A spectacular view of Central Park greeted her. From this height she saw the entire park as a small garden in the middle of the cityscape. The greenery cutting a stark contrast to the gray concrete, black asphalt, and silvery glass before her.

The room was long and wide with seven long couches strategically placed so people could hold conversations. That is, if there was anyone there. She walked around and found the kitchen. It was gleaming in polished stainless-steel décor. Bathrooms of rose marble, white ivory, and black tourmaline were intermingled with sitting rooms, media room, and one with a grand piano. *I hope Maria can play; I know Morris can't carry a tune in a paper bag.*

She continued her tour up the grand stairway, one of two on each end of the main salon. The second floor had another kitchen, more bathrooms, and various other rooms which could be for anything except sleeping; there were no beds. On the third floor she finally found bedrooms, five in all. Each with a bathroom attached. They were arranged around a central circular common room. Each bedroom had a balcony and a skylight. She went up the last set of stairs in the lounge and found herself on the rooftop helipad. She took a moment to look around at the city before the wind chased her back inside.

Christina made her way back to the observatory by way of the kitchen. To her surprise the refrigerator was well stocked. As were the pantries. Although, there were clothes in the closets and linens on the beds, it didn't appear that anyone had been living there. She began to wonder why Maria told her to come here.

SHE WAS ACCUSTOMED to a comfortable life. Morris made sure her bank accounts remained full. Every year she received a letter from Senator James with a new identity and bank account number worth in the tens of millions. And it didn't matter if she changed her name and moved to a different location, his letter always found her. Except for a four-year period, when she felt for sure, her little boy had died.

She scoured the papers from every continent looking for the news she hoped she would not find. She went to Aruba, then followed Elizabeth and Maria back to New York. She had just about given up hope. Was about to call Elizabeth and ask to meet her and Maria when a letter arrived by courier. She had a new name and a hundred million dollars. It also told her to leave New York. She did.

That was when she realized the letters weren't coming from Senator James. She was beside herself about the money too. She didn't know exactly what her son did to get it, but it had to be bad. She never read his name in the newspaper, but that didn't mean he wasn't behind some of the worst stories she read. Assassinations, bombings, killings, government overthrows… she could not prove it, but had a feeling Morris was behind or involved in all of it. *How else could he make so much money?*

At first, she donated a lot of it to charity. But that brought problems of its own. Even when she tried to do it anonymously, it always summoned a police investigation. For a couple of years, she travelled around the country stuffing poor boxes with a hundred thousand dollars every Sunday. One Sunday she saw a couple of parishioners in Shawnee, Oklahoma, who didn't look like the bible-carrying type.

Christina had been driving back and forth on Interstate 40 in an RV, making her weekly deliveries. Although she stopped at random churches of any denomination, the word was out to be on the lookout for the Good Samaritan. Luckily, no one knew who they were looking for, it could be a man or woman, young or old. One local paper reported, "The Feds said they could be looking for Jesus, Himself, for all they knew." The men in the Shawnee First Baptist Church were probably FBI, and even if she wasn't breaking any laws, she thought she better find another way to appease her conscience.

She started getting creative, dropping a bag of cash off at a food bank during the holiday. Donating clothes to homeless shelters with pockets loaded with a wad of hundreds. Christina thought it funny to send the Police Benevolent Fund one hundred one-thousand-dollar money orders she bought on her travels. Finally, she went to the senator's office one afternoon to seek his help. He was surprised to see her after more than a decade. He helped her set up a charitable foundation where she could funnel money to worthy causes. The money always came from offshore shell companies that could not be traced back to her. It was important for her safety as well as her son's.

She kept enough of the money to buy houses and follow Elizabeth and Maria around the world. She always kept her distance, and never showed up when Morris was with them, which wasn't too often. He was either away on business or locked behind the walls of some palatial estate. Although she rarely saw him, she knew he had a watchful eye on her. Always.

BARRY PULLED into a parking space a half block from the Dorian's garage entrance. He pulled out his car phone and punched in the numbers. "Let me speak to the Director… Yes, of course I'll wait… Hello, Sir, I am outside their headquarters."

"I read your report. Are you sure Morris Johnson is dead?" stated the gruff voice. "He's been dead before. This guy has more lives than a cat."

"At some point, every pussy gets fucked," Barry's dry wit was not lost on the CIA Director as he heard a chuckle. "I saw her shoot him in the face… point-blank. You don't walk away from that."

"Are you sure? Not a body double."

"His double was still in Washington wrapping up testimony. She did him, alright." Barry wanted to allay the Director's concerns, "before they transported his body, I slipped into the cold room. He had his own mortician on staff. I was really surprised she didn't have him cremated there. I managed to sneak a peek at the three bullet wounds on his chest and the whip marks across his back."

"Did you get a DNA sample? We could compare it to his daughter's."

"Couldn't. Didn't have that kind of time," then he reaffirmed his findings, "but the wounds were real."

There was a moment of uncomfortable silence. "They could have been medically created. I am sure Morris spared no expense on these body doubles."

"How much do you think you have to pay someone to take a bullet to the face?"

"Nothing, if he didn't know it was coming. Alright," acquiesced the man on the phone. "Get in there and make sure she understands we are still her number one client. Nothing has changed from our point of view."

"So, just to be clear. You want me to go in there and coerce the girl who just killed her father to play ball with us, or else."

"Coerce, charm, whatever it takes. I put you on this assignment because I was told you could charm a snake out of its skin." The Director's voice deepened, "do you want me to reassign you?"

Barry knew reassignment was never a good outcome. Forget about going from the frying pan into the fire, it was more like, being in a shithole getting shitted on. "No. That's not what I want. But this snake doesn't shed her skin. I just want you to know, if you want her cooperation, we are going to have to force it out of her."

"I don't care how you do it, keep her in the loop." The Director's voice was as dry as kindling wood. "Put a gun to her head if you have to. She is much too valuable of an asset to lose now. Maybe, working with her will be easier than with her old man. He already set our Southern Agenda back ten years."

"Okay, I'm on it." He cut the phone off before the Director could make any more unreasonable demands. Barry seriously doubted his bosses knew who they were dealing with. Morris was difficult because he always had his own agendas he followed, Maria was only interested in one thing and one person. Revenge on Sgt. Warren. He checked his Kevlar vest for the umpteenth time and headed for the underground parking.

Maria was on the second floor of the BSA's headquarters. One monitor on her father's desk, that was now hers, tracked Christina's every move the next floors above. The four-foot-thick concrete pillar off to the left of the desk held six more displays of the apartment. Maria was going over reports from field agents when Russell Mills walked in.

"How are you holding up?"

"OK, I guess," she answers without looking up from the papers in one of the folders. "There is so much stuff to go through in here. Morris was never a neat and tidy record keeper. I think he did it on purpose to keep me from finding shit."

"I don't think he wanted anybody to find shit," Russell sighs, "but he could put his finger on any piece of information in a moment. He kept it all filed in his head. He was a remarkable man."

"Yeah, of course he was, he will be sorely missed," Maria says without feeling. "What I'm missing right now is who do we have in Brazil, Colombia, and Venezuela?"

"I can find that for you," Russell gives her a smile as she finally looks up. "What I came in here for is to tell you, your boyfriend is here."

"My boyfriend?" Bewilderment momentarily softens her face. "BARRY THOMAS. What the hell, I thought I was done with him in Greece. I guess he thinks I need a shoulder to cry on and is hoping a dick to jump on."

"Want me to deny his access?"

"No, let him up. I'll come down in a few minutes and let him down hard." Maria's face twists to an emotionless mask, "if you refer to that government man as my boyfriend again, I'll shoot you."

Russell throws up his hands and backs out of the office. He goes through a doorway near another huge concrete column and heads down the stairs. He enters the large office floor of the BSA as the elevator doors open.

Barry steps out of the blandly decorated elevator car and starts to look around. He sees Russell and quickly approaches, "Is she here? I need to speak with her right away."

"You know it is customary to give the family a time to mourn."

"Maybe, but not so much when they are the cause of death," he quips loud enough for the girl at the receptionist's desk to hear.

"So, what? You are here on official business... Oh, wait, you're not a cop. You are a spy," Russell responds louder. "Why don't we go into the conference room and wait?" He heads down the corridor expecting Barry to follow.

Barry stands at the receptionist's desk as the thin, gray-afroed Russell in his three-piece charcoal suit walks away, his shoes clicking regimentally down the hall. He doesn't like him, and he knows the feeling is mutual. He shouts, "so, how is she going to know where to find us?"

"I will inform Ms. Johnson, you are in conference room A when she arrives," snarks the receptionist.

"Oh, great, now you don't like me either." Barry starts to walk slowly down the hall. He looks around like it's his first time there, "I'll be waiting in conference room A when she comes down from the second floor. Maybe you guys will do some redecorating now that... you know... the boss has retired."

"Ass." He hears from behind him and picks up his pace. He doesn't want to earn his star on the wall from a receptionist putting a bullet in the back of his head. He turns into the lighted room at the end of the corridor and sees Maria lounging back in one of the chairs with her feet on the table.

MARIA'S long black skirt is split up to her knee. Her black heels are pointing dangerously at him.

"Don't sit down. I won't be redecorating," she seethes, "I like the place as it is, nice and cheery. As you can see, I am still in mourning. So, let's get down to it... What the fuck do you want? You were my father's boy; I have no need for you."

"Nor I of you," Barry takes a seat across and behind her to force her to sit up.

She doesn't.

"My bosses inform me that their business with your father didn't end with him. They have invested a considerable amount of resources in this endeavor and they intend to see it come to fruitions."

"Run back to Langley and tell them I am in full command, and it will be business as usual. Nothing has changed. A Johnson is still running the show."

"Amen to that," chimes in Russell who is seated directly across from Barry.

Barry quickly recalculates his options as he feels very close to becoming a star on the wall. It is the anonymous end of a career in the Agency that they all try to avoid. Time to turn on the charm. "Look, I'm sorry I was crass out there. I know this must be hard on you. Morris was a good guy. As I said back on the island, I liked him. Let me help you."

"Help me with what?" Maria sits up and spins her chair around towards him. "What can you possibly do for me, that my own guys here, can't?"

"I can help you find your Sgt. Warren," Barry offers softly, "or prove that he's dead."

"Oh! So now I'm not a crazy woman chasing phantoms."

"You might still be. But I can pull strings at the Agency. Get them to investigate what other connections Warren may have been working through. You know a good asset has more than one avenue. You know everything went to hell in the explosion, then the senator and congressman… Well, their deaths slammed the door on the whole affair. You know the government isn't all gung-ho about exposing black ops deals. His or Morris'."

"Oh, wow! Really? You would do that for me," Maria gushes as she comes across the table towards him batting her eyelashes. "Go fuck yourself! If he is still alive, and I know he is, we will find him. I am quite good at finding what I'm looking for. Always have been."

Charm isn't working, time to put the gun to her head. "I am trying to help you here. The Agency wants to know how the US's top military weapons ended up in the Sudan. Right now, it looks like your little trip was to cover up your dad's involvement in an illegal transaction. A deal breaker. And a good chance all those involved go to jail."

"My dad always warned me about trusting people who are only looking out for your best interests. It is usually them who are getting paid."

"Your DAD didn't trust too many people…"

"He trusted me!"

"And look where that got him," Barry tensed for a slap or a shot. He got neither. He felt lucky, maybe he could push another button and get her to come around. "If we work together, we can get Gavril Avakian."

"Who?" Maria regains her composure. She knows she almost let this guy get to her.

"Oh, come on," Barry says frustratedly, "now who is playing games? Avakian, the Armenian arms dealer you ID-ed in the camp. You think he's your lead to Sgt. Warren, and we want to know how he got his hands on those Javelins. If Warren is still alive it would explain a lot of things for us. Us being the CIA, not me and you, just to be clear."

"Not to worry," Maria laughs, "there is no YOU and ME, but I will work with you for now. Obviously, your boss thinks you have an inside track. You've probably been exaggerating your worth in your reports."

"Why don't you take me upstairs?" Barry decides to go all in while he has a seat at the table. "I would love to see what we are working with."

"I bet you would, Mr. Spy," Russell jumps in.

"Yeah, that's never gonna happen," Maria agrees. "We will send you an address where you can operate out of. This is a respectable business here. We are in the business of saving lives and righting wrongs in the world. Can't have the likes of you hanging around."

RUSSELL TAKES Barry back to the elevator, which takes him back to the garage. In her office they watch him get in his car and exit.

Russell hands her a file with a dozen names, "these are the people we have on the ground in South America. What are you planning to do?"

"We are going to kidnap somebody. Somebody big; we need us a whale. If we want Ahab to come out of hiding, we need a White Whale, a Moby Dick of a tycoon for him to chase."

"What makes you think he will be looking to rescue anybody?"

"He's a merc and a kidnapper," Maria says sullenly, "what better business to be in than rescuing kidnapped victims."

"What about your boy… Barry? Are you going to work with him?"

"It can't hurt," Maria muses. "We let the CIA grab the Armenian. That way if he is connected to Warren, we keep him off our scent. I'll get the information out of him. My father believed we are in the same businesses. Arms dealing, security, kidnapping, and rescues. You know, all the big money games."

"Speaking of your father," Russell points to the monitors on the columns, "are you going to go talk to her?"

"Yeah, I guess so. Go! Find me someone fat... no, huge." Maria looks back at the monitors, "and I want you to pull those damn cameras out of the apartment."

"I don't think that is a good idea," Russell objects, "we need to maintain a level of security."

"Ok. But pull the ones out of the bedrooms and bathroom," she orders. "You know the bathroom ones are illegal as fuck."

"Those cameras only display on that monitor," he points to the desk.

"If I am the only one who can see them, then I don't need them." Maria gets an oddly queasy feeling hearing that bit of information. Was Morris spying on her or the other women in his life? He never gave the impression he didn't trust them, so why the cameras in the bathroom for his eyes only? Maybe because she had been abducted from a bathroom, and he was leaving nothing to chance. She felt better when she rationalized it in that light. But it was still creepy.

6

THE REINS OF POWER

Nicky is in his office in the Sons of Italy bar. It has been a week since the funeral and two days since he stopped drinking. He is recovering slowly from the binge. The bar has been closed all week. Everybody cleared out days ago, only the Russian Dolls remained. Drinking with him, passing out, waking, and drinking some more.

Rosalina stands in the doorway, "the girls are ready to go. It's time to go home, my love. We have given MoJo the sendoff he deserved."

"Ok, I'll be along in a moment," Nicky is drawn and gray. "Send Yana in for a minute."

"I don't think that is a good idea. She is hurting more than you. Please just let it go."

"I know what he wants," Yana says and slips into the office. Her body looks broken down as she slumps into a chair across the desk from him. "I have been asking myself the same question since it happened. Why?"

"Exactly," Nicky sits back, "why would Maria shoot him? What could they have been fighting about?"

Yana shakes her head. She is tired of thinking about it. "The

68

same thing they always fought about, Akilina. But why she would shoot him this time, I don't know. You will have to ask her. I did. Her mother did. She never answered."

"I have another question. Think before you answer… What should I do about her?"

"What do you mean?" A gasp came from Honey, standing just outside the door.

The girls file into the office. All taking a hard look at Nicky.

"There is nothing you can do. This was a private matter between Morris and his daughter. No matter how badly it turned out."

Nicky looks at the girls' glaring faces and realizes what is going through their minds. "Oh, no! I'm not thinking about killing her. I had an offer to make her, but now, is she ready to take over?"

"I do not know," Yana says, "she has taken control of the BSA, so maybe you are putting too much on her shoulders too soon?"

"That's what I'm worried about. Youse go on home, I'm going to call her over and have a talk with her. I gotta see where her head is at."

The women reluctantly leave the bar, not sure if Nicky is telling the truth. Yana worries that if Nicky pushes Maria too hard, he may end up like Morris. Killing a mob boss will have a much different outcome than killing her father. The gang remained loyal to her. The Mafia would not.

MARIA ARRIVES at the bar late that night. She enters through the back door; she's surprised her key still works after so many years. The place is dark, only Nicky's office light is on, "hey, you never change the locks. You know how dangerous that is?"

"Not really. No one is coming in here to kill me, and if they did, they would come through the front door. When we are open. Take a seat." He pulls out a bottle from his desk drawer. Pours two shots.

"You look like you've had more than enough," Maria waves off the drink. "Have you even been home?"

"No. These are for after I ask you two questions," Nicky slides one glass to her side and folds his hands on the desk. His face is long and pale, his eyes black like a shark's. There is a lack of warmth coming from him.

Maria straightens up and prepares herself for the question everyone has asked her. When he doesn't say anything, she prompts, "Go ahead Uncle Nicky. It's okay, I know what you want to know."

"Do you now? Ok, why did you shoot him twice?"

She is caught off guard by this question. Everybody wanted to know how her father was shot. And for the most part, she told them it was an accident. Which, for some part of what happened, was true. She told the first men into the office that day, Arthur Penn and Eli Boston, Yana's bodyguards, that she was arguing with her father. "When I said, 'I wish I was dead,' he tried to grab my gun from its holster… it went off. And then again when it hit the floor."

He heard what happened and didn't believe it. Maybe others didn't either, but no one wanted to know why she fired twice. That was the one question nobody asked. They just accepted whatever story she told.

She can't lie to Nicky, not now, not without knowing why he called her there. Nicky and Morris were brothers in every sense of the word. There was no one closer to him than Nicky, and no one closer to Morris than the man who sat across the desk from her now. She knows her life hangs in that moment.

She answers truthfully, "I guess he wasn't going to die fast enough from the first shot."

"Makes sense," Nicky says without judgement. "Now, the

big question. Are you ready to take over the family business? My family business."

Again, she is surprised by the question. She had a feeling Nicky was going to reprimand her for her actions. Maybe even have her killed. She didn't bring any weapons with her, ready to accept whatever fate her Godfather deemed appropriate. But being made Don, she, a woman, that is crazy. He has to be out of his mind with grief. She sits with her mouth open.

"Say something before you swallow a fly."

"What are you, crazy? Why me? The other families will never accept a woman as Don. Your own guys won't accept me."

"They will accept whatever I tell them is acceptable," Nicky says indignantly.

"Not this," she protests, "you are going to push them away. Worse, you are going to drive them to take you out. Me too."

Nicky nudges the glass towards her. "I have been thinking about this for a while. Been working with my Consigliere Joe; the Mafia isn't what it used to be, but it's yours if you want it. It is what we, MoJo and I, been training you for all your life."

Maria stares at the glass for a moment. She looks Nicky in the eye then drops her head. "It might be what you were training me for, but my father, he just trained me to be a killer. From the day I was born, I was nothing more than a weapon he could use."

"Morris trained us all to be killers," he takes hold of her hand. The pain and remorse she suffers oozes from her like a bullet wound in the gut. "But he had higher aspirations for you. We both did. This day was always in your future. Did I ever tell you about the day I joined his gang?"

Morris took the blindfold from Nicky's eyes. He was in a basement apartment somewhere in the South Bronx.

Morris said, "are you sure you want to go through with this?

Once it starts, I cannot stop it. What happens when you walk into that next room is all on you."

"You are making a big deal out of this," Nicky laughed, "I heard about people getting jumped into the gangs before. I can take a few kicks and punches."

"It is more than just a few kicks and punches, if anyone doesn't want you in the gang, that person will kill you." Morris put a hand on his shoulder and looked him in the eye, "I won't be able to do anything about it, it's their right to reject anyone they feel isn't worthy of brotherhood."

"Then I'd better prove myself worthy," Nicky responded earnestly, "I want them to know they can count on me in a fight. I'll have their back, and if needed, they will have mine. You said I can fight back, right?"

"You are expected to," Morris confirmed, "and fight hard. But no killer blows. You are trying to become their brother."

"But what if they are trying to kill me?"

"Then all bets are off. You fight to stay alive." Morris walked towards the next door. "Wait here, I'll see if they are ready for you." He entered the room devoid of furniture.

Russell was there and five gang members of various stature. He approached Morris. "So, you brought him," he said, "is he crazy? Why is he doing this?"

Morris shrugged. "He is looking for your respect. I guess that is the best way I can explain it. Ok, everybody, get over here." Morris eyed them critically, he knows three of them personally, Black Ice, The Hammer, and Crazy George. The five gangbangers were all bigger and better built than Nicky. "Jesus, Russell, you couldn't have picked some guys who were less likely to beat him into a coma?"

"These are the only five who would come. Everyone knows your friend is a Made-Man," Russell revealed, "no one wants to take on the risk of the Mafia finding out about this and winding up in the East River. Again, why is he doing this? He is part of the Mafia; he can't be part of the gang. They will kill him if they find out, and us!"

"I know. And he knows it too." Morris looked hard at each man. "I am not throwing a punch, so he will not actually be a member of this gang. That being said, if anyone throws a lethal blow, I will handcuff you to his body when I drop it off at his father's—the Don—house. And you can explain why you killed his son before he dismembers you. Understand?"

All nodded.

And with that Morris marched Nicky into the room. The fight began with Russell's shot to his gut. Nicky threw some wild punches and elbows, striking The Hammer in the face. It wasn't much of a fight as Black Ice sent him to the floor with a karate kick to the chest. A few more kicks to the body and Morris called it done.

The guys helped him up and slapped him on the back. Then exchanged a few words and left.

Morris stood back as he heaved up his gut and some blood. He said, "You don't look too bad. You did well. They do respect your bravery, if not your intelligence."

"What do you mean?"

"To take a beating for no reason is not the smartest thing you ever done."

"What do you mean, NO REASON? I got jumped in!" Nicky protested as vehemently as the pain would allow.

"No, you didn't. I did not throw a punch; everyone present must participate." Morris said philosophically, "A man can't serve two masters, you are mafioso. But they do respect your wanting to be part of the brotherhood. They will stand with you when needed."

MARIA IS IMPRESSED by her Uncle Nicky's story. She never heard he tried to join her father's gang. It took a few days for the black and blues to disappear from his body and he could show up at his father's place. The gang members had been extra careful not to hit him in the face.

She says, "It was a bit different for me when I joined the gang."

"I remember when you returned to New York with Morris. I told him it was too soon after all that you went through. But he said you insisted."

"I did. I had just turned fifteen and was feeling like a prisoner. Morris was trying to protect me by hiding me away. I was determined not to be the victim or to be victimized ever again." Her eyes tear up as she goes back to that warehouse in Queens. "I demanded to get jumped in. Go in as a soldier. I wanted to go in anonymously, but he thought it would be safer if they knew I was his daughter. He was wrong."

MARIA STOOD in the school gym of P.S. 285 near St. Mary's Park in the heart of the South Bronx. The building was erected in an old gothic style with reliefs and arches over the entrance. The large gray stones gave it the appearance of a fort, just the sort of place to hold a battle royale. The gym bleachers were filled with gangbangers from across the city but only members of the Flaming Stars were going to be part of the initiation crew. Getting jumped in was usually a secret affair, however, Morris wanted everyone to know Maria was his daughter. It was also unusual for a girl to be jumped into a gang.

"Who will challenge Maria Delitanni's right to the brotherhood of the Flaming Stars?" Morris booms. "Let all those who would test her mettle in the fires of combat step forward. But know you this, you risk life and limb to prove her unworthy."

Maria knows the proclamation is mostly for show. Her trial will be physical but not deadly. She will either fight and give a good showing of her toughness or be forced into submission and not accepted into the gang. One section of the bleachers rise in unison, dozens of guys file down onto the gymnasium floor.

"Oh, you are in for it now," Morris says with a smile, "just remember, if you get knocked down get to your feet as quickly as you can, or they will kick the shit out of you." He throws a tight-fisted right hook that she lets land on her left cheek. Her head snaps to the side, and it is on.

At first it's a parade of boys, some younger than her. They punch her with weak jabs to the stomach or chest. Mostly because they don't have the power to hit any harder, and some because they just want to be part of welcoming the queen into their ranks. She is royalty, everyone knows her story. They saw on the news the night a Queens highway was destroyed to free her. They have heard how she launched the attack that demolished a Washington D.C. neighborhood as payback for her kidnapping. On the streets of the South Bronx, she is a goddess.

Then, a circle begins to form around her of older men, some, twice her age, clad in leather or cut-off denim jackets, with chains and spikes adorning them. They wear various insignia of yellow stars, blazing red meteoroids, and one has a binary star of gold and white with flames flowing in arcs from each. It's Russell, wearing the same emblem on his back as her father. Now the trial starts in earnest.

They attack her three or four at a time. She blocks the punches aimed at her face and absorbs the body blows when she has to; she is well trained at fifteen to block out the pain and concentrate on the fight. She also makes herself pliable, rolling off the fists to minimize their effectiveness. She steps into the men and uses her elbows and knees to throw more powerful blows.

Each man throws a couple of punches before stepping back

to form the ring. Maria, hyper aware of her surroundings, catches sight of a flat, four-knuckle, tiger-fist swing heading for her throat. Her split-second reaction lets only one boney knuckle graze the side of her neck. She tracks who the assailant is and catches his arm as he tries a second punch. She spins him around and tosses him into the body of men.

At once the circle of onlookers step back as the young man has decided to challenge Maria to a lethal duel. Maria does a little boxer's shuffle then settles into a karate stance. The rest of the gym rise to their feet in silence.

The man, a dark Puerto Rican, is a couple of years older than her, a few inches taller, and about fifty pounds heavier. The gang know him as Guao, Puerto Rico's Poison Ivy, because he's thin, dark-skinned, and proves himself to be deadly. He takes a similar stance, then steps forward and leaps into a flying roundhouse kick.

Maria ducks the kick and moves forward, throwing a series of jabs. He blocks them all and catches her arm. He attempts to break it, but she throws her hip into his side and flips him to the ground. She kicks him in the face and dances away. She thinks that is enough.

Guao bounces to his feet with a backflip, fire in his eyes. He charges her and she counters by once again flipping him a couple of feet across the hard wood floor. He rolls, twists, and comes to his feet. Maria doesn't wait for another attack. She lands a flying kick to the side of his head. The gymnasium echoes with the sound of Guao's neck snapping. Quickly followed by the roar of an appreciative audience.

"I LATER FOUND out he wanted to kill me because my father had killed his brother years previously." Maria states coldly, "that wasn't the first time I killed for him either. I wanted to join the gang to get away from him, instead, I spent three years here in New York and sank deeper into his world. That's when I realized there was no escaping Morris."

Nicky drinks his shot even though hers still sits on the desk. He begins to explain his motives and actions. First, there was the Commission Trials. Maria had followed them on the international news, the heads of four of the five New York Mafia families faced numerous conspiracy and racketeering charges. She had worried he was going to get caught in it too.

"When you called me in those days," Nicky recalls, "I told you not to worry about me. What I couldn't tell you then was that I initiated the whole thing, as my ascension to the Commission wasn't going as planned. I had tapes from my father, and some I made myself, that… let's just say, found their way into the right hands. They helped the New York District Attorneys' office build their case again the other Dons. Now, I sit alone as the head of the Mafia in New York."

Nicky had never revealed this information to anyone, not even Morris. Although, he suspects MoJo knew where the DA got their initial information. It was one of those things between him and MoJo, they never had to say much to know what the other was thinking or doing. He missed that. He never had a friend like MoJo before, and now he knew he would never find another.

He is feeling old and tired; looks it too. The gray at his temples quickly climbs up his head. His hair is mostly gray with streaks of jet-black running through it, but it's his face that exhibits the life of crime and the toll it has taken on him the most. The puffy bags under his eyes, the deep lines that define his mouth and forehead, all put there by years of dirty deeds. With MoJo gone, and all the money he would ever need, he just doesn't feel like he wants to live the life any longer.

"I have another, less selfish reason for making you my successor," Nicky continues, "it concerns your mother."

"What about Elizabeth?" Maria's voice shows real concern.

"She doesn't look… Well, she's not happy," Nicky thinks for a moment. "Not that I expect to see her smiling and laughing considering the circumstances. What I mean to say is she hasn't been at peace in this life. She has paid a terrible price for what we did, MoJo and I, years before you were even born. I'm going to take her upstate with me, we can retire on my family farm. I don't think she's ever been there, so there will be no memories to haunt her."

"I don't know what to say," Maria confesses. She has never considered how Elizabeth feels; they have always been distant and there is a coldness she doesn't fully understand. It's also why she was devastated by Akilina's death. Even though Morris was by her side ever since that day, losing Akilina was like losing her mother. She doubts Elizabeth's death would have phased her at all. Morris' didn't. "I guess I never noticed, as Elizabeth was always depressed. I just thought it was having to share my father with the others. I don't think she was into that lifestyle, but I know Morris didn't care if any of them liked it. It fucked up her head."

"Well, maybe it did," Nicky concedes, "but that still leaves you and me. I need you to take over for me. Of course, I will be available to counsel you if and when needed. What do you say?"

"What can I say? Yeah, of course, I'll do it… But there is something I want you to do for me."

"Drink your shot, then we discuss business."

Maria downs the drink and turns the glass upside down on the desk. "Okay, this is what I'm thinking. Instead of telling everyone you are putting me in charge of the business, I want you to put a hit out on me. Say it's for killing my father. Say I'm trying to muscle you out of the business."

Nicky's face turns ghostly white. His eyes widen, removing almost all the age lines around them. He shakes his head emphatically. "No way! Are you crazy? Why would you want me to take a contract out on you? I…"

"Hear me out, Uncle Nicky," Maria pleads.

"No! This is beyond madness."

"If you put a contract out on me, I am sure Warren will come after me. And when he does, I'll nail his ass." Maria tries to explain her plan rationally, "My father said he would not come out of hiding while he was alive. Now, he's dead. Warren won't want to pass up on an opportunity to finish me off too."

Nicky runs his hands through his hair, rubs his eyes, and stares at her. He can see she is completely calm and very serious. "Is that why you shot your father? For this insane plan of yours?"

"No, Uncle Nicky, it really was an accident," Maria starts to cry. The first time since Morris' death. "I don't know, he went for my gun. He must have thought I was going for it. That I was going to kill him. But now that he is dead, I just want to get this over with. As quick as possible. I have another plan in the works, but it never hurts to have a backup. Isn't that what you taught me?"

"Yeah, but not one this insane," Nicky isn't convinced she knows what she's asking him to do. "If I put a hit out on you, anybody and everybody will be gunning for you."

"I know, and I am willing to take that risk. But one of the hitmen will be sent by Sgt. Warren, and he will lead me right to him."

"You hope." Nicky sees she won't take no for an answer. He pours another drink for himself.

Maria turns up her glass, gets her shot, and seals the deal. "Man, it is late. Well, at least I don't have to deal with my so-called Grandma tonight. Warren was probably waiting for something like this to happen to get someone next to me."

"Wait," Nicky laughs, "you don't know she's your grandma?"

"My father told me his parents were dead."

"That asshole! He sent his mother away to protect her when we were at war with the Banoas. You know, I never asked him what he had her doing after all that settled down. I assumed he put her up in a nice villa somewhere, and youse guys had Thanksgiving dinners, and Christmases, and all of that stuff. What an asshole."

"Are you sure? You know she really is my grandmother?" Maria's eyes become misty again.

"Of course I am," Nicky feels himself getting emotional too. Then he shakes it off, "I sat at her kitchen table as close as I am to you. Ask her to make you lasagna, she got the recipe from my mother. I'm going home. You go to her, youse have a lot of catching up to do."

MARIA ARRIVES at The Dorian at 1:42 AM. She greets Derrick, the night doorman, and Owen, the night concierge. The middle Valkyries slide silently open, and she steps in. She presses the white number 81 image on the black glass display panel, and in a few minutes, steps out into the blue lit control room of the BSA. The monitors around the room display the vast worldwide holdings that fall under the Bright Skies Agency's domain. Some are monitoring computer traffic, others display people in their offices, while others show ominous tactical readouts from the Black Strike Army, the other BSA under the umbrella.

Maria points to the heads-up display labeled Alpha One, "what's going on there?"

"Mr. Mills has initiated a surveillance and snatch operation on a banker in Venezuela. You may have seen him; he lives down on the fourteenth floor when he is in the United States."

"Are they about to make the grab?"

"No, Ms. Johnson. Just setting up the bird's nest. We have

two more teams scouting other targets. Do you want to see?" The young man looks eager to show off his knowledge of the equipment.

Maria hates to dash his enthusiasm; she nods. A few keystrokes on his computer and the screen switches to another house. It is an infrared picture, but it is late, and the multiple red figures are motionless and horizontal.

"That's good enough for tonight. Okay, have the reports on my desk in the morning. I want good pictures, high resolutions. You get me?"

He nods vigorously.

She feels better and heads to a back stairwell. The door only opens for a select few. She leaves the perpetual night of the control room for the actual night of her bedroom three floors above.

She stops in the kitchen for a light snack. She doesn't bother turning on the lights, just reaches in the fridge and pulls out a bowl of strawberries. As she turns around, she hears,

"A late eater, I see. May I join you?"

"Yes, of course, I hope I didn't wake you."

Christina notices the softness in her voice. The gruffness of the bar is gone. Maybe she needed time to think, or maybe she had been tired. "I was on the couch over there. I took the bedroom with empty closets, I thought it would be alright for me to use. I wasn't planning on sleeping on the couch tonight, just force of habit, then you showed up."

"Sorry about that," Maria's facial expression is softer too, "a million and one things to do. When did you get here? Do you like strawberries?"

"How do you know those are still edible? Obviously, no one lives here on a daily basis. I debated if the offer was genuine for a couple of days, before taking you up on it."

Maria laughs, "Oh, they are fresh. When anyone plans to be in town, we call ahead and have the fridge stocked. There is a good amount of food in the deep freezer that will keep, too. After we are done, I'll show you to Morris' room. Don't worry about ghosts, I don't think he's ever been here." She slides the bowl across the counter. "So, what do I call you? Grandma or Granny?"

"Don't you dare!" Christina mocks offense. "You can call me Grandma if you like, or just Christina. I see you don't mind calling your father and mother by their names. What brought you around? If you don't mind me asking."

"Nicky," Maria answers bluntly, "I think he wants you to bake him a lasagna."

7

A RAY OF SUNSHINE

M aria is up early the next morning. Christina had already made breakfast. The smell of bacon is what got her out of bed. The sunrise over Manhattan is glorious. No matter what kind of night she's had, seeing the city's skyscape bedazzled in gold and silver reflections cheers her up. It's what she loves about New York. There is no place like it on Earth. She picks up a single piece and munches down on it. "I hope you didn't go through this trouble for me. I don't eat big in the mornings."

"No real trouble," Christina says, "I made something for myself, I just made extra in case you wanted some."

Christina is wearing the same blouse and pants from yesterday. Her black hair is done up in a tight bun on the back of her head. Around the edges loose stragglers are trying to break free.

Maria looks her over and says, "Hey, didn't you bring any clothes with you?"

"I wasn't sure if I was staying the night. But the nice man at the front desk tells me you expect me to move in here. Is that still the case?"

Maria picks up another piece of the crispy bacon. "I thought we settled the question of who you are last night. Christina, you are welcome to stay for as long as you like. Unfortunately, you won't have much company. Gisella and Yana already left for the island. And Nicky has taken Elizabeth to his family's farm."

Christina smiles, "Ok. I guess it's just you and me then. I was hoping it would be, I really didn't feel comfortable dropping into the whole menagerie. Oh, I'm sorry, that came out all wrong."

"No, you are right on. Morris did live in a kinda zoo environment," she laughs. "Guess you know more about me than I know about you. We will have some time to get to know each other better. But I am sure I'm going to have to take off soon. I got to get things in order."

"No worries, that will be fine. I will get the nice man…"

"Victor."

"Yes, Victor, to have my bags brought over from the Excelsior."

"Ooh, the Excelsior," Maria puts on an air, "fancy schmancy. You might fit right into our little zoo."

Christina finishes her breakfast and moves back to the lounge. She runs her hand around one of the five marble pillars that rise from the floor to the ceiling. She admires the Doric column style and the life-sized statues along the walls. "I recognize the early Greek column style and a couple of the gods in here, Zeus, Athena, Hermes, but not those guys on that wall. I didn't know my son was so into Greek mythology and culture. But I guess living in the Greek isles for so long he was missing it."

"I don't know if that had anything to do with the décor in here. The columns are needed to support the helicopter landing pad on the roof. I guess if he had to put four-foot columns in the middle of the place, he might as well make it look nice. Like I said last night, I don't think he's ever been in here." Maria eats the rest of the breakfast on the platter, eggs and pancakes, and brings a glass of orange juice to the couch facing the window. "Morris built or purchased a lot of places he never stayed in. His way of hiding in plain sight. He would let people think he was in New York or LA or Fiji, but he rarely left the island."

Christina sits next to the young woman and studies her face. Her dark golden complexion and natural black curls give her goosebumps. Realizing she is staring she quickly says, "How do you make people think you are somewhere when you are not?"

"Body doubles," Maria blurts out. "What are you looking for? This is the second time I notice you staring at me. Are you trying to see if I am really your son's daughter?"

"Oh, no, that's not it at all. I'm amazed at how much you look like her." Christina thinks for a few moments, deciding whether she should bring up the subject. "Do you know who Maria Marino is… was?"

"Oh, her." Maria pouts and huffs.

Christina feels bad for mentioning the name. "I'm sorry, this is probably a difficult topic for you. I am sure it must have caused some trouble in your life."

"You have no idea," Maria laughs heartily. "I believe she drove Elizabeth crazy. I also think Morris never really buried her and that is why he never could truly love Elizabeth. Or any of the women. And probably why he loved me too much." Her facial expression changes instantly with the last sentence, as if a curtain dropped in her head, cutting off her emotions. She goes into a blank stare, but a second later she is back. A big smile crosses her lips. Not a joyful smile, but one that takes pleasure in pain. "It almost floored me when Uncle Nicky said the thing at the gravesite. I thought Elizabeth was going to keel over into the grave. That was hilarious."

"That's awful," Christina is shocked. The funeral was a dreadful affair by any account. She had been to a few where families broke down in hysterics, and some that were so stoic to the extent of being uncaring, but Morris' was like everyone stood on a glacial cliff. One word too many and they would all crash into the icy sea. "That's a pretty mean thing to say."

"We are being honest here, right?" Maria doesn't wait for a reply. "My MOTHER… she never wanted me. I was a mistake. No, worse than that, I was a crime. My Father, dear old dad, raped her. And nine months later, the family's disgrace was born."

"That can't be true," Christina's rebuttal is calm, "my son…"

"YOUR SON WHAT? He's a good boy? Would never hurt a fly? Morris raped my mother and killed my grandfather that very same night." Maria stares at her with those icy-blue, unblinking eyes. "I may have only been a baby, but my grandmother told me that every single day of my life. And told Elizabeth too. Right up until the day she died. It was her mantra. And I am certain he killed my grandmother and her brother too. The story is he got me to kill them. HE TURNED A THREE-YEAR-OLD INTO A MURDERER. I was nothing more than an instrument of death to him. Your son, my father, was a monster, but he loved me…" cynicism drips from her lips, "because I reminded him of his dead girlfriend."

"I know my son was a killer, and he killed a lot of people before he ever met your mother, but he was not a rapist. I don't know how he felt about your mother, I guess he loved her as much as he could. He did love Maria, that I do know. And if he did become a monster, something more than the killer he already was, it was her murder that pushed him over the edge." Christina wipes the tears away. The memories of those days coming flooding back as vivid as ever. "I knew your mother; she was a sweet girl. Elizabeth didn't have anything to do with Maria's death, but she carried the guilt as if she did. Sometimes people blame themselves for things that were out of their control, or other people blame them and then do horrible things to make them pay. They unwittingly pass that guilt on to the next genera-tion. And while we are being honest, why don't you tell ME HOW MY SON DIED!"

Maria hears the gunshots go off in her head. Should she tell her the truth? The fact that she killed Morris; not by accident, not out of anger, but as part of her plan to get revenge on the person who killed the one person she loved? It was by his own admission that he needed to die. Like he was asking her to kill him so she could get the revenge she desperately needed. It was her only chance at happiness. Her chin sinks down to her chest and she stares at the floor. She studies the red veins of blood in the white marble. For the first time noticing how they flow from her feet out into the city.

She turns to face her grandmother. "We were in his office. I went in there before going to the gun range in the dungeons. I just wanted to tell him I planned to leave that day. I had business to attend to. He didn't want me to go. We argued. I am a grown woman; I can make my own decisions." Maria looks for understanding in her grandmother's face. She finds none. "I guess I interrupted him when he was cleaning his gun. The magazine was on the desk, but he hadn't ejected the bullet from the chamber. Morris always told me when I loaded a pistol, 'rack one in the track, you may not have time later.' He was mad. I saw him turn the gun towards himself. He shoved the pipe cleaner into the barrel hard. Then the blast." She cries.

Christina does not. She waits for Maria to wipe her eyes and compose herself. Christina's eyes narrow, looking through the young woman next to her.

Maria's skin tightens, as if a sudden frost overtook the room.

In a harsh and disapproving tone, Christina utters, "you're telling me, he shot himself?"

"He didn't mean to. It was an accident and it was my fault. I distracted him, made him angry. It is all my fault Morris is dead." Maria puts her face in her hands and starts crying again. This time real tears.

Christina never had the chance to see her son's body. She demanded but everyone told her it was not worth the trauma she would suffer, 'better to remember him as he was.' She does not know this woman. She doesn't know what she is capable of, or how genuine her reactions are. However, she recognizes something familiar in the moment, she had seen it many times in her son, when he lied. Christina does not know if Maria is lying to her or herself, if she can't face the truth or doesn't want her to know what really happened. She knows this is the closest to the truth she will ever get. She decides to leave it at that.

THE PHONE RINGS once and Maria picks it up, "Yes. Bring them up." She turns to Christina, the two of them had spent the rest of the morning reflecting on better times, "that was Victor. Your bags are here. He's sending them up with one of the boys."

The private elevator opens and the boy who exits is a thirty-year-old man. He wheels a large luggage cart with seven, full-size suitcases on it. "Where should I take them, Miss Johnson?"

"Leave them by the door, we will take care of them later." After the luggage is arranged neatly in the atrium and the man descends in the elevator, Maria says with a smile, "I'm glad to see you travel light."

"It has been some time since I lived in New York. I am planning to stay a while. At least until it gets cold, I do not miss the winters." Christina pulls one of the bags into the lounge. She lays it down and fishes two small keys from out of her bosom.

"Do you really think that is a safe place for them?" Maria laughs. "Besides, they could just pry the lock open if they wanted to steal your jewelry."

"I wouldn't advise that," Christina says. She turns the two steel lock bars up and inserts a key into each one. With a slight twist of her wrists they pop open. She smiles and opens the olive-green suitcase. The bag is neatly packed with twenties, fifties, and hundreds. "A little walking around cash."

"What would have happened if someone pried the lock open?" Maria is curious.

"If they did, or didn't turn the locks to the safe position before inserting the keys, I'd be out five hundred thousand dollars," Christina pauses for effect, "and the person would have no hands… Or head for that matter. The fella in Queens told me if I could afford to lose the money, I wouldn't have to worry about being robbed twice. At least not by the same person."

"There is more to you than I suspected." Maria is finding more to like about this woman than she anticipated, although, she never expected to find she had another grandmother. She only has faint memories of the other, and those haunted her nightmares for years before her vile visage faded with time. Christina's face has a permanent underlying smile, even when she is annoyed. The face one would expect a grandmother to have.

"I told you, I'm Morris' mother. Do you want to know where I got this money?"

"Morris gave it to you."

"Yeah. I guess that wouldn't be a big surprise," Christina likes her granddaughter. She knows Maria doesn't trust her, but she is also aware the world she grew up in wouldn't have encouraged much trust. It couldn't have been easy living surrounded by murderous men. The secrets she would have to keep. Never knowing when someone would come after her. Maria told her a small bit about being kidnapped, the pain showed up a minute or two into her story and she ended it abruptly. Christina isn't sure why she went into it, she knew nothing about it, it was never on the news. Maria ended it with Morris' dramatic rescue of her.

The morning is good, and they seem to have settled into a mutual respect for each other and Morris.

"Let me tell you why I carry around so much cash." Christina tells her all about her mission to put Morris' money to good use.

Her way of saving a little piece of her son's soul. She gives money to everything she thinks Morris may have harmed; addiction programs, women shelters, widows and orphans' funds, and through her charitable foundation things he probably never touched. She does spend some of the money on herself.

She has a home in Madrid, a chalet on the outskirts of Paris, and various beach houses around the world. Keeping up with Maria was a fulltime job. After a couple of years, she came to terms with her son's ill-gotten loot. And once he became a weapons manufacturer—not that she liked that side of his business any better, but it was legal—a telecommunication giant, and whatever else he was into, she felt less guilty.

"I kind of paid it forward in some instances. And some things were just a good cause."

"Uh, not to dampen your spirit and sense of generosity, but what you are doing could technically be called money laundering."

"No. I don't think so," counters Christina, "I'm not getting anything back for it. I think the real crime here would be tax evasion. But I am okay with that."

Both laugh.

"You know, I really like you, and I am sorry I didn't get to know you sooner, Grandma." As much as she is having fun with Christina, she has business to take care of. She wonders if her grandmother will be okay knowing how deep in the business she is, and how much deeper she is going. "It has been fun, but I have a board meeting to go to. I'll be back for dinner. No one should have to eat alone."

"Okay, that's fine. But I have one more thing I want to show you." Before Maria can respond, Christina pulls a photograph out of one of the open suitcases on the floor. "This is the only picture I have of Morris. He wasn't much of a picture-taking guy. Most guys aren't, but the girl there with him, is Maria." She watches as the young lady studies the photo then hands it back.

"I guess I can see the resemblance," Maria states. "My guess would be she was of mixed race; very pretty. I suppose Morris had a hard time losing her. She looks like a killer with black blood."

"Hmmm, maybe. I knew her mother briefly back then but never knew who her father was. Go to your board meeting, I'll be here when you get back. And I'll put away all this stuff."

"If you like, I can send someone to help you," Maria offers, "Morris never liked having servants or anyone like that around. But I can send a girl up to help you. At least someone to take his clothes out of the room. I'll have them sent to charity; they are brand new, never been worn."

"Okay, please do."

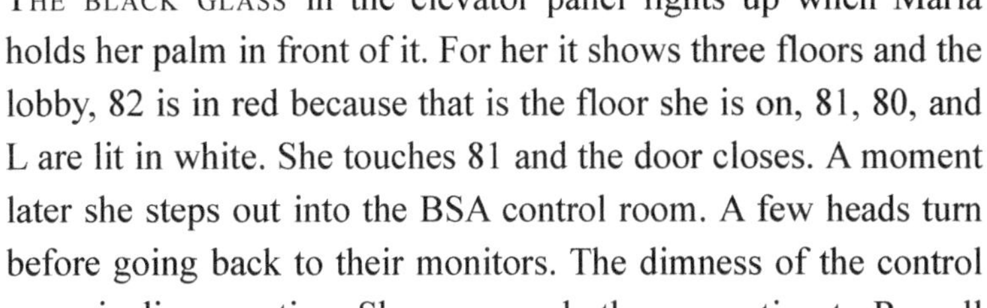

THE BLACK GLASS in the elevator panel lights up when Maria holds her palm in front of it. For her it shows three floors and the lobby, 82 is in red because that is the floor she is on, 81, 80, and L are lit in white. She touches 81 and the door closes. A moment later she steps out into the BSA control room. A few heads turn before going back to their monitors. The dimness of the control room is disconcerting. She once made the suggestion to Russell to change the lighting, but he informed her it was like that to avoid eye strain.

"The men and women working in here spend hours in front of monitors. It would be detrimental to their eyes if we brightened the place up. I worked in a fire control room when I was in the navy, you get used to it after a while."

But she never has.

When she reaches the sunny office in the back there are three folders waiting for her on the desk, and Russell. "And I hate that black glass in the window too. I can never tell who's in here waiting for me."

"My bad," Russell quips, "I'll wait outside from now on, but I actually just got here myself."

"Have you read the reports? Who do we have lined up?" She looks out of the clear side of the glass to the control. She spots a tall blonde woman at the far end of the room, who appears to be taking a coffee break. "One minute, I want to tell Karen to go to the apartment and help my grandmother clean out Morris' room."

"Wouldn't you want to do that yourself?"

"Why? It's not like he ever touched the stuff. He's never even been in the apartment."

Russell gives her a look of disbelief. "Of course, he was. Many times. Why do you think he had them put a helipad on the roof? So, he could fly in and out without anybody knowing it. And by anybody, I mean customs. Did you think he just came to the office when he was here?"

"Yeah, I thought he stayed out on Long Island or that place in Connecticut." Maria begins flipping through the pages of one report. She feels comfortable around Russell, he's another one of her uncles. "It's just that I never saw him in there. I thought he bought it for us 'girls.' You know, a place where we can get away from him. And he from us."

Russell mulls the thought over in his head. He was Morris' oldest friend, had run the streets together, and built this empire from the age of fourteen. If anyone knew Morris, and not many did, it had to be him. And as he recalled, Morris never did spend time in the apartment when 'his girls' were around. He was very protective of them and never let them out of his sight, but they were safe here; he could relax knowing there was an army below to thwart any attempts on their lives. He often left the office and took the helicopter out of the city. "I guess you're right. Maybe he did want to give you ladies a break."

Maria smiles, Russell is being diplomatic. She picks up the

phone and dials Karen's desk. She spins around in her chair and looks at the black glass.

"Yes, Ms. Delitanni."

"Karen, when you get a moment, I want you to go upstairs and help my grandmother pack up some things."

"Yes, Ma'am. Things are slow, I can go now," she replies cheerfully.

"Thanks. Oh, Karen, leave the sidearm. No need to upset Morris' mother." She hangs up the phone and turns back to Russell, "The banker from Venezuela, I don't recognize him. How much is he worth?"

"Five billion. I think it's listed there on the third page," Russell tells her. "He controls a large amount of the oil that flows in the country. You wanted a whale; he will make quite a splash. We also targeted a Colombian shipping magnate, and the Brazilian Foreign Minister. So, which one do you want to take?"

"Which one? All three, of course," Maria laughs and tosses him the folders. "If we are going to smoke the Sergeant out, we are going to need a forest fire. But I don't want to tip him off. We go with three different groups, at three different times. Nothing closer than… oh, a month of each other."

Maria flips through some other folders on her desk and scans the pages with lackluster interest. Earning reports, market shares of network shows, government acquisitions, and the latest R&D from the various science departments. Morris' empire is world-wide, had a hand in everything from agriculture to zoology. Some of the companies are fronts for his less than reputable businesses but most are legitimate. He had an honest interest in the world, not just a money-making mentality. She recalls him saying, "crime can make you rich. Investments will make you wealthy. But knowledge will make you invaluable."

"Do you think they know my father is dead?"

"Everybody knows your father is dead." Russell laments. "Don't let the low turnout at his funeral fool you. I didn't publicize where it was being held because those were his wishes. He only wanted his true family there. His death sent shockwaves throughout the world. Both the underworld and so-called respectable businessmen mourned his passing."

Maria gathers up the folders and prepares to go downstairs to the BSA headquarters, it is nearly time for her board meeting. This is the first one she will hold since Morris' death. All the CEOs of the companies have RSVPed that they are coming. And those who couldn't make the flight, are teleconferencing in. She figures these well-thought-of people, men and women, are coming with their knives sharpened. For the last three years she has handled these people with an iron fist, today will be no different. She smiles wickedly at the thought of wearing the Ball Buster to the meeting.

"What's so funny?" Russell is still in his mournful state. "These businessmen are nothing but crooks in nicer suits. You remember that."

"Don't you worry, I know. Hey, before I go into that den of thieves," a new thought flashes through her head, "what's going on with my boyfriend and our Armenian?"

"Oh, he's already on the ground with a strike force. We gave him the location and he high-tailed it over there," he reports. "The government is most anxious to find out where he got those missiles from. I thought you'd shoot me if I called Barry your boyfriend."

"And I still will, so don't slip up," she jokes. "Have the jet ready to go when I'm finished with these fools downstairs. I want to be there when they grab Gavril. I don't want the CIA to bury him in some black site before I can have a talk with him."

⌐ ᴎᴡ┌

MARIA STARTS down the back stairway to the public offices of the BSA. That's when it hits her, she promised to have dinner with Christina after the meeting. She stands on the steps debating, "meeting then flight, meeting then dinner, then flight." She finally decides, she isn't going to be like her father, it is going to be meeting, dinner, flight. She will just make it a short meeting. Tell everyone it's business as usual, shut the fuck up, and go home. That should work and show them who is in charge.

Now, she wishes she did bring the Ball Buster. Then she'd be sure there would be no backlash. She walks into the large conference room and drops the stack of folders down at the head of the table. The bright light is blinding from the western sun. *Don't any of these morons have sense enough to pull the shades down?* She goes to the control panel and lowers them halfway. The room of forty-two looks relieved.

There are men and women from around the world. Maria thinks it's like the United Nations in there. Everyone has a nicely carved wooden nameplate, complete with the company they head. They have their thin folders, with reports of extremely urgent business, to them, in front of their folded hands. Very democratic of her father, everyone knows who everyone is at the table and what they represent. Her nameplate just has Maria Delitanni. It is all that is needed.

They all wait respectfully for Maria to take her seat. This is only the third time she addresses the entire board of director. The first, three years ago when Morris announced she was taking over. And again, when she had to quell a coup in the form of a stock buyout. The second was designed to give some of the board members a controlling interest in their companies. Like she would ever fall for that.

The monitors on the wall opposite her come to life with another dozen faces. She remains standing, "can everyone hear me?" She asks those who are teleconferencing in. When everyone in the room and on tv affirm they can, she says, "Good. The company is doing fine. It is in good hands. Nothing has changed. Everyone go back to whatever it was you were doing and have a good day."

There is the start of a clamor in the room and from the monitors.

Maria says in a loud voice, "in case I wasn't clear. I said shut the fuck up and go the hell home. Meeting is adjourned." She stands, waiting.

The monitors go black on her command and reluctantly people pick up their folders and stuff them into their briefcases.

She watches like a schoolteacher as her pupils file out of the room. *Okay, now for a nice dinner.*

8

LIES AND SPIES

The onset of winter weather is abrupt and swift. It's mid-October and the temperatures have already nosedived into the thirties. Overnight, people went from short sleeves to short parkas. New Yorkers know that once that cold air sets in, it is there to stay. Not thin-skinned, but Maria finds herself packing for the Caribbean Islands. It gives her the perfect excuse to slip away for a while.

Christina is more than happy to accompany her. Although her original plans were to reacclimate herself to her hometown, the first cold windy morning and Maria's announcement at dinner that she is leaving for business changes all that. She packs two small bags, leaving her money case in the apartment's safe, and boards the helicopter.

It is a short flight to a private airfield on Long Island, then onto another small three-engine jet. Christina eyes the other passengers suspiciously, four large brawny men, very clean cut. Two are African Americans, one is African, and the last one she can't place his accent. She guesses somewhere in the Eastern European countries. It is a little after midnight, but no one thinks it's a strange time to fly, except for her.

Over the years, she knew Morris moved abruptly around the world. One day they were in one house, the next, the place was vacated, and the family was across the globe. Her son lived a nomadic life for years before settling in the Mediterranean. She thought maybe he was trying to give Maria a stable upbringing.

"I'm sorry for the sudden change of plans," Maria says as she swivels her chair around to face Christina. They are sitting across the aisle at the back of the main compartment. The four men sit on the other side of the bar in front of them. "Things came up at that board meeting and, well… that's the business I'm in. It's drop everything and run to head off the next catastrophe. We will make a stop in the Caribbean where you can stay at the beach house, and I will come there as soon as possible."

"Where are you dropping me? In the Bahamas?" Christina asks with a bit of sarcasm.

"The Bahamas? No, that's for tourists," Maria's face twists as she tries to smile and ignore her grandmother's displeasure. "We have a plantation on the island of Nevis. It's lovely. Morris bought it a couple of years ago. He said Nevis will be the next hot spot in the Caribbean. He started building a hotel and resort on the other side of the island."

"I take it, that's not where you are going."

"No, I'm taking Karl and Fumu, we are going to Germany."

Christina raises an eyebrow; it's the word Germany that catches her attention. She won't mention it, but Morris would speed up the end of his sentences when he was lying. Like he couldn't get the lie out fast enough. She knows people never caught on, but a mother knows, and so does a grandmother. "So, who are the other two Americans? my bodyguards?"

"Oh, we left in such a hurry, I never introduced the boys; Diego and Palmer." Maria stands up but Christina puts a hand on her arm to stop her from getting their attention. "I guess you can get to know them on Nevis."

"That's not why I stopped you. I don't need bodyguards. I have been getting along on my own just fine."

Maria sits down, takes Christina's two hands, and leans in close, as if she's about to reveal an earthshattering secret. "But now you are in Morris' world. There is danger all around us, all the time. I used to hate all these guys shadowing my every move, but I found out the hard way, there is no escape."

Christina knows that even though Maria is holding back on what she really has planned, she is deadly earnest in what she is saying. It's obvious Morris immersed his daughter in the under-world. She is as much a part of his criminal life as his friend Nicky Rocci. She wonders if she should have stayed out of it. Then she gets her answer.

"You should have stayed in the shadows," Maria confirms as if reading her mind. "But once you stepped out into the light, there's no going back. No more hiding. And trust me, there is safety in numbers. Even when it is only two." Maria watches as the full realization of who she is sinks in. She does not want to overwhelm Christina, but for her own safety she must know what possibilities await her. Morris hid her because she could be a weapon used against him. She now has become a risk to Maria and herself.

Christina's face goes from bewilderment to shock and finally settles on horror. This sweet young woman with an angel's smile is a heartless killer. Had to be to keep up with the company she travels in. The four men on the plane have the same disarming demeanor. People one wouldn't look at twice. But if you watch them longer, you notice the precision movements, their hyper awareness, and sharp reflexes. She had seen men and women like these around Morris, Maria, and his women for years. She was just never close enough to look them in the eyes. But now that she has, she is disheartened to see the same look in her granddaughter. *Morris, how could you do this to her?*

Maria again rescues her grandmother from herself. "You look tired. There is a bed through the door there. Why don't you get a couple hours sleep?"

"I could use a little rest," Christina tries to put on a smile, "I'm not as young as I used to be."

"None of us are," Maria stands up and holds out a hand, "that is the sad fact of time."

THE PLANE LANDS on a private airfield and Diego and Palmer are properly introduced. Bags are loaded into a waiting jeep and the short predawn drive to the beach house is completed. A full staff of people wait on the porch of the four-story colonial house. When Christina heard beach house she thought of a small cozy hamlet. When she heard plantation, she imagined a sprawling mansion surrounded by fields, and that is what she got. Several small one-story stone builds dot the property, two are large round structures off to the left of the main house, and there is a two-story cannon tower to the north facing the sea. The ocean is her front yard and sugarcane fields the back. Behind the ten-foot-tall sugar canes is the deep green mountain that dominates the island. The house sits on a small black hill, a semi-dormant volcanic dome overlooking the area.

Diego tells her as they drive up the coast road that Morris restored it to its original eighteenth-century design, not its function. He says Morris had a thing for taking what was once a bad piece of history and making it a good part of the future. At some point he was planning on turning the place into a museum.

Christina likes the idea.

The head of the house, Mr. Saven, shows her to her bedroom by way of the natural hot spring, the spa room. "You are really going to enjoy that. They built this house here because of the fresh hot water that rises up through the vents. Sea water goes in under the island, fresh hot water comes out," he says in a delightful English accent.

She makes a note of where the room is before collapsing on the large fluffy bed.

CHRISTINA AWAKENS to breakfast in bed just before noon. Afterwards, she wanders around the house taking in all the amenities, bars in several rooms, movie theatre in another, a couple of spas smaller than the one she saw that morning. She doesn't see anyone working in the house, not even Mr. Saven, until she sees Diego watching television in a sitting room.

He is a big guy, easily two hundred and fifty pounds tucked neatly in a silk suit. He is young, his jet-black curly hair cut short, and a close shave doesn't add any years to his appearance. When she enters the room, he quickly stands up and closes his jacket to conceal the nine-millimeter Glock in his shoulder holster.

"Please, don't get up for me," she tells him. "You can be comfortable, and I have seen guns before." She looks him over closely and finally asks, "where are you from? I've been all over the world and can't place your looks."

"I'm a mixture of an Egyptian father and Colombian mother. Not a usual combination, so I get a lot of inquisitive looks," he admits, trying to put her at ease. He motions her to take a seat next to him. "Can I make you a drink?"

"It is a little early," she replies, sits down, and crosses her legs, "I'll take a white wine." As he goes behind the bar, she checks out the television show. It is playing The Simpsons. "I didn't picture you as a cartoon man."

He looks up quickly, "I love Homer. He means wells, he's

just so stupid. The funny thing is, I can't tell if he knows how dumb he is, or if he thinks he is smart." He returns and hands her the glass. "You won't see much of the staff. If you need something, there is an intercom in every room, either on the wall or like this one here on the table." He points out the small silver speaker box with two buttons on top. "Push the black one on the right to call the household staff. When they answer, just speak naturally. Only push the white button if there is an emergency. Palmer and I will respond, in person, immediately."

"What emergencies can there be on an island like this?"

Diego turns to her, "I was told by Maria to give you all the information you want. Answer any question about the business you may have." He senses the question that is gnawing at her insides. The question he hopes she won't ask. "But the most important piece of information I can give you is this, your son's major business is weapons development. He manufactures guidance systems and software for missiles and guns."

"Guns?" She doesn't understand the relationship, "What kind of guidance do you need for a gun?"

"Oh, not like a pistol or rifle, I'm talking about armaments on a battleship or aircraft." He clarifies then tries to justify his concerns for her safety, "it is a very dangerous business. You can imagine the number of foreign governments that would want to take advantage of anyone they can. And not just foreign agents either, this is a multi-billion-dollar industry, that kind of money invites all kind of unsavory people."

"Ok, got it," Christina assures him, "white button for emergencies only. Anything else I should know?"

Diego thinks for a minute. "The other buildings on the estate have not been fully renovated yet, so stick to the main house. From the outside they look perfectly fine, that is the thing with these old, gray stones, they hold together well, but the wood inside gets eaten away by the weather and bugs. The main house was well-cared-for, but the other quarters were cared for as much as the people who were forced to live in them." His smile is warm and charming. "We know everyone on this island, so any newcomers will be watched closely. I ordered extra security to the island. You won't see them, but they will be around as backup. My only job is your safety."

"I thank you," Christina says humbly. "I'll try not to be any trouble."

"Oh, no, Ma'am," Diego comforts her, "I have been the personal bodyguard for Yana, and then your granddaughter for years. Morris wouldn't have trusted your life to anyone else but Palmer and me, I am sure Maria knows that. Palmer… well, he's a more solitude type of guy, you won't see much of him, but rest assured he is there protecting you. You live your life as normal. We will take care of everything else."

"Diego," Christina smiles weakly after what she has heard, "my life hasn't been normal for years." She does remember seeing Diego with the family in the past, but now that he mentioned it, she can't recall seeing Palmer around. A chill runs through her as she can only imagine what his job and talents must be. They both turn their attention to Homer Simpsons' antics on the screen. They laugh meekly.

MARIA ORDERS her pilot to immediately take the jet to its maximum altitude and speed. It's not the same plane she arrived on, this one is sleeker, longer, with two engines mounted to the rear of the spotless white fuselage. The powerful plane reaches supersonic speed and high altitude with ease. She wants to get to Armenia while it is still night. Barry Thomas had not only gone there without her or connected with her people, but he also moved in and grabbed the arms dealer, Gavril Avakian.

She revealed Gavril's location, but Barry was supposed to execute a joint operation. There are concerns the Russians are protecting Gavril. He is an asset for them, getting technologies they would otherwise not be able to get their hands on. She planned to take him on the street with the help of the CIA. They would face less resistance than an in-home assault would bring. The risk of his capture getting out was a problem to her but one she was willing to take it. She is not concerned if the Russians know he has been taken, as long as it does not get back to Warren. Maria is sure the Russians will bury the news. The plan they devised meant nothing now, she receives the report Barry made the grab without opposition. Without her. That is troublesome.

Fumu ends his call and turns to Maria, "We have the location of the black site. Our people are using ultrasonic technology to map the structure. We will have a team ready to go when we land in two hours."

She is clearly upset by the developments. She trusted Barry and now it seems he is working against her. But who is he working for, the Sergeant or the Russians? "Did you give instructions on what to do if they tried to move him?"

"I did. If they try to move him, use deadly force to acquire the target. But try not to kill Agent Thomas. Avakian will not get away from us."

"I wouldn't mind it too much if Barry Thomas caught a bullet." Maria ponders how that would weigh on her position with the Agency.

She doesn't want to start a war with the US government as they finally have a good working situation, but this is going to upset five years of cooperation. After Washington, and the two congressmen, Morris left those in the government looking to execute him. He delivered the missile technology in the worse way imaginable, by striking Washington D.C. in the middle of the night. She remembers pushing the button that launched the rocket designed to kill Sergeant Warren. Senator Carter called it a treasonous act in his Arms Subcommittee's closed-door hearings. Too bad he didn't know Morris put a target on his back also. *Five years and we still cannot trust these bastards.*

"He's going to have a few hours of questioning before we get there. He may kill him after he gets what he wants."

"There is nothing we can do about that," Fumu admits.

Karl joins the two and they begin putting together a preliminary action plan. They will need the layout of the black site before they can finalize their strategy. "The location will have few guards, who will not want to draw too much attention. If it's not heavily fortified, we can take it down with less than a dozen men. However, there are a lot of places in Eastern Europe that are heavily fortified, we just won't know until we get there."

Maria says, "it has to be big, fast, and decisive. I know you are worried about drawing attention to us, but we cannot let Barry kill our only lead. We can deal with the local police if they get in our way." She paces up and down the aisle of the jet, willing it to go faster. She runs scenarios in her mind of Barry and Warren conspiring against her. She imagines getting to the site and finding Warren waiting to kill her. The more she thinks about it the more she wants to kill Barry. *I could kill him. Not like the CIA haven't lost agents in the field before. If he steps in front of a bullet, so be it. We don't need the CIA anyway.*

"We don't know if Avakian is connected to Warren," Fumu says, sensing the growing anger in Maria.

"Oh no?" Maria blasts, "Why do you think Barry moved on him without us? He knew why I wanted Avakian. This proves he is connected to Warren, and it proves Barry Thomas is too."

"Maria, it proves nothing," Fumu rationalizes, "Avakian could have been on the move. Barry may have been forced to make the grab early. Let's wait until we are on the ground and have a clear picture of what's going on."

"Ok, we wait until we are on the ground, then we go at them hard."

Maria recruited Fumu three years ago and he has learned

that when she's in this state there is no sense reasoning with her. The only person who could ever talk her down off the ledge is dead. He returns to the cockpit and radios more instructions to teams in Azerbaijan, Georgia, and Turkey. He also radios a freighter they have in the Black Sea, it has missile-launching capabilities. He wants to be ready if things go horrendously wrong. He does not want to start a war; however, he will do anything to keep Maria from being captured or killed. That includes starting a war between the United States and Russia. The collapse of the Soviet Union has left all of Europe walking on eggshells; one feels it's just moments away from all-out war.

Fumu is well aware of Maria's obsession on getting revenge for Akilina; he heard the stories dozens of times over the three years. It is also why she recruited him, as a hunter. He worked in the Nigeria's National Intelligence Agency, the country's CIA. Although, it was Maria who recruited him on one of the joint missions with the BSA as they interrupted a plot to kill his president, Morris convinced him to work for him. Maria had a feeling, deep in her soul that Sgt. Warren escaped execution, Morris had proof.

What had begun in South America was spreading to Africa. The US was pulling the strings of some upheavals on the continent, and it looked like Warren was dancing at the other end. Tactics were similar. The difference in Africa was that Warren seemed to have a free hand in how operations ran. And it was a little obvious his old crew went to great lengths to remove their tattoos.

Fumu told Morris, "Not surprising, you seem to be a man who will go to the ends of the earth to get revenge."

"Yeah, but I am not after his men, just him." Morris contemplated Fumu's view, he wasn't wrong. "Only Warren would be so driven to erase any traces to himself."

Fumu countered his argument, "I believe your daughter will

not stop there. I would cut off my arm rather than let either of you find me with that tattoo."

Fumu did not find proof that Warren was alive. They found a few of his men around the world, not one led to Warren. From his tactics, Fumu figured he was an intelligence operative, CIA, or darker, and would be hard to track down. After Washington, he would give no one a direct line to him. There would be at least three levels of separation, even from his oldest and most trusted operatives. Fumu felt that if he were dead, that would have been easy enough to ascertain. Since it wasn't, Warren had to be alive. The government, any government, doesn't give up an asset like Warren.

MARIA ENTERS THE COCKPIT, "How're we doing up here?"

"Good," replies the pilot, "I just switched the transponder to the Turkish Airline code and slowed down a bit."

"You slowed down? Don't slow down," yells Maria.

"Miss Delitanni," the pilot responds calmly, "we are already flying too high to be an airliner, continuing at our previous speed would be a dead giveaway. We might fool a few civil air traffic controllers. You realize there are dozens of newly freed air forces down there, with boys not much older than yourself, sitting on former Soviet air defense rocket launchers thinking tonight is the night I die. When I said, we don't want to be a dead giveaway, dead was the operating word. Don't worry, I will get us there in good time."

As the pilot is reassuring his passenger, miles away from him a young man sits staring at a radar screen watching the numbers float by, his finger on the button. The numbers don't add up. The altitude, the speed, the plane's call sign cannot be an airliner. It has to be something else, something clandestine, something nefarious. He is terrified. Should he push the button, alert everyone to what he's seeing? The only thing more terrifying than being wrong is being right.

What if he brings down the plane and it is an airliner? Merely a skilled pilot riding the jet stream trying to get to his destination a little early? If he pushes the button, a hundred people die. And if it is not a jet airliner, but another type of jet, and he brings it down maybe thousands of people die. If he lets it go on its way, maybe everyone onboard gets to their home safely, maybe it drops a bomb on someone's home and tomorrow is quite a day for everyone. One push of a button, a few minutes, five at the most, a rocket blasts off into the night and the world changes forever.

The numbers glide across his screen. They are not heading towards his home. On its course it will be a hundred miles from his hometown. His finger eases from the button. Sweat runs down his face and he wipes it with his gloved hand. He flips the switch down and disarms the missile's warhead. He leans back in his chair, in the three-ton armored mobile rocket launcher, with its four two-ton rocket at his back, hidden deep in the woods and calls out to his buddy in the driver's seat, "hey, turn on some rock and roll."

As music floods the truck, he reaches up and takes his girl-friend's picture which he stuck in the corner of the radar screen down. He kisses it and thinks of the things he will do when he gets back home in four months. He hopes the world can hold on for that long.

MARIA TINGLES WITH EXCITEMENT. Hands fidget with bottles in the bar. Her fingers stir the ice in her drink. The display map on the cabin wall shows the plane icon inching closer to their destination. She hasn't been this close to Warren since she started the hunt years ago. Back then she was alone, working in secret, afraid, convinced her father would not understand.

Now, she has a team, if not his blessing, and Gavril, the first solid lead since the Mardi Gras Man. She will not let him slip through her fingers.

9

DOWN THE RABBIT HOLE

Two years after joining the gang, Maria had her own chapter. They operated out of the North Bronx, close to Nicky's territory. The old bangers, who had been with the FS since its inception, were answering to her. Not because she was Morris' daughter, although no one forgot that fact, but because of her ability to create positive income for the gang.

Like her father, she was not afraid to use force to get what she wanted; territory, members, business partners. Like her Uncle Nicky, she used bribery and payouts to forge alliances with those more powerful than herself. She had multiple dealers working the cities, which she kept a couple of the more lucrative ones from the gang. That money and connections went straight to her. Cocaine, crack, and heroin trade was strong in New York and the Tri-state area. As was illegal guns and stolen goods. She learned dealing wasn't so much about the commodity as it was about the marketplace. No matter what you dealt in you must control the supply and distribution. It was a cutthroat business that she stayed on top of by using both the gang and her Mafia connection to put down any challenges.

She also handled herself well in a fight. She wasn't afraid to take an iron pipe to a rival's head in front of his boys. She was known to be armed at all times. And she was known to beat a person to death for the slightest infraction. It earned her the street name, Mother May I, as her would-be victims were often heard begging for their lives saying, "Mother, may I say I didn't mean to offend you." The Mother part came from her young gang-bangers who never used her name, referring to her as their mother.

Maria ran them as robbery gangs. Sending a dozen at a time into stores to do quick snatch and grabs. They would roam the subways during rush hour pickpocketing businessmen. Or they would take over a subway car and violently rob the passengers. They would pull the emergency brake and escape through the tunnels before the train reached the next station and the awaiting police.

If any of her boys got caught, they would rather die than rat on their brothers and mother. A year or two in the youth house, 'baby jail', as she called it, was a badge of honor to them. Those who graduated from baby jail went to running more sophisti-cated operations, warehouse break-ins, car-jackings, running dope houses and needle galleries. Those who proved themselves loyal, moved up, those who did not, were buried.

She employed a special tactic with the girls in her crew. She stripped them of their colors, freed them from a place of servi-tude. Unlike in other gangs, her girls moved about the city as an extension of herself. She instructed them on how to work their way into other gangs, and men of power orbits. In the male dominated world of crime, women were often overlooked and invisible. She taught them to use that to their advantage. To live in the fringes, exist in the in-between spaces where men were blind. They were her eyes and ears. And she taught them the value of information, how to use it, and when.

All these things she had learned from the best, her father, and her uncle. By the time she went to join the FS, she was years beyond any of her peers. The Flaming Stars was graduate school for her criminal education. Morris and Nicky knew she had to be street smart, she could only learn by being on the street and living on her feet. Two years and she was a boss. That's when Morris called her home.

———

"IT'S TIME, LITTLE GIRL."

I cringe at the sound of his voice and that name. I want to drop the receiver, hopefully it will sound as obnoxious to him as he sounds to me. Instead, I said, "time for what, Morris?"

"Well, time to come home. I enrolled you in a very good university in Rodez," Morris says. "Your mother would like to spend the summer with you before you go off. It is a very nice area in the southern countryside. I know how much you like France."

"You said Mother wants to spend time with me," Maria hisses, "how about you, Dad? Do you want to spend time with your Little Girl?" The last two words leave her mouth like bullets.

Morris lets the slight go without reaction in his voice, as this is the way he envisioned the conservation going anyway. "Teenagers." He waits a moment then continues, "I thought you didn't want me hanging around in New York. You said you wanted to prove yourself without any help or influence by my presence. So, I stayed away for the last two years, but I always had my eye on you. You graduated top of your class, straight A's, just like your dad, I might add. And running a top-notch crew. I am extremely proud of you."

I wonder what is really going on. In the last two years I had the customary calls on my birthday, Christmas, end of the school year. Now, all of a sudden, he wants me home so he can ship me off again. "If I'm doing such a good job, why pull me out? I can go to school right here. They have the finest colleges in New York. I know you can't come to the US, considering all that you've done the last time you were here…"

"Don't be silly, I come to the States quite often," he brags. "There is more to being a boss than cracking heads and paying your way out of trouble you can't bury. It is because you are doing so well that you need a change of scenery. You can only run the street for so long before the street runs you over."

Ah, there it is. He's afraid I'm becoming too powerful. He fears his gang will fall into my hands. Well, there is nothing he can do to stop me. I am not his Little Girl anymore. It's time he realizes I have my own plans.

Morris knows she's preparing a counter argument and decides to cut her off. "Why don't you talk to your Uncle Nicky? I know you run everything I tell you past him. See what he thinks about my idea."

"Nice try, Dad," I shoot down that suggestion like the trap I know it is, "you and Uncle Nicky agree on everything."

"Not everything. Just the things I am right about." Morris says lightly, "I just happen to be always right."

"If I leave now, I will lose all my influences that took me this long to build. I don't need a college education."

"You don't if you want to run a street gang…"

"I hear a but coming!"

Morris laughs. "Ok, here it comes. But if you want to run an empire then you need all the training you can get. And if you have any real influence over people, that sphere of influence and control will only spread as you do. But… that's a second one, don't take my word for it, go ask your Uncle Nicky. You will see I'm not trying to trick you. But I am right. Ok, that's the last one."

The phone line goes dead.

Not even a goodbye. Typical, I am just one of his underlings. Not his daughter. This call is an order carefully disguised as fatherly love. I'll go see Uncle Nicky, then I will do what I want to do.

━━━━

MARIA WALKS into the Sons of Italy around eight o'clock, hopefully before the Guidos and Goombahs get drunk, and she has to break an arm. She doesn't know why Uncle Nicky lets these wannabe gangsters hang out here. Half of them couldn't pull off a decent job if their lives depended on it. There are one or two regulars who make good stickup men or muscle to back him up if there was a hit on the bar, but most of them are wasting their time if they think they are going to become mafioso.

"Is he in the office?" I ask Rosalina.

"Where else would he be?" she says and puts up a hand, "but he's not alone. Have a seat, I am sure he will be done soon." She slides a drink to me.

Some greaseball nudges one of his friends off the stool next to me. Before he can start his bullshit, I pull my left sleeve up revealing the dagger I wear strapped to my arm. He wisely goes in search of another girl to hit on. Then the office door opens and a guy about as old as the greaseball comes out with a big smile on his face.

Rosalina shakes her heads and with a comical look nods for me to go in.

"Hey, Uncle Nicky," I greet him as I close the door.

"What brings you around this den of iniquities?"

"I'm sure Morris told you to be expecting me," I roll my eyes to show I'm not going to fall for the surprised look on his face. "He wants me to leave New York and go to school in France. And I know you are going to agree with him. You always do."

"That's not true. I only agree with him when I'm right. Can I help it if I am always right?" He laughs. "Sit. We talk. Man to man. Uh, woman…"

"Ok, here's the thing. I am just coming into my own here. My crew is pulling down serious money… Uh, is it ok to talk business here? I mean, you have a lot of wannabes out there. Don't want anybody talking about you and the gangs."

He laughs harder. "This place is a front for a front."

"What's that supposed to mean?"

"Well, the wannabes want to feel like they are close to the action, so they come here. The cops, and the feds, want to get something on me, so they try to bug the place. They will occasionally send in someone undercover. They will hear some BS from someone out there and they will be happy. But actually, nothing goes on here. It is all just a show. But me and you, we can talk freely here, this room is always clean."

"It's like I was saying, Morris wants to pull me from the streets just when I'm making my mark. He's afraid I'm going to replace him." I lean forward, "why else would he order me to leave my crew? Once I'm gone, they will fall back into the fold, and he will take control of them."

"Teenagers," Nicky says and shakes his head, "I hope I wasn't that paranoid when I was your age. Or so sure I knew everything. But I probably was just like you are now. First, you are making a name for yourself on the street and that's not good. I always taught you to stay out of the light."

"But—"

"But nothing!" Nicky cuts me down quickly and I can do nothing but listen. "People who make a name for themselves on the street either end up with a number on their back, or that name carved in stone in the graveyard. Is that what you want?" He is thumping his index finger on the desk in front of me. "If you think your crew will turn on you when you are not there, then they were never yours. And you are not the boss you think you are. Go to school! You know how we operate, the smart ones we send to school. We always can use another lawyer. The others, they get educated by the state. We also need good morticians, and you learn to cut up a body working in the kitchens. Like that fool who just left here… you know what I mean."

"I do." I look down at the desk, avoiding the condemning glare. Nicky can be hard to take when you get on his bad side. I can't tell him what I really want to do so I come up with the best excuse I can think of, "I don't want to be a lawyer."

"Then study something else. You are smart, like your father. I suggested he send you to business school. You can learn finance and how to be a real boss. You want to be a crook, the biggest crooks come out of the ivy league, not the South Bronx. Your father is one of the smartest people I know, and so are you. It's in your genes. Go to school for a couple of years, and when you come back, you'll run the city, not just the streets."

I know I can't win. But that doesn't matter, I already have a plan in mind. I will let Uncle Nicky and Morris think they won, but I fire one last shot before I give in, "My father is smart and successful, he never went to college, and neither did you. Both of you are at the top of the mountain as far as I can tell."

Nicky sighs, "Morris probably had a degree in chemistry before he finished high school. He could cook up explosives I never even heard of. I am sure he got degrees in engineering and physics along the way. He reads textbooks like other people read comics. As for me, I was born into this life. I was trained since day one. We have trained you too, but now it's time for you to take the next step. Go to school, give it a try, if you don't like it, you can always leave. The streets will always be here."

WE HAD a glorious Fourth of July celebration in New York. It was the best one in years, Uncle Nicky, Morris, my mothers, and the Russian Dolls were all on hand for the firework display. We lit up the Island, our fireworks could be seen from Manhattan, and it made the news the next day. It was meant to be a combination of welcoming Nicky back as the Godfather, a belated eighteenth birthday for me, and my farewell to New York. I arrived at the castle July 6th, early in the morning, and spent one more day with Morris going over what I should study at the Université de Rodez, and who I shall be.

"Naturally, I cannot just be myself."

"I did not pick a university in France because it is a good school," Morris explains, "I picked it because no one will have heard of you, or me. You will be safe there under an assumed name and with a couple of bodyguards."

"If you really want to keep me safe, don't send bodyguards to draw attention to me," I complain. "I took care of myself for three years in New York without your protection."

"Do you really believe you were on your own? you were surrounded by about a hundred people loyal to me and devoted to you. You will not have that kind of security in France. I just want to have someone close by…"

"Come on, Dad." I only call him that when I'm angry or being sarcastic. He always knows which one I mean. "Even without bodyguards or weapons, I can handle myself. You know that."

Morris nods his head. He's giving up, which I know means he isn't really giving in. He will send someone I don't know to watch over me. Which is perfect because I already have a body double to take my place. The bodyguard has never met me, so he or she will only have a picture to go by, and my double looks like my twin once she puts in her contact lens.

My mothers interrupt our debate with the announcement that we are going clothes shopping in Milan. Yana had made some comment on the plane ride back about washing the gang filth off of me. Yana and Gisella forced Elizabeth to join them because they didn't want to leave her alone with Morris—although she was as distant as ever—and had the jet warming on the runway. According to Yana, who was the go-to person concerning fashion and appearance, I could wear some things from New York. But to really standout, I needed the latest Italian fabrics and designs.

"Doesn't that defeat the purpose of me being incognito?" I question.

"On the contrary," Yana replies, handing me a glass of champagne as we take off, "you are the daughter of a Louisiana oil tycoon. You need to shine. How's your French?"

"Je peux parler un peu," I tell her. "After four years of high school I can say some phrases and hold a simple conversation."

"That's good enough," Gisella chimes in, "they won't question you too much if you take too long with your answers. And they will expect you to speak a bastardized dialect anyway." She drinks her champagne and slides in the lounge chair next to me. "After Milan, we go to Paris for a few things. I am so glad to get you out of New York. We fought with Morris every day to bring you back home. Even Elizabeth got on his case to bring you back when he returned from his business with Nicky. Isn't that right, Liz?"

As usual, she is sitting as far away from me as possible. She mutters and nods, not really giving an answer. I think she was happier while I was gone. Back in New York and on the plane, I look her over for signs of abuse. There is nothing physically showing, but the vacant look I saw all my life is present. Every now and then I catch a glimpse of her when she doesn't know I am around, and she seems full of life. She looks that way when it's just the three mothers, as I refer to them. Even at times when I catch her alone with Morris, she sparkles. I came to realize; it is me that reminds her of her great sin.

WE TRAVELED ACROSS EUROPE. A week turned into a month, and a month into a summer. It was the four of us and of course, Diego and the mysterious Mr. Palmer, who I only saw on the plane. The three mothers were shopaholics. We bought clothes, jewelry, furniture for my dorm room even though we had no idea what it looked like. They bought me a car to get around in, then a bike when I told them I didn't know how to drive. That was a bit of a lie, I drove getaway cars back in New York, but just a few times.

What we couldn't take with us on the plane they shipped to the castle or the university. They were trying to spoil me, like I was a kid again. I knew they were trying to rid me of the gangster I had become. I played along. It was fun. It made them happy, even Elizabeth cracked a smile or a joke a few times. Once school started this would all be over, and I would get down to business. I couldn't let them in on my plan, not because I didn't trust them—Yana would understand—but I didn't want to put her in the position of hiding what I planned from Morris.

Uncle Nicky once told me, "The only secret you can keep is the one you keep to yourself." Between him and Morris they held the secrets of the Sphinx.

I spent the first week of September at the castle. Packing was a chore as we had just got back and unpacked everything. It was then that I realized how unnecessary the trip had been. I couldn't possibly take all of it with me. Yana and Gisella arranged everything by seasons, starting with the fall which I would take with me.

I opted to take the winter things too, "It will make my traveling home less hectic in a few months."

"Thinking like a college kid already," Morris said, poking his head into my room. "Diego will be going with you…" then added quickly, "just to get you registered and settled in."

"I don't need—"

"Humor your old man," Morris insisted, "he will be there for less than a day. He'll carry your bags to your room and be gone before anyone knows who you are. You have your emergency phone?"

"Yes, of course," I sighed, like I ever went anywhere without it. "I won't ever use it."

"Well, you know it's not for you to order pizza. It's a private satellite network. It calls one number, and an emergency response team will be there in minutes. I have set them up in town. Don't worry, they will not be anywhere near the university or you as long as you don't call them. Outside of that, you are on your own."

TWO DAYS LATER, Diego was delivering my trunks—all eight of them—to my apartment in one of the residence halls on campus. It was a two-bedroom, two-floor flat in a building that housed four other apartments. My car was in the garage and the bike in the foyer. None of the other students, or perhaps professors, had arrived yet. I made sure I got to the school a week early so I could look for Morris' spies.

The next day, Ahnri Shepherd arrived at the apartment, to put my plan into action. I had Morris enroll me with the alias, Ahnri Shepherd, as it would be easier for her. No chance she wouldn't remember her own name. It was the American spelling of a French name she believed had been passed down from her Louisiana roots. I got her a secured line on our network so she could warn me if anything happened. It dialed one number, which went to an answering machine in the walls of an apartment in the Bronx. The machine was hard-wired to the building's electrical system.

"I will check the machine twice a day. If there isn't a message, then I know everything is good."

"What if something does happen," she asked, fearful of being caught, "like a surprised visit from your father."

"My father will not come here," I assured her, "although, he may send someone. Or my mothers may drop in. You tell them you are house-sitting, and I have gone with friends. I will be back in two days. No matter what day it is, I will get back here in two days."

"If they find out I am lying, they'll think I have done something to you. Your father will kill me!"

"Not before the two days have passed," I jokingly calmed her fears. "They probably won't arrive unannounced, so if they call here, you call me, and I'll be back. You just study, get good grades, and nobody will be the wiser." I didn't tell her about the tracking device in my back as I had a plan to block the signal. Morris would be concerned but he knows I know how to do it and have done it before. I had gone dark for months at a time.

The last thing I did was pack an extra set of textbooks. I had to learn everything they are supposed to be teaching me while I am gone. I was sure I would have a lot of time to read while I executed my plan. That night I boarded a plane for Atlanta under one of the dozens of aliases I have. I picked out a topless bar called Cat Tales near Fort Benning. That was where I'd get a job tending bar. That was where I started my search for Sgt. Warren.

THE MANAGER of Cat Tales is a weasel of a guy named Taylor. He looks like he spends eighteen hours a day in the club and out of the sun. He probably doesn't spend much time out in the night air either. Taylor speaks with a wheeze, a lisp, and a hacking cough every third sentence, that makes interviewing with him for a job an excoriating pleasure.

"How old are you? and don't lie. But I don't really care, just have to know if I need to hide you from the sheriff when he makes his rounds." He coughs without covering his mouth.

I slide back a few inches from the desk. "Eighteen."

"Hey, don't get all squeamish in here, I can guarantee you will get a lot more than a little spit on you. OK, take it off."

"What! No, I'm here for the bartender's job."

"Take a look out there, girly," Taylor points to the one-way window behind me. "Do you see any of the girls, bartenders or not, with their tops on? These guys ain't interested in your sparkling conversation, they don't care what sport is on the TV, and they do not give a damn for the cheap-ass overpriced piss water beer we serve. They are here to see some tits. So, let's see yours."

Angrily, I pull my sweater over my head, then my bra straps down my arms, "will these do?"

"Now, was that so hard?" he grins triumphantly. "I'm not interested in how you look as long as you don't have some disgusting scar or deformity that will freak out the customers. You start tomorrow, twelve to four behind the bar. I will give you a week or two, college girl. If you work out, I'll give you more hours. And if the guys take a liking to you, I'll let you work the poles sometimes. The girls will teach you what you need to know." He goes back to looking past me out the window.

I put my top back on and start to leave the office.

As I open the door, he says, "Hey, this is a business. Act like you like it, or you won't make a dime out there. You need to leave who you are at the door and become a completely different person when you are in here."

Two weeks is all I need. I know how these places operate, any girl who is in one for more than a couple of weeks will find herself on her knees in the alley or bent over a table somewhere, either by force or drugged. I know better than that, I just need a couple of days to see if anyone comes in with the tattoo. Warren's men look like ex-military, so I figure I'll work my way around a couple of these places.

Behind the bar is a good place to operate from and I have a couple of my girls already working other clubs across the South. I made sure we stayed out of Mob bars, didn't want Uncle Nicky finding out what I was doing. I taught the girls how to conduct an interrogation, so they won't give themselves away.

Find a guy with a couple of tattoos and start a conversation. Compliment him, such as, "I like the colors on that one," or, "That looks so real. Can you make it move?" Then I let them talk for a while before faking wanting to get one myself. "I was thinking of getting a small one, right here over my heart." I touch my breast to reel them in. "What do you think, maybe a bird or something?"

The guys will say, "Yeah, you could get a bluebird or a hummingbird."

"Hell, no! I want something badass. Like an eagle, fighting, bloody claws, or carrying a weapon. You know, a 'don't fuck with this bitch' tat. What do you think?"

"Yeah. Yeah. I know a guy," or, "hey, I've seen one like that, but on a guy," or, "I know where you can get that done."

Another couple of drinks and the guy gives me all the information I need without ever knowing what I'm looking for. If my girls find out anything, they call my dead drop number and leave the details on the answering machine. Two weeks and I'd be on my way to the next seedy bar. I worked my way across the South and then up the Midwest. Then I got lucky.

A message comes in a week before Thanksgiving. "Hey, I found a guy with your tattoo. Eagle clutching a sword, bloody talons, the works. It's on his left forearm, he keeps it covered but some drunk grabbed him and ripped his sleeve. He owns a bar in the French Quarter called Sweet Black Bourbon on Bourbon Street. I didn't ask him about the tat, but another guy I have been liquoring up said it was an army platoon insignia. I'm out of here before anybody catches on to me."

That is the break I was looking for. I'm there the next day. I don't do the usual, apply for a job, or try to get to know him, I don't have time for that because Ahnri calls and says Morris left a message for me to come home for the holidays. I debate, shall I have a team grab the guy and beat the information out of him? Shall I go home and come back in the New Year? I size him up for a couple of days; he is retired and broke, except for the bar he owns. He isn't going anywhere.

I STOP at the college first, to get a breakdown on my professors from Ahnri. The usual things my family will ask, like, who is tough or easygoing, which subjects I like, how are my grades. She has prepared a small booklet with pictures I can study before returning home. I tell her to go wherever she wants for the next few weeks and thank her for helping. She knows not to ask where I have been.

Diego shows up a day later to help me with my luggage. He has that look on his face, the one that says he wants to warn me of something but was told not to. I have seen it before and am sure Morris is up to something. I also know, I will find out soon enough.

It is shortly after dinner after my mothers, even Elizabeth, have sufficiently grilled me on school and the young men in my life. The latter, I have to fabricate, as most of the men are horny drunks at least twice my age. Not suitable for dinner conversation and none that I share anything with. Morris takes me into the bar, "I see you are wearing the necklace I gave you."

I clutch at the gold cross hanging from my neck. I forgot to take it off when I returned to France. "Yeah, well... I have become accustomed to it."

"I gave you that cross so you could block the signal from your tracking device from time to time. Not for you to go off the grids for months at a time." Morris is furious, even if his voice remains steady. "You may not have time to press the panic button on your phone, provided you still carry it. Your implant is the last link to being able to find you in an emergency."

"If I am in an emergency situation, the kind you fear," I bolster my words by holding up the cross, "this will be ripped from my neck, and you will instantly know where to find me."

"Yeah, but will we be able to get to you in time? That is the question."

"I thought you had a team, minutes away in Rodez."

"I do," Morris walks right up to my face, "but were you in Rodez? How would I know?" He walks past me and leaves the bar.

The next couple of days are filled with family stuff. It has been a long time since I spent the holidays with them. Thanksgiving dinner, decorating for Christmas, going shopping with the mothers to escape Morris' glare. I have forgotten how preceptive he is. He doesn't trust anybody and that makes it hard to fool him. I wonder if he knows where I've been. Should I tell him what my plan is? No, he'll put a stop to it, I am sure of that. He'll say it is too dangerous or, he'll handle it. Like Uncle Nicky, they always say, "If Warren is alive, we will find him and kill him."

It is the "if", that disturbs me. They have doubts whereas I have none. I know in my heart, deep down in my soul, he is still out there. He needs to pay for what he has done. I especially feel it around this time of year, and I know Yana feels it too. Akilina was her sister. If I need her to run interference for me, I'm sure she would. I will just have to see what turns up in New Orleans.

Before I left, I ordered several of my crew, both guys and girls, to stake out the bar. They are to work their way close to the Mardi Gras Man. During our conversations and dinner talks, all I can think of is getting back to New Orleans, and my target.

MARDI GRAS MAN pins me down with his left arm across my neck. He rips the chain and cross away, his eagle with its bloody claws reaching for my face. I feel my flesh tearing apart and the fire from his massiveness entering my body. Tears flood my eyes, but I hold them back. I see Warren standing there, laughing, enjoying my suffering, his words echoing in the darkness, "That's my little girl." I wake covered in sweat. The pain in my abdomen is as real as in my dream.

I cannot wait any longer. It is the witching hour, 3:00 AM, December 30th, and the devil is calling me to do his bidding. I take a car and drive to the docks then a motorboat to the nearby island where there is an international airport. I am in the air before daybreak.

The Sweet Black Bourbon is not like the other bars we had canvassed. It is a normal touristy nightclub. There are tables and chairs set up around a bandstand and a small dance floor off to the right of it. A couple of pool tables are farther towards the back of the bar, which runs the length of one wall with the plate glass window at its end by the door. The name of the place is emblazoned on the window in red letters with a whitish outline. Hanging on the wall over the bar, dead center, a wooden plaque carved the same as the tattoo I am seeking. It was what led Tracie to this place and the owner.

I arrive at ten, find a table near the door and start sipping the house specialty, Black Bourbon. The place is packed with New Year's Eve celebrators. Mardi Gras Man is working the bar alongside two of my crew, both hulky dudes experienced in breaking bones. Two girls are waitressing, and I have a bunch of people in the crowd. They will wait until the place empties before making a move.

Mardi Gras Man, all six-two and two-forty of him, pulls out a chair at my table and sits down. "Well, it's 1991 and you are back."

My mouth falls open.

He continues, "you were in here a couple of weeks ago. Hung around for three days then took off. I was wondering when you would be back. You are the young lady behind the Washington incident?"

"So, you do know who I am. Then I guess you know why I am here."

"Because of this," he pulls up his sleeve and displays the tattoo. His arms are well defined, his white hair and beard make him look old, but not his muscles. He is a big black linebacker of a man capable of taking on the guys in the bar. He notices five of them his size milling around. "The crowd is thinning out, how many of those who are left are with you?"

I look around, "most of them."

"Ok. Let me get rid of the rest." He stands up and shouts, "Happy New Years to one and all. This may be the place you are at, but it's not the place you want to be, there is more action down the street."

About a dozen people slowly, drunkenly, make their way out onto the street. Twenty people, mostly guys, remain. They spread out through the bar, two guys check the bathrooms for passed-out partiers and find none. Then they lock the doors and pull the shades.

I speak slow but loudly, "So, how do you know who I am, Mardi Gras Man?"

"My name is…"

"I don't need you to tell me your name," I cut him off, "I know it. How do you know me?"

"I didn't the first day, but when I looked in your eyes as you stared at the plaque, you had the look of unimaginable pain. I have seen it many times. The pain that was caused by this tattoo." He pulls down his sleeve and buttons it. "About six years ago, some colleagues, I guess you would call them that, came to warn me about what happened in Washington. They told me it was probably over and done, but in this business one can never be too sure."

"So, your friends warned you."

"Not friends, call it a professional courtesy. I used to work for them, but was retired long before whatever led to Washington ever took place."

"Yet they still warned you about Sgt. Warren and me. Why didn't you run when you saw me? Were you thinking you could finish the job?"

"What was the sense of running? if you found me here, you would keep looking until you found me again." He looks around the room at my crew. "I started noticing my new regulars the day after you left. If I ran, how would I convince you I have nothing to do with your... Sgt. Warren? You do know that's an alias, right? I worked for a guy called Captain Pike, he was big into science fiction. Took his name from a Star Trek show. My only chance is to meet you face to face and convince you I can't help you find the guy you are looking for."

"Can't or won't," I demand.

"Can't. You see, when they let you blow up those headquarters, they were burning Sgt. Warren. I don't know him, never worked with him, and all the information I have about this regiment has long since been changed. Headquarters, safehouses, teams and their members, passwords and networks, all that I had access to was swiped clean years ago."

"You know what I think?" I ask, "I think all that information is really hard to flush down a toilet. I think your friends may change names, but the places remain the same. I think you really don't know what you do know, but we are going to find out. If you want to live, you need to cooperate with us."

"No matter what, I'm not coming out of this alive," he whispers to me, "here's what I can tell you of my own free will. I was proud to wear this tattoo at first. I was doing bad things but for the good of my country and the world. Then I started to learn that my orders were as much for making some people rich as it was for keeping other people down. You will do what you want to do to me, but I still cannot help you."

"We will have to see, won't we? Felix, I think he is ready to begin."

"OK, MARDI," Felix says, "now that you are all tied down and strapped up to the lie detector we will begin. I have some truth serum here; we are going to start with the chemical interrogation just to loosen your tongue. Maria, you may want to leave, this is going to get ugly."

"Mardi is rolling his eyes at you, Felix. I am sure he had sodium pentothal before. And I have seen worse. I am staying for as long as it takes. Are you boys finished prepping the place?"

There are three video recorders set up and a microphone pinned to his shirt. One of the guys gives the thumbs up, "we are recording. The boys across the street hear everything loud and clear."

"Good." I look over at three others who have sprayed black paint on the windows and are finishing putting up steel-plated plywood on the door and windows. I had them bring in the rein-forcements in case Mardi is lying about no longer being a member of the elite military unit.

While I was away, my guys followed him home every night and he didn't seem to make any dead drops or receive secret messages. They tapped his home phone while he was at the bar and the phone in the bar after he closed. In the few weeks since I had been there, he didn't receive or make a single call from home. Only general business calls came into the bar. He lives alone and is alone in this world.

Felix injects Mardi's vein and removes the rubber hose. "We will give my special juice a minute or two to take effect. He may have had sodium pentothal before, probably sodium amytal too. But I kick it with a little psychotropics, Methylin and for good measures, LSD. Our friend will be talking out his ass in a few minutes."

Felix begins asking him questions immediately. He asks simple things, where did he live, what is his name, what day is it. After five minutes Mardi's speech starts to slur, and Felix asks more pointed questions. "What is the name of this military unit you belong to?"

"It's a secret. We don't have names."

"What is the name? What do you call yourselves?"

"Free eagles... First eagle squadron... Blood eagles reporting for duty, sir."

"Take your pick, but I like Blood Eagles," Felix says, "It has a nice ring."

The questioning goes on for hours. Mardi answers some with absolute clarity and others in gibberish. He slips in and out of time, speaking in Vietnamese, probably about things he did in Nam. Other times in Spanish, talking about Nicaragua. He speaks Russian and German too. I figure most of the foreign language stuff is of little use, but we will get it translated later.

He is untied from the chair and laid naked with a girl on the pool table. She whispers her questions, and he responds favorably to the stimulus.

As Felix puts it, "this is a true honeypot. Hopefully, some of these trips down memory lane will be of use." He mostly tries to get him to give us names, dates, and places. He asks, "who did you report to in 84?" or "where were you stationed?" and "when was your last mission with your eagle squad?" After fifteen hours he passes out and we all figure we can get some sleep.

Day two begins at sunup. Although no daylight is visible in the bar, we hook up flood lamps and shine them directly at Mardi from five feet away. The heat is intense, a proper beginning for physical interrogations. We turn loudspeakers to the door and play a tape of construction sounds. We hang signs outside the windows reading, "Under renovations, will reopen soon."

Headphones blast a combination of classical, rock, and disco music into his ears at jet engine levels. Mardi, tied to the chair with a board up his back and rope around his neck, is unable to turn his head or shield his eyes. Felix instructs one of his guys to alternate the sound from left to right as he takes turns hitting his kneecaps. Sometimes the strike is in sync with the music, other times not. The rubber baton has an iron core and tiny steel thorns. After a workout on his legs, Felix goes back to asking question about New York and Washington.

Mardi maintains he knows nothing of the operation. He says he doesn't know who ordered it, who was involved, or where they were headquartered. His left eardrum shatters and blood runs down his neck. Felix places one of the flood lamps inches from his right eye and he screams as it cooks in its socket.

Three hours go by, and I walk up to his reddened, burnt face, "You could still get out of here alive if you give up the people you know."

"You have moved to stage two torture," Mardi moans, "there is no hope now."

"Don't give up so easily."

"I'm saying there is no hope for you. You have gone down the rabbit hole. You are looking for someone you know you may never find, but you will not stop until you are dead."

"Oh, yeah, I have a game we can play, maybe two. Do you want to play little piggies or ten little Indians?" I pull out a bowie knife and hold it up to his good eye? I start singing, "This little piggy went to the market. This little piggy stayed home." I wait for a reaction. "Ok, then ten little Indians it is. Ten little Indians jumping on a bed. One falls off and ends up dead." I take the knife and chop off a finger. "Now, there are nine little Indians jumping on the bed. One falls off and ends up dead." Sherump.

After I chop off five fingers from his right hand, Felix cauterizes it with a small blow torch and bandages him up. He tells

Mardi, "Just tell us everything you know about this Sgt. Warren guy, and we can end this."

"I have been telling you all along, I don't know this Sgt. Warren. I've looked at the drawing and I don't recognize him." He sighs then lifts his head slowly, "If we were in the outfit at the same time, we were probably in different units. Our paths never crossed. In a black operation like the Blood Eagles, one unit did not know anything about another unit. Hell, I can't even tell you how many units there are. You can kill me fast, you can kill me slow, it doesn't matter. I can't tell you what I don't know."

"Ok. I tried to help you out here." Felix places his feet in a tub of ice water. He sparks a pair of jumper cable clips in front of him. "You know what comes next. Last chance."

Mardi Gras Man drops his head in resignation. The sound of electricity fills the room, and the weak sound of a painful scream. Then the cycle repeats itself.

Nighttime has come and the crew of a dozen men—mostly armed against an attack they realize isn't coming—and Maria are eating at the bar. Mardi is unconscious, his burnt and mutilated body loosely tied to the chair. He is too weak to stand or attempt an escape.

Felix speaks up, "we got everything we are going to get out of him. He is not being brave or heroic, he's been out of the game too long to be of any use."

"You're right," I say and smile, "this has been a couple of fun days though, right?" As I look around, a couple of the guys shrug and continue eating. "Ok, let me take one more crack at him then you can wrap it up here."

I walk over to Mardi and shake his head until he wakes up. "Hey, the boys are tired of playing games, so tell me something good."

Mardi's voice cracks, "You are in Wonderland now… and I wonder what kind of mark it's going to leave on you. I wear mine to remind myself of the pain and shame I have caused others through blind obedience to a so-called righteous cause. I wonder what your tattoo will come to represent."

"Ok, well, that's it I guess." I take his left arm and lay it on the table. He is too feeble to pull it away. I take the cleaver from the table and hold it up for him to see. "As a favor to you, for the hours of joy you have brought me, let me repay you by freeing you of your shame and guilt."

Then I chopped off his arm below the elbow and above the eagle perched on a sword with bloody talons. The arm lies motionless on the table. Mardi's head drops to his chest for the last time.

The guys sit staring at the sight.

I say to the air, "Ok, stop the recording now. I'll be over in a second to get a copy of all this."

Felix walks over, "we will clean up here and get rid of the body."

"No, don't do that. Leave everything as is and burn the place down. There are a couple of barrels of Black Bourbon in the cellar, it ought to burn really good, send a bright and vivid message," I inform him, "maybe when his guys sift through the ashes and find out what happened here, our friend will come out of hiding."

"What are you going to do now?"

"I am going back to school and going to go through the tapes. You guys return to New York and analyze them too. Follow up on any leads you find, look into any names and places he mentioned. Keep me informed."

10

PAYBACK IS A BITCH

This is a black ops mission and arriving at an airport will not be a secret, not in Armenia. Maria and her two men, one Russian and the other Nigerian, land in a field in the Armavir Province. The area is rocky and inhospitable to air traffic, the perfect place to put down unnoticed. Her team on the ground ran a tractor across the terrain and cleared a landing strip minutes before their arrival. Then they'll cover the plane with camouflage netting, to disguise it from the air but not from ground traffic. Maria knows they only have a couple of hours; she leaves the pilot with instructions to fly to Turkey if they aren't back in four. Or if the plane is spotted.

They take a two-car convoy into the city of Yerevan. Like any other capital city, it is bustling with activity and tourists even at this late hour. The first car pulls up to a disco and three of the four Armenians get out. They flash their badges at the door and walk in unquestioned. Pounding techno music, which sweeps the European cultures like a tidal wave and flashing multicolor strobe lights, obscure their entrance. They fan out and take positions near three doors, one just outside the men's bathroom, another by the far end of the main bar, and the last off to the right of the DJ's booth. They scan the crowd, looking for and spotting their counterparts.

Maria's driver goes two blocks past the club and turns left, down a narrow street. They stop in front of a café, jump out, and rush into the small shop.

Fumu Akombi jumps over the counter and tackles the barista before he can draw his gun or press the alarm. Karl's pistol whips another man sitting by the entrance. The driver quickly makes his way to the back room and draws his gun on the three men playing cards.

Maria follows the driver into the room. "Hands where I can see them," she orders. When they don't respond she says, "oh, come on, I know you guys speak English."

Karl has locked the door and is now in the room.

"You don't want to have happen to you what just happened to the other two agents out front, do you? Hands on your heads."

This time the three men comply. Maria's men take them and zip-tie their hands behind their backs. All five men are sitting on the floor in the back room of the shop.

The driver goes to the back, punches in a code on a keypad hidden in the wall, and a door slides open. He says, "there will be another iron door down the stairs at the other end of the tunnel. I do not know the access code to it. Also, there may be sensors or cameras in the tunnel, so be prepared for anything down there."

"I am always prepared. That is why I brought this." Maria pulls out a hand-sized bundle of plastic explosives. She jests, "do not worry, the guys down there are old friends. They will be happy to see me."

"How long should I wait?"

"Until we get back, of course!"

"Madame Johnson, this is a CIA black site," the driver says, "they will send a response team."

"Yes, but they should come from the club upstairs, and that's why your men are there. Have a coffee, this will all be over very quickly," she assures the nervous Armenian driver. Then she and the two men disappear down the dark stairwell.

It is a World War II tunnel. It has not been updated since the cold war. A dim yellow light every hundred feet illuminates small sections of the narrow passage. Black areas separate each section, a spot where a sentinel could be waiting. There is a dampness to the walls and small puddles on the floor. It is the type of place one would expect a black site to be.

They reach the iron door; it isn't much of a barrier. Maria places the package on the door below the lock carefully, keeping the magnetics from making a sound. The black cardboard box contains a shaped charge inside, a high-power V-shaped plastic explosive backed by a water bladder. They put on their goggles and earmuffs, then Maria attaches the leads to the detonator. They retreat about twenty feet, the length of the wires, she hopes no one is standing on the other side of the door. She turns the key.

Not knowing what type of barricade they would find at the site, they brought a heavy-duty door knocker. The force of the blast is directed forward and punches a hole in the door a foot in diameter. The water sprays back at them, and some gets sucked into the hole. The blast is strong enough to rattle the coffee mugs in the café a block away. Several of the lights in the tunnel blow out and half of it goes dark. Warning lights flash in the DJ booth above as the door twists and recoils back.

Maria slips past the old iron door hanging half off its hinges. The outer room of the secret cells is in darkness. Two bodies blown out of their seats lie on the floor. The inner door opens and two men with guns drawn emerge.

Maria sees Gavril Avakian tied to a chair in the other room. "Barry, how rude. You started this party without me. And here I thought we were going to be lovers."

FIVE AGENTS PUSH through the crowd to make their way to the doors in the club. The three Armenian police officers pull their badges from inside their shirts and let them hang from the chains around their necks. They also pull their nine-millimeter pistols from their holsters as they block the door. The fourth police officer is at the entrance to make sure no one leave the club.

The partiers keep on dancing, unknowing of the intrigue unfolding around them or beneath their feet. The music over-powers the sound of the explosion below. The rattle of glass and liquor bottles, is an unusual occurrence, but not a cause for alarm. Those who do notice the police presence sum it up to the usual drug raid. All part of a fun night in Yerevan.

The five agents realize whatever is going on in the interroga-tion room three floors below will take place without them. A shootout in the club is not a risk worth taking. The site's cover is already blown, but it's not them who are the target. Whoever is held down there, which they are not privy to, alerted more powerful people than the East European Agency's field office.

"WHAT THE HELL, MARIA?" Barry demands. "You kill two agents and breach a top-secret site. You could have been killed. What the fuck is the matter with you?"

"Doesn't look that way to me," Maria says, still pointing her pistol at his head. She takes a quick glance at the two agents on the floor. There isn't any blood, but they aren't breathing either. She surmises they died from blunt force trauma. The crushing of their internal organs, kind of injuries a person sustains in close proximity to an explosion. "Sorry about your men but I didn't have good intel on the security down here. I guess the door knocker was a little too strong."

Barry walks up to her and lowers her weapon. The other agent with him moves to check on his fallen friends. Barry nods to Fumu and Karl. He takes Maria by the arm to a corner of the outer room. "How did you even know about this place?"

"You're joking, right?" she asks. "We gave you the whereabouts of Avakian. Do you think we were going to let you walk away with him? Get your information and then he drops off the face of the earth? I thought you wanted to help me go ghost hunting."

"I was going to share everything we got out of him with you!" He breathes deep to regain control. "After this, it is going to be hard to convince my boss to cut you in on anything."

"You don't have to cut me in," Maria says playfully as she begins emptying her backpack, "I'll just get what I need myself and then you can do what you want with him." She looks inside the room. Gavril has been worked over and there is a medical kit open on the table. "So, you couldn't beat it out of him and now you are going to give him the soup. Rattle his brains and see what falls out?"

Barry is about to give the fifty-year-old arms dealer a shot of hallucinogen drugs. He is worried the beating was killing him. The soup, as it's known in the trade, is less brutal but not truly reliable. People tend to ramble about anything, one has to be skillful to question a person under the influence. Barry is very skillful.

"It may take a little longer, but I will get the information. We have plenty of time, or at least we did. Since my men haven't arrived, I'm guessing you burned this place."

"I wouldn't do that to you," Maria says innocently, "those are my men upstairs. But I guess you are right about not having a lot of time. Am I also right to assume the regional office is sending a team to secure the place?"

"That would be my guess."

"OK, I'm just gonna take a couple of minutes and ask him

one question." Maria holds up the iron rebar she took from Derreon and walks into the room.

Fumu sticks his pistol in Barry's chest as he tries to stop her.

GAVRIL LOOKS UP. His hands are chained through a ring welded to the table. Maria walks around behind him, cuts the strap around his chest holding him to the chair, then cuts the straps around his legs. He looks at the two-way mirror, the bottom half of the mirrored side has cracked and fallen but the thick, clear glass is still intact. He sees the two agents and two other men watching him.

"Well, I'm guessing this isn't a rescue attempt," Gavril says in clear English.

"A rescue attempt?" Maria asks. "Are you expecting someone to rescue you?"

"I have money. I have friends. I have business partners," Gavril says wryly, "I was hoping one of them would get me out. I didn't think anything as dramatic as this, you know, a friendly payment to the right people and I walk."

Maria rolls the rebar back and forth on the table in front of him. "You are never walking out of here. I promise you that."

"Little lady, the CIA trained you very poorly. You never start an interrogation threatening to kill the informant. Leaves you nowhere to go. Give your—"

"Hey, I'm not the CIA. And I didn't say I was going to kill you. I said you are never walking out of here." She picks up the rebar and slams the edge of the table then points it at his face. "You need to listen more carefully because I'm going to ask you one question and you need to answer truthfully. Am I clear?"

Gavril doesn't answer, he stares at her and tightens his body. Maria circles the table again and on the second time around kicks the chair out from under him. He slowly starts to stand when she swings the rebar and connects it with his right side. The blow sends him to his knees on the floor.

"You didn't answer my question," Maria states calmly, "so, that was a warning shot to your kidney, I think. But that's not the important one. Now, if you don't answer the next one, I aim for your spine." She looks in the broken mirror, where part of his face is reflected. *There is no fear showing, but there will be.* "Tell me where I can find your boss, Sgt. Warren."

"Who?"

Maria raises the bar and in a big arching swing strikes him from the ribcage to his hip on his left side. The sound of breaking bone follows. He grimaces to hold in the pain, his silence allowing him to stand in defiance.

"Your boss," she tells him. "I know you work for him. You see, you have a scar on your left forearm where you burned off the eagle tattoo. I know all about him and you. What I don't know is where to find him. So, where is he?"

"Oh, you are his daughter, aren't you? I hear your father died a particularly horrible death."

"He did, I killed him," Maria admits bluntly. "But that's not the answer to my question." She swiftly switches back to the right side and delivers another blow, harder and closer to the center of his back. This time he does yell and collapses back to his knees. "Let me tell you what happened to two of your brothers who burned their tattoos off. I threw the second one out a tenth-floor window. He landed on the one I threw from the fifth floor. He was still alive when the second guy hit him. By the way, the second guy begged me not to throw him out the window as we walked up the next five flights."

Maria watches him contort in agony and enjoys his discomfort. He will soon be begging for his life. She wishes she had more time, but the strike force will arrive way too quickly and she needs answers now. "How do I find your boss?"

She doesn't wait for an answer and makes a big looping

tennis swing across the middle of his lower back. His spine explodes. The men in the outer room hear it and the chilling scream that follows. Gavril is hanging by his arm, unable to stand. The pain causes him to blackout.

He regains consciousness when Maria pulls him onto the table by the collar of his bloody shirt. He lies across the table from the waist up, his legs limp and lifeless drooping to the floor. She is on the other side of the table, lying face to face with him. She looks at him with absolutely no emotion, no anger, no hate. She says quietly, "I told you, you are not walking out of here. In a minute, you won't be able to pull a trigger to shoot yourself. I know exactly where to hit your back. This is a thing my dear old dead daddy taught me, dying is not the worst punishment. Not being able to die, when you so desperately want to, that is hell. How do I find Sgt. Warren?"

Gavril can barely speak. She is wrong about not feeling his legs, they feel like they are on fire. He has both feet in hell and the flames are rising in his body. He knows she isn't going to kill him until he tells her what she wants to know. He whispers, "I buy bearer bonds and an English courier picks them up. That's how I pay my share. The courier firm is Dunn and Welsington. If you want any more information, ask your Russian friend."

MARIA COMES out of the interrogation room satisfied. Her men had packed away their goggles and other equipment in her backpack. She is about to leave when Barry asks,

"What did he say about the javelins?"

"You know, I forgot to ask him about them," she turns back to the room with the rebar still in hand. The four men watch as she walks around the table. Stands behind the beaten man still draped over the table and with all her might rams the rebar in his ass. She sidesteps to pull the iron bar from the dead man's rear end. She tosses the rebar on the table and exits the room.

"What the hell did you do that for?" Barry screams at her.

"I just remembered," Maria says, wiping the blood from her hand on a towel Karl holds out to her. "He got them from Morris. The whole Sudan mission was set up by him to bring Warren out of hiding. Dad figured a score that big would get his attention. He was right. Who knew?"

"So, now… what do I tell my boss?" Barry complains, looking at the mess in the other room.

"Tell them not to worry," Maria reassures him, "we won't be selling any more black-market missiles now that I am in charge. Now, I really have to run."

MARIA and her men pull away from the café moments before three black Volvo sedans arrive. They can see the strike team storm the building as they speed down the street. The other half of the team calmly gets in their police car and drives away without incident.

The sun is coming up when the car reaches the makeshift airport. They quickly get the jet in the air. Maria calls ahead to London, to begin surveillance of the courier service. They will have to break into the office to discover where the bearer bonds were delivered to. They have to move quickly before the trail goes cold. Once word gets out that Gavril Avakian is dead, everything he touched will be burned. Maria is sure that Barry will make Gavril's demise look like an accident. At best, she will have a week before he turns up in a fiery car crash.

She stares at Karl. Did Gavril out him as a spy within her ranks? And for that matter, why did Barry rush to grab Gavril? She doesn't buy the urgency of finding the source of the missiles. He wanted to get to Gavril before her, that was for sure.

MARIA LANDS AT HEATHROW AIRPORT, her plane quickly diverted to a secluded terminal. She is met by her team of BSA mercenaries, and surprisingly, Barry. He has his own team of six agents which equal her forces.

Barry greets her fondly, "hey, welcome to Merry Ol' England." He whispers in her ear, "do not let this thing turn messy."

"What are you here for? Going to try to take me in?" asks Maria loudly.

"Of course not," Barry is still smiling and speaking softly, "after what you did in Yerevan, my boss doesn't trust you. He thinks you are losing your grip and wants me to babysit you. Just between you and me, you are lucky he didn't put an order to terminate on your ass."

"I'm not so sure he didn't," Maria complains, "you are travelling heavy. But for what it's worth, I don't think your boss would do that. He needs me and my company."

"He needed Morris," Barry turns to his men and signals for them to get in their vehicles. "And you killed him. You have yet to prove yourself to the Company."

"I killed him?" Maria says with shock in her voice. "Where did you get that idea from?"

"Isn't that what you told Gavril?"

"I was just rattling his cage. Trying to get him to give up his boss. And it worked," Maria insists. She circles her hand in the air and her men climb into their cars. She looks at Barry innocently, "I loved my father. We fought now and again, but he was everything to me. You know how he died, he shot himself while cleaning his gun. It was my fault for distracting him with a stupid argument. I'll never forgive myself for what happened that day, as I learned later his plan was right on target. So, are you going to follow me to my headquarters?"

"No, I'm riding with you. Tell one of your guys to ride with my men," Barry orders.

"Wow, full babysitting duties," Maria laughs cynically, "that must be eating you up inside."

"I do whatever it takes to get the job done."

"Exactly what is your job now?"

"I think it is to keep you out of trouble," Barry mocks her. He recalls the conversation he had with the CIA Director on his flight to London.

The director was emphatic that she stays out of their way, and told him, 'Help her find Warren if that's what she's after. Do whatever it takes to find him or prove he's dead. You keep her busy but quiet.'

"We put a team on this Dunn and Welsington too… Don't look so shocked. Obviously, we recorded everything that went on in Armenia. Langley knows everything, and they also want to know if Warren is still alive. And if he is, who's he working for or with?"

THE FOUR CAR convoy heads across the River Thames and goes into a middle-class residential neighborhood. Only Maria and Barry get out, then the drivers and the other three cars continue. The two walk into the den and Maria greets her team of techs working around the room.

Carla Grant, a woman twice her age, reports, "we are in their systems and combing through the data now. We should have the courier who handled the package in the timeframe we are looking at within the hour. I am sorry for your loss, we all are."

"Thanks, Carla. Thanks everyone," Maria looks around sympathetically. She is always amazed at how many people loved and respected her father. From the looks she receives back his voice pops into her head, 'you want your friends to love you and your enemies to fear you. But it is most important that everyone respects you. If they respect you, your friends will never betray your trust, and those who fear you will never test your resolve.'

"Carla, will we know who he delivered the package to?" Maria asks.

"It will be on the order with a signature. More than likely it will be a fake, but it's a start. We will also look for any other orders that fit the pattern. I think you will still need direct contact with the courier to find out what he knows."

"My men will handle that," Barry interjects.

"OK, fine," Maria agrees grudgingly, "as long as I am in the loop this time."

CARLA PROVIDES A SOLID LEAD. Gavril, using the same alias six times in the past two years, sent packages to a brewery in London's East End District. The same courier took the envelope and the same man signed for it. Barry's and Maria's men make up two joint strike teams and grab both men at 4 a.m. from their respective homes.

The courier lives alone. He is young, fit, and an amateur boxer. It doesn't matter. The six-member team of professionals hit him with a stun gun while he is still in bed. They bind, blindfold, and gag him before putting his body in a duffle bag for removal.

The brewery supervisor's kidnapping is trickier. He has a wife and three kids. It's clear to the team they can't take him at home. They call his house and tell him the brewery is having a major problem with the water pumps; he needs to come in immediately. Once his car is out of sight of his residence, two cars box him in and attempt the grab. Because of The Troubles, Arnold, the brew master, suspects something isn't right and brings a revolver with him. Although the fighting is mainly contained to Northern Ireland, some prominent people are targeted in parts of London. Arnold doesn't think of himself as an important person, but a 4 a.m. call worries his wife enough for him to pack his gun. His job at the brewery isn't important enough to make him a target, but his other affairs do. He lies to his wife, "Go back to sleep. This is probably a busted pipe or something mundane I must sign off on. I am sure I will be back in an hour or so."

A shootout ensues and Arnold is taken alive but badly wounded. The gunfire awoke startled Londoners, and it is sure to make the morning news. Maria's men commandeer Arnold's car and him.

She is pissed. "I knew I shouldn't have agreed to work with you. Your men can't even pull a simple grab and go."

"Your men were involved too," Barry counters, "they didn't help matters by shooting the man."

"Three gunshots are better than a raging battle on the street," she defends their actions. "And my men wanted to take him in his home…"

"With his wife and kids."

She slams her fist on the table. "Yes. He wouldn't have put up a fight there."

"Oh, but his wife and kids would have known he was kidnapped. That would have been better?"

"What, you think they don't know now? We could have handled it much better with his family as leverage."

"The Company would not green light a family kidnapping and hostage-taking," argues Barry.

"Look, this isn't a good guy bad guy situation. And by the way, you boys haven't necessarily been the good guys all the time. Now, we have a guy upstairs who probably won't be able to give us any answers for at least a day. Maybe two. Warren will be in the wind by then."

"It's not that bad," Barry lies. "We got the messenger."

"The messenger," Maria yells, "what the fuck is he going to tell us? He only delivered the package. We need that asshole upstairs to tell us what he did with the bonds."

"Maybe he did deliver the package to him," Barry's mind is working like a spy, "and maybe he delivered another package to the brewery. And he delivered the bonds to someone else. My guys will get the information without butt-fucking the guy."

"They better get something, or it won't be his butt you need to worry about."

"Just for the record," Barry looks at her hard, "I have no intentions of cleaning my gun around you."

THE MESSENGER IS TIED to a chair with his feet in a bucket of ice water. He has wires attached to his head, a heart monitor on his chest, and a metal handcuff on his right wrist which has a car battery cable attached. The handle of the metal ice bucket is attached to the black battery cable.

One of the men administers a shot to his left arm and tells him, "that is a chemical like adrenalin, it is going to make you feel everything ten times worse. So, the electric shocks won't kill you, but you are going to wish it did." Then he turns the switch.

The messenger's body tenses, and he screams. The current is turned off and he relaxes.

The same man comes back. "See what I mean? Now, ordinarily, we would put a leather strap in your mouth to keep you from biting your tongue off. But we need you to tell us what is in the package you deliver for Mr. Asus. And who you deliver it to."

Duffy, the messenger, sweating profusely already, is thinking hard. He feels the motion, hears the noise, and knows he is on a train. His screams will go unheard. He has little choice but to cooperate, he wants to know if he gives them what they want will he be allowed to live. "I'll talk, but you will kill me. Or Mr. Asus will, once he finds out."

The man shakes his finger at Duffy and another man turns the switch that sends the electric current down the wires. Duffy bites deep into his tongue and blood spurts out, falling into the bucket. The power is cut off.

"I told you to be careful with the biting. You don't get to dictate the conditions of your testifying here. But you don't have to worry about Mr. Asus, his part in this affair is over. Now, tell us what we need to know."

"Yes, I will, just don't kill me," Duffy pleads, "I had nothing to do with anything. I took the envelope to the KRB... the King's Repository Bank. I give it to Michael Stephen, and he gives me another envelope to deliver to the brewery. I don't know what is in either envelope."

The man at the switch whispers into a microphone, "did you hear all that?"

"Yes, I did," Maria replies, "shock him again and then get a description of the banker."

THE TORTURE GOES on for about an hour and Duffy repeats his story over and over. He gives a description of the banker, a middle-aged man, pudgy, and nonthreatening. Maria is satisfied when she sees the banker walking towards the bank. The man at the switch opens the freight train car door and the other man throws Duffy out of it. They watch as he tumbles down hundreds of feet off the mountainside as the train speeds on.

Maria follows the banker into the bank and then into his office.

He turns around abruptly, "Excuse me, Miss, may I help you?"

"Yes, as a matter of fact you can," Maria flashes a gun under her coat. "Now, don't think of this as a bank robbery. Because it's not."

"You will never get away with this robbery," Michael says calmly. "May I sit down?"

"No, it won't take that long. And as I said, this is not a robbery. I just need a little information. Tell me about the bearer bonds."

"Excuse me! Who are you?" Michael asks indignantly.

"I'm the woman who is about to bust a cap in yo ass," she lays on the ghetto accent. "The security cameras are offline. I have a couple of men in the bank, and if you tell me what I need to know, then this will not turn into a bank robbery with just one victim."

"What is it you want to know?"

"A courier brings you an envelope with bearer bonds. I suppose you deposit them into an account. I need to know who that account belongs to."

"That is really… uh… very illegal," Michael says and realizes how foolish he sounds.

Maria confirms it, saying, "so is murder. But I'm willing to risk it. How about you? You wanna take a little risk? Give me the information and don't say nothing to no one."

Michael sits down at his computer, prints out the information, and nervously hands the paper over.

She smiles and thanks him. "Remember, if you tell anyone about this, I kill you, I kill your wife, I kill your children. Clear?"

Michael nods.

Barry opens the car door and Maria gets in the back. "So, did he buy it?"

"No. He said he triggered the silent alarm on the floor, so we better get out of here."

"If he set off a silent alarm, why would he tell you?" Barry questions.

"I guess he didn't want me to shoot him when the police show up. Which, it would be a good idea if we weren't here when they do."

The driver takes the hint and pulls off slowly, then makes the first turn he comes to. He speeds up, as he wants to put as much distant between them and the bank before an APB—all-points bulletin—can be issued.

Maria tells him, "Take me to the airport."

"The airport? Where the hell are you going?" asks Barry. "You know I'm going with you."

"I'm outta here," Maria states angrily, "and I'm going alone. You already fucked me on this Armenian operation. I am not giving you the opportunity to fuck me over anymore. We are done!"

"We're done when I say we're done. If you try to fly back to the United States and I'm not on that plane, I can guarantee the Company will shoot you down."

"Who says I'm going to the US?" Maria counters his threat, "I'm going to see my grandmother. I told her I wouldn't be gone long, and it's already been four days. There is nothing more to do here."

Barry takes a softer tone, "Hey, I didn't try to screw you over in Armenia. We had a small window of opportunity, and I took it. I'll put some tech guys on the bank, and we will get a lead on the money. What do you want to do with the brew master?"

"I don't care. He and the messenger were just canaries in a coal mine. Just a way for the Sergeant to know when someone was on his tail. He's your problem now. Dump him on the street somewhere, kill him, whatever lets you believe you're still the good guy here."

They ride the rest of the way to the airport in silence. As Maria exits the car in the hanger, Barry says, "if you hadn't killed him, we may have been able to get out in front of the Armenian."

"Gavril gave me all he had. He was no use to me anymore."

"I'm not talking about that arms dealer," Barry remarks and shuts the door.

Maria is seething as her jet roars down the runway. She pounds several vodkas as the plane soars into the clouds.

Minutes later the pilot says over the intercom, "We are at cruising altitude, it is safe to use the sat phone."

Maria picks up the phone and punches in the numbers.

Russell answers immediately.

Maria says, "did you get her?"

RIGHT AFTER MICHAEL STEPHEN handed her the printout in his office Maria made a call from his phone. "Yes, I want to put in an order for twenty-four long stem American Beauties. Send it to Ezabel Williams at 6526 Palms Rd, Miami. The message reads, 'Best wishes. Here's to your success.'"

The banker did not believe for a minute that this beautiful girl with a snub nose revolver pointed at him was ordering roses for the name on the list. He didn't know what she was ordering, but he feared for the woman's life.

On the plane, Maria pulls the list from her pants and reads the three other names to Russell. They are businesses, each received thirty percent of the money deposited into the account and Ezabel Williams' ten percent was transferred to the First Bank of Miami.

THE FLORIST'S van pulls up to the house facing the Little Arch Creek. At 3 a.m. the street is dead silent. Each house is well lit in the affluent North Miami neighborhood. One of the three men approaching the Williams residence is carrying a long white box.

He places it on the porch. The second man slips around to the back. As he passes the phone line on the side of the house, he slices it with his switchblade.

The delivery man studies the security panel on the wall through the glass inset in the door. He's seen its type before, *piece of cake*. He sees his partner at the back door and jimmies the front one open. He quickly goes to the panel and rips the face off. He clips two wires and pulls the battery pack from the device, rendering it inoperable before it can sound the alarm.

The two men go upstairs and find two women sleeping in their bedrooms. The daughter's room has a red, carved, wooden picture frame with the black-haired beauty hugging a very happy young man. The bottom of the picture frame has the name Ezabel with the 'E' and 'L' forming the sides.

The delivery man softly touches the diamond stud earing in her ear. As she turns over the back-door man comes down fast on her mouth with a large swath of black duct tape. Her eyes pop open. The two men roll her in the sheets and quickly secure her arms and legs with canvas straps; the kind one uses to move furniture.

It only takes a moment for the girl to realize what is happening and begin kicking frantically. She can only flail on the bed like a fish out of water and be just as silent. The men wait for a couple of minutes until she has expended her energy in a futile struggle to get free. They take her pink pillowcase and cover her head, then back-door man, the larger of the two by a lot, heaves her over his shoulder.

They quietly make their way downstairs. The delivery man checks the street and grabs the box of flowers from the porch. Back-door man climbs in the side door of the florist's van and delivery man takes shotgun position in the front. The driver pulls away quietly.

"I just got the word. They took her clean. No witnesses," Russell reports.

"Did they scan her?"

"Yes, she's clean. No tracking devices on or in her." Russell goes on to ask, "who is this girl?"

"I have no idea," admits Maria, "but the Armenian deposited millions of dollars into her account. Or at least an account in her name, so she must be important to someone. I am willing to bet she is Sgt. Warren's daughter."

"I don't know," Russell doubts the plan, "if she is Warren's daughter, why didn't he have security for her? The florist said it was a piece of cake making the pickup. Not how I think someone worth millions would live."

"Maybe she doesn't know she's his daughter," Maria offers, "or he's keeping her profile low key. Hell, she might not know the money exist."

"That's what I was thinking," he agrees with her last statement. "She could be nobody and they are just using her identity to stash the money. I think, when the bank opens, we should make a withdrawal."

"Set it up. Where is the girl now?"

"On her way to New York in the back of the van. They already changed color and logo. There is a car a quarter mile ahead and two trailing at a quarter and a half mile. They are taking her to a safe house in the Bronx. She should be there by tomorrow morning."

"I'm going to the island for about a week. Just sit on her for a while and let's see what happens."

● **11**

CHECKMATE

Maria lands in Nevis around midday. The hot tropic air greets her unkindly, rivers of sweat run down her body. It is the one thing she hates, among the many other things she dislikes about her life, the drastic change in climate that comes with jetting around the world. She would rather stay put in her nice cozy castle in the Mediterranean Sea.

But there was always some business trip Morris had to go on. And a lot of times he dragged her and her mothers along. She believed it was his way of legitimizing his lifestyle. Yana brought the paparazzi, and it was as if he were saying, "see, I'm not that bad man you all hear about." Then there was Gisella, she added a professional air; a doctor and head of a children's health organization. "What a good man he has to be to care for all the sick children in the world." And last was Elizabeth, she was always last; his so-called wife. And Maria, the tag along kid. "A true family man who could do no wrong."

Whenever things went bad, he was looked at in that way. Constant whispers about this unseemly deed, or that questionable deal, we got on the jet and flew somewhere very public. He made sure to be seen with a senator, minister, president, or king, then the rumors would die down for a few months. We would go back to our cozy little castle. And he plotted his next nefarious plan.

MARIA AND CHRISTINA sit on beach chairs looking out at the ocean. The sun hangs halfway above the water and slowly drops down. Their shadows stretch out behind them as they sip afternoon cocktails.

Christina asks, "did it go well in Germany?"

"Where?" Replies Maria.

"You said there was an emergency in Germany. Did you get the matter resolved?" Christina doubts the answer she'll get is the truth.

"Yes, I think it turned out better than expected." Maria cheerfully replies. Recalling her cover story, she adds, "these things seldom go as planned. Or end up where you think they would."

Christina feels Maria is being as truthful as she can be. She changes the subject and takes a different tact. "Diego is a nice man. He told me you are worried about my safety, the arms business being what it is. He said you hired extra men to patrol the island. Will I be able to spot them when I go into town tomorrow?"

"If you can then they are bad at their jobs and I will fire them," Maria jokes. "Don't worry, they will blend in like the flora."

"I get the feeling Diego knows there is more you are worried about than just an arms race. He is really uptight."

"It's his job to be," Maria says without showing any concern. "But Diego knows only what he should know. We have many avenues of business, and this corporation only runs smoothly if people stay in their lane. As the government describes it, operating on a need-to-know basis." She sips her cocktail, thoughts rumbling around her head.

She wants to keep her grandmother safe, but the recent events make it hard. If Barry is working against her, as he clearly is, then whoever he's working for can put her in harm's way. The island is the safest place for Christina right now. Only her most trusted people are here; those she brought into the BSA. People loyal to her, not her father, not her uncle. Except for Diego and Palmer, whom she trusts like her father and Uncle Nicky. She must persuade her to stay here.

"Christina, how much do you know about what Morris was into?"

"At the time of the club shooting, not a whole lot. But as time went on, I came to know that Nicky's family was heavily involved in the Mafia. And my son, with his gang affiliations, fit right in. He and Nicky were two peas in a pod. Knowing the kind of things the Mob is known for, gambling, loan sharking, extortion, prostitution, and let's not forget drugs, I figured my son had his hands in all of it." She looks at Maria, not for a denial but confirmation, and a confession. What she gets is a little of both and a lot of neither.

"Let me tell you a story my father told me many times," Maria begins. "It's the story of Adam and Eve in the Garden of Eden. They were living a blissful life, a childlike existence, and God wanted them to stay that way. But then they ate the apple.

"They didn't learn right from wrong, good and evil, or sin that day. They learned life and death. They learned that they were growing older each day and one day they would die. They learned no matter how beautiful life was in the garden, it would all end one day. As it would for every living creature, plant and animal.

"They weren't kicked out of the garden. After that day, the garden was never that idyllic again. Morris told me it was better not to know too much, but knowledge is unavoidable. And once we see the world for what it is, it is never as beautiful as it seemed."

"Do you know who told him that story?" Christina asks.

"He never said," Maria says, awaiting revelation.

"His father."

The look on Maria's face reveals she didn't expect that answer, or what would come next.

"He told it to the boys two days before he was killed in a subway accident. Morris never accepted his father's death was an accident. He spent the rest of his life looking for someone to blame, and for revenge."

"But you say it was an accident. How did it happen?"

"They were working on the tracks and were supposed to have been finished. Someone turned the power back on. Another man dropped a pry bar used for moving the heavy tracks in place. It was long, five feet or so, and iron. It hit the third rail; you know, the high voltage one. The men were standing in the water in their steel toe boots. There is always water in some parts of the tunnels. Five men, my husband included, were electrocuted." Christina wipes away tears. The wounds reopened again. "No one admitted to turning on the power. They think one of the five may have done it, accidentally or on purpose."

"On purpose?" Maria's voice jumps in disbelief.

"For the insurance money," Christina tells her. "The five families got paid. There were all sorts of nasty rumors flying around, suicide… murder. There were many questions, some unasked, all unanswerable. After five years the city finally paid and called it an accident. But by that time the damage was done."

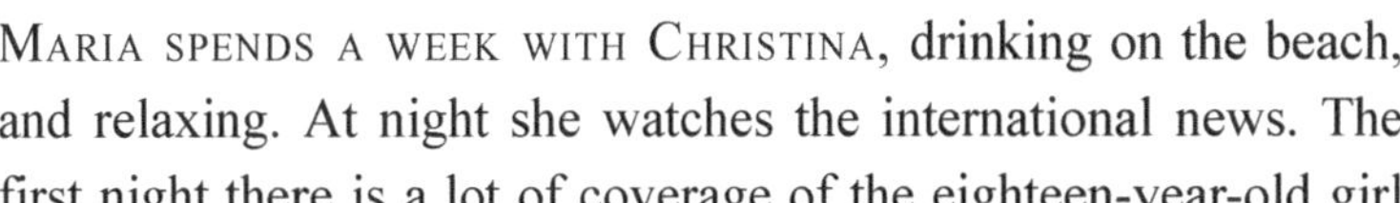

MARIA SPENDS A WEEK WITH CHRISTINA, drinking on the beach, and relaxing. At night she watches the international news. The first night there is a lot of coverage of the eighteen-year-old girl kidnapped from her bed in Florida. The police deem it a targeted home invasion and kidnapping because the security alarm was disabled, and the phone lines cut. Some label it the Teddy Bear Kidnapping because the young girl, Ezabel, was wearing a night-gown with a teddy bear on the front. It brings back memories of the infamous Ted Bundy, and the reference is quickly dropped.

Sonja Williams, Ezabel's mother, appears on television several times pleading for her daughter's return in her heavy Brazilian accent. The pictures of the girl in her cheerleaders' outfit and closeups of her face framed by her long, flowing, silky black hair are more like glamour shots than that of a search for a missing person. Mother and daughter can easily pass for movie stars or runway models, and for a while the news media is all over it.

The whole thing makes Maria sick. By the end of the second week, the story gets less than a five-minute mention on the local news stations, just to report the police has no clues, no leads, and no suspects. And she is grateful when the news moves on to the next hot topic of the week. What does interest her is that Ezabel's father is away on business and cannot be reached. The news doesn't even show a photograph of the man as they read a press release from his oil company. The mysterious Jonas Williams, as she dubs him, is worth looking into.

Maria has another heart-to-heart talk with her grandmother before telling her she is leaving for New York. Christina complains that she has nothing to do on Nevis; they don't even have proper stores. But Maria insists she remain on the island until the situation surrounding Morris' death settles down, explaining as best she can about power struggles within the underworld and legal boardrooms, and that now that Christina is in the limelight, she is not safe from either. She assures her grandmother the university prepared her well for the corporate world, and Morris trained her for the other.

"How does one train for a life of crime?" Christina asks.

Their afternoon drinks and tête-à-tête have become a true bonding experience. A time when any question or topic can be explored. She feels Maria wants to let her into her world, even if it is at baby steps.

"Well, to start, he allowed me to get jumped into his gang."

"Oh, no! How could he? How could he let those boys… men… do that to his own daughter?" Christina feels the wine rising in her throat. The thought of Maria being sexually assaulted by who knows how many guys brings a look of horror to her face.

"No. Wait! I wasn't a Fuck Me Girl," Maria snickers at the thought of how most girls get inducted into the gangs. "I wasn't gangbanged. Morris would have never gone for that."

"Thank God for that," Christina sinks down in her beach chair, "because if he wasn't already dead, I would kill him."

"No, I went in as a soldier," Maria laughs. "Like one of the guys. Then there were the usual gang things one has to do. Beat people up, a little breaking and entering. Selling drugs, guns, whatever else." She catches herself being too honest by the look on her grandmother's face. "It prepared me for the worst people I would deal with and gave me friends I could count on in the toughest of times."

THE TWO-STORY, brick safehouse in the Gun Hill Road section of the Bronx is unassuming. As a corner building at the top of a hill, it is a great tactical location, a view of approach from all four directions. It had been up for sales for months and just recently been renovated. Within the last two weeks moving vans and delivery trucks made a few visits to the young couple who bought the house. A working pair, both leave early in the morning and return late in the evening. Not unusual in the working-class neighborhood, but it gives the neighbors no chance to get to know them.

Maria arrives late in the night when all the other houses have long since gone dark. She immediately goes to the back bedroom where Ezabel is gagged and tied to the bed. She slaps the girl's face to wake her up. The fear in her eyes is like a drug to Maria. It sends her into euphoria.

She removes the gag and says, "if you yell no one will hear you. The windows are inches thick and soundproofed. But I will hurt you, do you understand?"

"Please let me go. My family has money, they will pay whatever you want," Ezabel replies frantically.

Maria slaps her hard across the face, "do you understand?"

"Yes."

"Good. I don't want your money," she sneers, "I am going to make you the same offer your father made me. With a few slight changes due to the circumstances of today, but basically, it is the same deal. Your father meets with me, and you go free."

"My father is an oil executive and was out of the country when they took me. But has probably returned by now. If you let me call him, I'm sure he will meet any demands you have."

"Funny, that's what I thought too," Maria sits next to the frightened teenager, "but your father has not been on TV, or done anything to seek your return. Maybe, he doesn't really care what happens to you."

"No. No. That's not it at all," she is panic-stricken. "You know they are just waiting on a call. I can make that call, and tell them no cops. That is why we left Brazil; the risk of kidnapping was so high. He won't try any tricks. You can trust me."

"You sound just like I did when your father kidnapped me."

"What?" Ezabel's mind reels. "My father would never kidnap anybody. He has plenty of money…"

"Stupid girl! Money isn't the only reason people take another person prisoner. He wanted something from my father that he didn't earn. And he hurt—"

"No! That was not my father. It couldn't have been him. He's a good person. Kind and—"

"Is this your father?" Maria pushes a sketch of Warren in her face.

Ezabel's eyes widen and she shakes her head, no.

Maria knows she's lying, her eyes say it all. She lets the drawing drop on the girl's chest then holds up another picture of an eagle perched on a bloody sword, "perhaps you remember this tattooed on your father's left arm."

"No, you're wrong," she pleads, "my father lost his arm in an accident at an oil refinery. And he was badly burned."

"Let me guess," Maria says coldly with a wicked smile, "about ten years ago. I'll let you call your father and you can tell him I have his arm; I want to give it back to him. But first, there is a little business between me and you."

Maria leaves the room and returns quickly, wheeling in a medical cart, too high for Ezabel to see what is on it. Maria checks the leather straps on her arms and legs holding her to the bed. She picks up a propane torch, turns on the gas, and lights it.

Ezabel struggles against the restraints, then starts crying and begging, "please don't hurt me. You don't have to do anything, my father will pay you. He will give you anything you want."

"Will he give me back my beautiful Akilina?" She rips the covers from the bed, exposing the young girl's naked body tied spreadeagled to the bed. "Good, they did just as they were told. Now, I can't expect you not to scream, so I am going to put the gag back in your mouth."

Ezabel tries to keep her mouth closed but the pressure of Maria pushing the hard, black rubber ball down on her is too much. Her eyes freeze on the black branding iron Maria holds in the torch's flame. Tears run down her face as she watches it go from black to red to white hot. She struggles and twists as the white glowing shape of an eagle on the end of a poker comes closer.

"Stop squirming. You don't want me to mess this up." Maria grabs a fistful of the girl's hair and pins her face to the bed. She laughs as the sound of searing flesh and muffled screams mixed with the smell of burning flesh. She is transported back to the Queen's warehouse where she watched her nanny suffer the same cruelty.

The black and red eagle rises, and the girl's once beautiful face is now grotesquely disfigured. The girl has stopped moving, but her chest is heaving violently as the pain pushes her into unconsciousness. Ice cold water brings her out of a nightmarish dream to see the fiery bird hovering above her. It sinks out of her vision and agonizingly lands on her left breast. This time, the black escape of unconsciousness does not come. Ezabel feels the fire spreading through her chest.

"Sorry, dear," Maria says kindly, "pain and shock is a very strange experience. You can only escape it once. Your body adjusts to it very quickly. It starts to expect the feeling that's coming, and you get to experience it in all its glory. Here, let me show you." She applies the white-hot branding iron one more time through her pubic hair right above her slit.

Her body heaves up violently against the burning metal, causing the tender skin to be ripped away as Maria withdraws the weapon. She collapses again. Maria says to the motionless figure on the bed, "I guess I was wrong. There is only so much the body can take before it gives up."

～

EZABEL WAKES to her body racked by the blistering of three areas. She dimly realizes she is no longer bound to the bed. Now she is in a cage, a kennel for a large dog, still in the same room though. She feels eyes upon her and turns to look behind her.

Maria sits in a chair, humming. "Ah, there she is," she smiles, "I thought I might have killed you."

"How long have I been asleep?"

"Long enough for me to build that cage and put you in it," Maria says sarcastically. "Long enough for dear ol' daddy to make an appearance and plead for his little princess' life. Sadly, only one of those things happened."

The cold steel bars of the cage take Ezabel's mind off the burning inside and make her aware she is still naked. "Can I get some clothes?"

"Why? Plan on going somewhere? Got some place you'd rather be?" Maria mocks. "Hey, not to worry, it's just us girls here. Your other jailers, the ones in the ski masks, are gone. I don't need them anyway, because if you try to escape, or if daddy mounts a rescue, that cage is wired, and you will be electrocuted."

Ezabel starts crying, her sobs becoming uncontrollable. She lunges forward and grabs the bars with both hands, prepared to die. Nothing happens and she sinks backs down to the floor of the cage.

"Um, silly girl, I didn't turn on the current yet. I didn't want you turning over in your sleep and ZAP!" Maria claps her hands loudly as she yells. She laughs at the frightened figure huddled in a fetal position. Was she like this when she was kidnapped? No. She was brave and full of fight. And she was only twelve.

Maria flicks a couple of Polaroids through the bars, hitting the girl in the back. "Here, take a look at these. I was thinking of sending them to the newspaper. Do you think they make you look dead? Don't want daddy to think you are already dead."

Ezabel picks up the pictures and glances at them, she is tied to the bed with black scars on her body and face. She tosses them out of the cage. "Yeah, I look fucking dead."

"Hey! There you go." Maria bounces up out of the chair. "That's the spirit. Show a little moxie. I'm going to get my camera. Maybe, we can get daddy to come out of hiding for his little princess after all."

"Please, can I get some clothes and something to eat? I am freezing and starving."

"Hey, you know, it's always give me… give me… give me. Maybe, that is why daddy is glad you're gone. I guess I can give you a bowl of dog food. Don't want you wasting away, and believe me, you don't have far to go. But no clothes, don't want to hide those beauty marks. By the way, you've been out for a whole day."

As Maria shuts the door, Ezabel hears a click and a low hum. She quickly touches the bar and gets a mild shock. She huddles on the mat in the center of the cage. She knows it has been over two weeks now and from the looks of it her father hasn't said a word about her. What did he do to this woman that drove her insane?

RUSSELL LOOKS up from Maria's desk as she walks into the office in the Doral. He stands, comes from behind the desk, and gives her a hug. "I don't know if you are just plain lucky, or there is divine providence guiding your path."

"What are you talking about? And go ahead and sit back down, I'm not staying long."

"Those three businesses you gave me," Russell hands her a report, "the Colombian shipping mogul we were going to kidnap is tied to one of the companies. It was a lot of shell companies, but he is the big pea in the end."

"Interesting," she says as she begins plotting her next move. "Did we grab him yet?"

"No. We got the banker and the politician but haven't seen any activity on those two yet. I was going to put the boys on him in the next couple of weeks."

Maria sits on the desk and crosses her ankles. She starts swinging her feet up and back like he's seen her do as a little kid. It's a telltale sign she is thinking of something very mischievous.

Finally, she says, "Let's keep him as our ace in the hole. We will keep a close watch on him and be ready to take him when we need to. But I came here today because I have another problem."

"The girl," Russell says.

"Yes, the girl," Maria smiles, "she is his daughter, no doubt. But he's not coming to her rescue, so I want to up the ante. How did he reach out to my father back then?"

"Through the Mob. Chicago, if I remember correctly. But Nicky Nails burned that bridge years ago. What about the CIA? Do they know you have the girl?"

"No, I didn't give them any information from London. Anything they get, they will have to get on their own." Maria continues swinging her leg then reaches into her coat pockets and pulls out six photographs. The three of Ezabel passed out on the bed and three closeups of her in the cage. Her legs stop moving and her smile straightens to a grim sneer. She hands them to him. "Make sure these are seen by the right people. Start in Queens, maybe he has some old contacts there who will recognize the marks. Let them know we want to talk trade."

Russell looks over the pictures, the black eagles perched on the sword prominent on her face, chest, and abdomen. He shows no outward sign of emotion, as he can feel her icy stare boring into his brain. "I'll tell them to contact Nails to set up a meeting. Is that, ok? Are you two still on the outs?"

"Yeah, it's fine. He'll be even madder if we don't include him."

"Hey, watch yourself," Russell warns, "word is out that he's not happy about MoJo's death. There is talk… whispers that there's a price on your head."

She hops off the desk. Her demeanor has changed back to the

happy-go-lucky girl from moments ago. "There is always someone trying to kill you. You just have to make sure to kill them first. Know who told me that?"

"Morris."

"No, Uncle Nicky. He told it to Morris. Then one day he told it to me. Anyway, I've got to get back to my little pet. Hey, you want to hear something interesting? My little princess says her father lost an arm years ago. Cool, right?"

Russell looks at the pictures again, "Maria, put some clothes on her. I wish you'd let me send some people over to help you keep an eye on things."

"She's not going anywhere," Maria waves him off the idea. "Not without clothes. It is as cold as a bitch out there. Besides, more people mean more attention."

Maria can't believe her luck, London yielded two big scores; the princess and now the Colombian whale. Even though they are going to grab him anyway, now she knows he has ties to Warren.

MARIA BANGS on the bars with a big metal spoon. She slides a dog bowl through the cutout at the bottom of the front of the cage then bangs on the bars again, harder and louder. "Wakey, wakey, sleeping beauty. It's time for breakfast, Princess."

Ezabel rises slowly and looks at the bowl of little brown balls suspiciously. In a raspy voice, strained from exhaustion and hunger, she asks, "you kept me in this cage for three days without food and now you expect me to eat dog food?"

"It's not dog food, silly. It's Chocolate Krispies or something like that," Maria says kindly. "The dog bowl is the only thing that will fit through the gate. What kind of monster do you think I am?"

"I don't know. The crazy kind," Ezabel tells her. "Can I have the spoon?"

"No, and for that crack you can eat it doggie style."

Ezabel picks up a rolled crispy ball, sniffs at it, and slowly puts it in her mouth. The flavor is unmistakable, and she grabs a handful of the breakfast cereal. Within seconds, she finishes the bowl. She looks at Maria sitting on the wooden folding chair staring at her. She seems to be looking through her, not at her. "Can you please let me out so I can go to the bathroom?"

"You know the rule," Maria snaps back to reality. "If you have to go, go. I will hose you down later."

"Please, my stomach really hurts! And you must be destroying this house by doing that."

"I'm not being mean or crazy. I built the cage around you, so there is no door," Maria explains. "The panels are riveted together. And do you really think I give a shit about this house? I'm probably going to burn it down. You just better hope you are not in it when I do."

"You are crazy." Ezabel states while wrapping her arms around her stomach. She lies back down with her back to Maria. "Why the fuck are you so crazy? You look like you have a pretty good life to me. You dress well, speak well, say you have money. So why are you doing this to me? What could my father have done to you that was so bad?"

"I told you," Maria snaps back, "your daddy kidnapped me when I was twelve and did horrible things to my Akilina. He made me watch everything." She stands and grabs the bars.

Ezabel scurries to the far corner of the cage, glad Maria can't get in. There is murderous rage in her voice and eyes. In a meek voice she asks, "Who was Akilina?"

"She was my mother," Maria replies with a cold, lifeless voice. Then she shouts, "I watched as three men ripped her apart. You better hope your father answers the messages I put out there,

I am getting tired of waiting. And if he doesn't, I am thinking of taking my eagle and burning your insides out!"

"Why don't you just call him?" Ezabel says softly. She can barely imagine the pain that is burning through this woman.

In the past three days, Maria has been exposing everything she knows about Warren; his mercenary business, other kidnappings attributed to him, and assassinations. Ezabel didn't want to believe any of it, but Maria revealed she had followed his path down those same dark and evil deeds to catch him. Ezabel is sure if it's true he did all that to Maria, she is prepared to do it to her, and worse.

Ezabel knows exactly the next place where Maria intended to stick her white-hot poker. "I told you, I have a number. You can talk to him if you give me a phone."

"Yeah, and he traces the call, then BAM," Maria kicks the cage, "you are free. I'm not stupid."

"I offered to give you the number, you can call from anywhere. He—"

"He will want proof of life," Maria says, "he'll want to hear your voice, or see a picture. That is how the kidnapping business works."

"But you have pictures of me…"

"Not the kind you use to prove someone is still alive. It's too risky." Maria slips back into the wooden chair, her mind going over the different scenarios. She abruptly storms out of the room then returns a couple of minutes later with a pen and paper. "Ok, this is what you're going to do. You are going to write down that fucking number. Then, you are going to write down a question and answer that only he would know. I'm going to call him; I'll ask him the question and one of my own. If he gets either of them wrong, you're dead. If he gets them right, he will give me a question and answer for you. The same thing, get the answer wrong and you are one dead bitch!" She drops the pen and pad through the top bar.

Ezabel starts writing.

"That question has to be a good one. No what was the name of my first dog. It has to be something only he and you would know. Like the first time he fucked you when your mommy went shopping."

MARIA LEAVES the house and walks quickly down the block. It's mid-morning on a Saturday and there are a few people out in their yards. She keeps her head down and doesn't look to either side as she makes her way around the closest corner. She needs to go two blocks to the nearest pay phone outside a pizza shop under the El. She doesn't like traveling in the neighborhood during the day. Too risky.

She calls Russell and gives him the information on the paper. He will give it to one of their guys to make the call from somewhere out of state. She suggests they make the call from Florida, and he agrees. She tells him she will call back in an hour from another location for the reply. An hour is all the time Ezabel had left. If she doesn't get the answer by then, she will move on to plan B.

It has to be that simple. Either he is her father and willing to trade his life for hers, or she is just another casualty, and the hunt continues. She has sacrificed many people over the years. She hopes Morris was right, that with him out of the picture, Warren will finally show his face.

She rides the train downtown, not really going to any place in particular, just needs to kill an hour. She smiles thinking about how Ezabel described Warren… no, not Warren, Jonas Williams, his left arm cut off a little below the elbow. Having to wear long sleeves and gloves to hide his plastic prosthetic, which fools no one. And the best part, the left side of his body, face and head, burned and scarred. Ezabel said she was terrified of him when he returned from his business trip and the year he spent in the hospital. Promising her food really opened her up.

"Hey, pretty girl, what's on your mind that got you smiling so pretty?" The young man stands over her, flexing the bulge in his pants in her face. He lets the train swing him close to her with a wicked grin. His friends across the car laugh.

"Just recalling a funny story that happened when I was a little girl," she says. *Everyone wants to have a little fun today.* "Sit next to me and I will tell you about it."

He turns back to his friends with a bigger grin and swings into the seat next to her.

Maria puts a hand on his inner thigh and rubs it lightly. "Ok. You can't tell this to no one."

He nods vigorously and she rubs his leg again, leaning into him, purposely arousing him. His legs spread wider, inviting her hand to go further.

"When I was about twelve there was this bad man who did very bad things to a friend of mine. My father built a missile and let me launch it. I recently found out it blew off his arm and burned up half of his body. I kidnapped his daughter and tortured her. Now, I'm going to burn the other half of his ass. Ain't that some cool shit?"

He looks at her in shock.

She pulls out a switchblade and stabs him in his crotch, the blade slicing through the bulge between his legs.

He screams and his friends rush her.

Maria leaps to her feet and meets them halfway. She slashes one of their faces and stabs another in the stomach before the doors open and she jumps out of the train. She holds up the bloody knife in one hand and the middle finger of her other hand in the window.

SHE RETURNS to the house later that night, her clothes stained with blood. She asks Ezabel her father's question, "what happened during the Marlins verses Cougars halftime show?"

"Joey Bosco missed the catch on my Toe Touch jump. I landed on my toes too hard and broke both my big toes. I continued the halftime show but missed the second half of the game."

"I was expecting something more substantial," Maria says, looking at the girl's feet for signs of injury. The toe on her left foot seems to be slightly curved outward. "But I guess for an eighteen-year-old that's big. Get some sleep. I will have my guys set up a meeting with dear ol' dad tomorrow, and perhaps in a day or two he'll be dead, and you can go home."

"You are not going to let me go. I have seen your face; I can identify you."

"I don't care about that, or you," Maria admits, "it's your father I want. And once he's dead, I have no reason to stay in the United States. So, I'm not worried about what you know or do. But if it makes you feel better, after I kill him, I can kill you. That way… I don't know… you don't have to live with the guilt of getting your father killed."

"Where did the blood come from?" Ezabel asks as Maria exits the room.

"Just passing time. And if you want my opinion, your father is a piece of shit, who's not worth your pity, or your life." Maria clicks off the light and the hum of electricity through the cage is reassuring. She stops outside the room and mulls over the idea of letting the girl live. The plan was, get Warren, shoot the girl, "no loose ends, right, dad?"

She heads down the hall to the other bedroom, flops on the bed, and stares at the ceiling. She still has doubts Warren is going to trade his life for Ezabel's. He'll have his men try to kill her first. *I'm going to need an ironclad trap.* Maybe use the girl, make it so he must try and rescue her, then kill them both. She smiles.

BOOM. Maria springs out of bed. That's not thunder. Even coming out of a deep sleep, she knows the sound of an explosion. Ezabel! They found a way to trace her after all. Maria grabs her gun and slings on her shoulder holster. She hears the girl screaming. It's a frightful sound, not one for help. Maria takes a knee in the doorway of the bedroom.

A head pokes momentarily at the top of the stairs with a set of night scope binoculars. It is visible for only a second, but that is too long. Maria fires and the intruder tumbles down the stairs. She charges forward and tries to reach Ezabel. A burst of machine-gun fire rips through the wall in front of her. She fires three low shots through the wall of Ezabel's room then turns back to the bedroom.

She slams the door and runs into the adjoining master bathroom. She notices the night table lamp is out and doesn't remember turning it off. She doesn't remember falling asleep. *Damn it, they cut the power.* The generator will kick in and send a thousand volts to the cage.

Maria reaches for the fireman's pole they installed in the bathroom and slides down to the bathroom on the first floor. They replaced the door with a wall, so no one knows it's there. She crawls into the hole under the sink and lies on a mechanic's creeper board. She pushes the lever on the front and the powerful electric motor winds the cable that is anchored at the other end of a tunnel. The steel cable zips her down a track in the black tunnel. A second later an explosion collapses the opening, and a small indentation appears in the backyard.

She wishes they had wired the whole house as she wanted, then she would be sure the girl and her rescuers would be dead.

A few small charges inside the bedroom were all she needed. Russell overruled her, 'they could go off with you in the room, or before you can make it to the escape tunnel.' She settled on electrifying the cage instead.

THE ASSAULT TEAM MOVED QUICKLY, the breaching charges on the front and back doors synched perfectly. The shaped charges were deafening inside the house and no louder than a small caliber handgun outside. Two four-men teams entered the house with lightning-like precision. Maria's shots and the girl's screams alerted the neighbors at 3 a.m. that something odd was going on. The second man from the front door team had a silencer on his custom-made Uzi. The gun battle was over so quickly that only two houses', the one next door on the right and the neighbor directly across the street, lights came on.

The men wisely cut the power first, they knew MoJo's daughter had learned some tricks from him. They wanted to limit the chances of attacking a house that was probably wired to explode. They fanned out to every room. One of the back-door team members cut the leads from the generator in the garage. The Uzi-carrying Man Number Two shot his way into the master bathroom just as the tunnel explosion sent dirt and smoke into the room below him.

He radioed, "She's gone. The little bitch had an escape tunnel."

The third man from the front door team radioed the rest, "Hey, get in here, you are gonna wanna see this."

Man Number Two and Four joined him in Ezabel's room. The pale green figure was huddled terrified in the corner of the cage. Man Number Three slowly approached the cage.

Man Number Two warned, "I wouldn't touch that. Remember who we are dealing with."

MARIA COVERS her ears and hides her face after she pulls the ring hanging from the top of the tunnel. It's attached to a wire that runs ten feet further down the tunnel to the wide circular end. A muffled explosion and soft gust of air passes her. Then water starts rushing down the hole. She crawls as fast as she can through the last few feet and climbs the steel ladder into the dark room above.

The noise from the downstairs bathroom jolts Leo out of bed. His wife hurriedly goes for her bathrobe as he runs down the stairs in his underwear. He flips on the light in the bathroom as Maria emerges from the hole in the tiles. "What the fuck?"

The man's wife and teenage son push their way into the bathroom, dumbstruck by the sight. A woman covered in mud stands in what is left of their guest bathroom.

Maria registers the shocked looks and draws her gun. "No time to explain. I need your car keys."

"What," yells Leo, his face turning red, "no fucking way!" he takes a step forward.

Maria holds the pistol higher, making sure he is looking down the barrel. Then she moves it slightly to the left, pointing it at his wife. "I would shoot you all and look for them myself, but I really don't have time."

"Joey, get her my car keys from the kitchen," the wife almost screams at the young boy.

The boy dashes off and returns holding a ring of keys and a little pink hair troll in his hand.

Maria fires three times, hitting the father in the forehead, his wife in her chest where her heart should be, and his son in the throat. "Sorry people, no loose ends."

She puts a new clip in the 9mm pistol and quickly gets in the car parked in the driveway. A few houselights are on in the block as she calmly pulls out and drives away. She makes a couple of turns and parks the car a few blocks away. She gets in her car and heads for the highway. Fire engines and police cars are racing across the intersections blocks away in her rearview mirror.

Maria reaches into the console compartment, pulls out the car phone handset, and presses number one on the sleek black receiver.

It rings once and Russell answers in a very sleepy voice, "what happened? Where are you? Are you okay?"

"Fucking Warren. That motherfucker sent a hit team. I want to know how he found us." She bangs the handset on the dashboard. "I'm sorry. I know that was probably loud on your end. I'm heading for the Lucky Catch in City Island. I'll be out to sea in about an hour. Time to go with plan B."

"What about the girl? Is she dead?"

"Don't know, but I hope so," Maria says uncaringly, "I couldn't get to her, and they killed the power to the house. I told you we should have wired the place. A couple of hand grenades is all I asked for. We wouldn't be talking about her now."

"Strange."

Maria can hear him moving around his house. And muffled sounds in the background. "Did I wake up Lucy?"

"No, that's the police scanner. You caused quite a stir in the Bronx. But the girl is alive and in police custody."

"Really," Maria almost drives off the road. "The men left her there… Why?"

"I don't know. The police say they found her in the cage. No one was in the house when they arrived. What exactly happened?"

Maria tells him the story. She killed one man. Doesn't know how many others were in the house. And left the family of three in their bathroom dead. She arrives at the marina and takes the car phone onboard. She plugs the unit into the console and calls him back.

"This is bad, Maria. She knows what you look like. The police are going to be all over you."

"She's not going to talk," Maria confides, "we had a real girl talk. She knows what a lowlife piece of shit her father is now. I think we are good."

"Are you kidding me?" Russell yells. "You branded her. Tortured her. And was going to kill her."

"Yeah, but she didn't know about the last part. I told her I was going to let her go after I killed her father. But keep tabs on her, we kill her if we have to. The boat is ready, get plan B started."

"We have to talk about plan B. There have been some interesting developments. I'll tell you at the rendezvous."

"Okay. But first, I must call Sgt. Warren and give him a piece of my mind." The forty-five-foot pleasure yacht rhythmically hums out of its berth into the Long Island Sound. Soon it will be out of US waters, then she will call Warren. Not sure what she will tell him, but this is not over. She will let him know that.

THE WAVES LAP against the sides of the Lucky Catch. Maria kills the engines and drifts southward off the coast of South Carolina. She's lounging on the deck, soaking in the sun, but not relaxing. She is running the events of the last few days through her mind. How did Warren track her down so quickly?

It couldn't have been through the phone call, that was passed to multiple people, and they wouldn't have known the origin of the call. She has to have a mole… no, a rat in her organization. Not Barry, he was cut out of the loop on this one. Her men confirmed the CIA turned the brew master loose the next day. And they didn't hack the bank's computers either. They were satisfied the missiles came from Morris. Barry was up to no good, but he was unaware that she had returned to New York.

She ponders the question for two days, the only way to get an answer is to make the call. Her hands are clammy, the thought of hearing his voice again sending a shiver down her back. She shakes off the fear, *you are a grown woman, not a little girl anymore. You've killed men more dangerous than this half of a man.*

She presses the number one on the radio phone, "let's do this." There follow a series of beeps, tones, finally a ringing, and then silence. She waits an extra few seconds before saying cheerfully, "Warren, you old dog. How the hell are you?"

"I am mad as hell," comes the gruff reply. "Why would you do such a thing to Ezabel?"

"What?" Maria plays innocent. "Giving her the lowdown on you. Telling her what a sick and psychotic bastard her father really is. She would have to find out some day."

"You know what I mean," he yells, "the marks. Why did you burn her like that? I never touched you."

"Oh, but you did. You touched me very deeply. Right down to my very soul," Maria says coldly. "It was the only way to convince her I was telling her the truth. How else could I do the crazy things I did if not for her crazy father forcing me to do them?"

"Well, you will never get the chance to do anything else to her," Warren's voice cracks with anger. "I have the best plastic surgeons working on her. They tell me the scars will not last."

"We both know that's not true," Maria chuckles. "The smell of burning flesh never leaves the nose, especially when it's your own. Or someone you love. The screams come flooding back into your head in those quiet times. You can cover up the scars, but you can never remove them."

"So, this was payback for—"

"NO! She could never repay what you owe me. Losing an arm and half a face doesn't even the score between us either."

"I'm glad you feel that way," Warren says calmly, "because now you owe me. I will kill you for what you've done to her."

"I suppose we both have our debts to pay. But you tried and failed. Don't think it's going to be that easy again."

Warren laughs heartily down the phoneline. "Those weren't my men who attacked you. You seem to have been building quite an enemy's list over the last few years. It seems none more dangerous than the one you added now. And for the record, I could have killed you anytime. In Angola, in Ecuador, in Kosovo, or any of the other places you thought you would find me. You weren't worth it to me then. Now, you are."

The line goes dead. Maria switches to the other channel, "tell me you got something."

"Nothing," Russell admits. "He was bouncing his signal all around the world. The same as we were. We got a dozen pings all over the globe. He could have been at any one of them or at none."

"Well, at least he didn't get a line on me either. Have you narrowed down the plan B team?"

"Yes. Only the most essential and trusted people are in on it." Russell pauses for a moment, clears his throat, and says, "you know, he was talking about Nicky. Johnny Nova, or Giovanni Boscoletti, his given name, turned up dead a day ago. He was a member of the Brooklyn family. They were trying to collect the price on your head. That's why they left the girl behind."

"I'll talk to Nicky, tell him to lift the contract on me."

"Why would he do such a thing?" Russell asks in disbelief. "I mean, put a hit on you in the first place."

"I asked him to," Maria admits. "I figured Warren would jump at the chance."

"That's crazy! Wait until I talk to Nicky. From now on, you run all your plans by me first. No more cowboying. We clear?"

"Yes, boss." Maria says sardonically.

"I'm not kidding," he scolds her some more, "putting a hit out on yourself… That's just crazy. And very reckless."

"I know, but that was before we found the girl. Anyway, meet me in Barranquilla, just the team. No one else knows the new plan, and I want it to stay that way."

"You are becoming paranoid," Russell warns.

"No, I don't think so," she retorts, "I think we are going to need to clean house very soon. You know how it is when someone dies, there are those who will always try and take advantage of the situation. Morris' death probably gave more than a couple of people ideas. Watch your back. People are your friends, until they're not."

12

COKE IS KING

The police and military forces in Bogota, Cali, and Medellin conduct simultaneous raids on warehouses, pharmaceutical companies, and shipping facilities. Fourteen sites are swept up, hundreds are detained, and hundreds of millions of dollars in cocaine seized. It's the biggest drug raid in a decade, and it targeted the businesses of one man, Sebastian Sánchez.

The midday raid didn't capture Sebastian, he was home at his estate in Barranquilla. But it gets his attention. Calls begin coming in before the handcuffs can be snapped tight at most of the locations. The lieutenants and captains of the cartels want to know how such a thing is possible. Sánchez has taken payments from them for years and guaranteed the security of their merchandise.

Since the fall of the major cartels in Cali and Medellin, multiple drug lords sprouted to fill the void. Although smaller in size and number of soldiers, they were no less lethal. Sánchez offered centralized shipping to the United States, Canada, Europe, and Africa for a hefty fee. One that included safety from the drug wars of the 80's. The drug wars Morris had fought so well.

Maria and Russell still hold a great deal of influence within the law enforcement of Colombia and the government does not want to see a return to the violence of the 80's that turned the streets into rivers of blood. But when Maria reached out to the Ministers and threatened to expose who was taking drug money, whether true or not, they were compelled to comply.

Morris had trained a great many of the people that took part in the raids. Some were young men when they worked with him. Now, they were in their forties and had spent the better part of their lives fighting the 'never-ending battle'. They comprised what he called his private army. From time to time, he would reach out to an army sergeant or police captain, and they were glad to perform a special mission for him.

The missions were usually small quick affairs, an assassination, kidnapping, or hijacking of somebody they were told was trouble and in Colombia. This was the first large scale coordinated effort in years, and Maria told them it was in retaliation for her father's death. His death, ordered by Sebastian Sánchez, who worked for the notorious Sergeant John Warren, who most thought had died. As it happened, just as Sebastian was becoming a multimillionaire shipping tycoon.

Maria waits for Sebastian's phone to die down before placing a call, "Sebastian, guess who." She waits a moment for an answer then continues, "Oh, come on, it's Corine Lassier. Has it been that long? You were a bit of a dirty old man the last time we met, but still charming. I think we need to talk, in person."

Sabastian had met Corine four years ago. She captured two men who worked on the docks where a lot of his ships sailed from. She wanted to know how well he knew the pair, and when he convinced her they were ordinary laborers, she dropped one from a five-story window and the other from the tenth floor. He knew why but didn't let on at the time. This time, he felt the meeting wouldn't go so well.

AT 2 A.M. the gates of Sabastian's walled city roll back as four black Mercedes Benz sedans barrel through. No headlights to illuminate the dark road or give away their position. They reach the first intersection, two go right and two go left, and speed through the streets. Even at this late hour, they must maneuver through traffic and pedestrians, not stopping or slowing down. The lead vehicle that took the street to the right hits a man and his cart as it tries to round a corner. A block later those two vehicles split up, taking two roads that lead directly to the ports.

The two cars that went left have less traffic to contend with as they head into the foothills. A mile into their journey, the lead car turns onto a road leading toward the airport. The second car continues into the lush idyllic green countryside.

A second wall rings the compound of Sabastian's home. One tall archway with a thick black iron gate is the only entrance. The passenger in the black Benz presses a button on a remote-control device and that gate spread apart. Before the gates at the estate can roll back, two motorcycles without lights lie down on the track of the gate. Another dozen bikes race through the blocked gates. Each bike carries two riders, one to drive the motorcycle and the other to shoot anyone who tries to stop them from reaching the house.

Gunfire erupts all around the house as many of Sebastian Sánchez's guards do try to stop the Uzi-armed bikers. Three bikers fire wildly at the house and ride right through the front door. The last of Sánchez's men die in the foyer as bikes slide to a stop in front of giant, double oak doors. The three black-clad passengers get off the back of the bikes and approach the door.

The figure in the middle pounds on the door. "Come on Sabastian, open the door already."

The lock clicks and the door slides open. A paunchy, middle-aged, balding man stands holding a shotgun in one hand.

Maria slings her Uzi around her back and takes off her helmet. Russell and Fumu lift the visors of their helmets but keep their Uzis trained on the man at the door.

"What's with all this cloak and dagger stuff? I told you we just needed to talk." She pushes him aside and walks into the study. It is a large two-story room lined with books, and seated on two sofas, is his family. Eight terrified people holding their collective breaths for what seems like an hour. "Look at what you are putting your family through. This was all very unnecessary. Here, I'll take that shotgun. We don't want any accidents."

"This was very necessary," Sabastian says clearly, handing her the gun, "Señor Williams is going to know I did whatever it is you are going to make me do. He has to at least see that I put up a fight."

"Yeah, that is not going to matter much to him. You lost about a quarter of a billion dollars in products which he is gonna have to replace. Or else your business partners are gonna be gunning for the good ol' Sarge. Now, my calculations show, and feel free to correct me if I'm wrong. I figure, he has a billion dollars in product that is ready to roll out the door. Is that correct?"

Sabastian doesn't answer. Instead, he stiffens and looks defiantly at her.

She raises her hand, Russell and Fumu step forward and flank Sabastian. They train their guns on the people sitting in front of them.

"If I drop my hand, your family is dead, and you will still have to answer the question."

Sabastian remains silent.

"How about this? I point to one person on those couches and that person dies. How many shots do you want my men to take before you answer a simple question?"

"One and a half billion dollars in cocaine. But only half of that is packaged and ready to go." Sabastian lowers his head.

"Hey, no shame," Maria says, staring past him at his wife and kids. "You have a lovely family. Three strapping boys, four beautiful daughters, and a very distinguished wife. They are all worth fighting for. But letting them get killed for a scumbag like Sgt. Warren, I would lose all respect for you if you let that happen."

"What do you want me to do?"

"Ok, now this is the hard part," Maria takes his arm and walks him over to a pair of overstuffed armchairs. "These are really nice! I assume a lot of your men are dead outside the house. So, I'm going to provide you with some helpers. You are going to move everything Warren has to our warehouse. And you are going to provide my men with the location of his cocoa fields and processing plants."

"I can't do this," Sabastian pleads, "he will kill me. My family…"

"I hope not. Because you are going to deliver a personal message."

"No! Please! Why don't I tell you where he is, and you tell him yourself?"

Maria tilts her head to the side as if considering the idea. "No, that won't work. He will definitely kill me on sight. It has to be you. And to make sure you deliver the message; I am going to hold onto your family." She stands up and motions for his family to come over. "Come, give your daddy a hug and say goodbye. This may be the last time you see him outside of a box. Hey, do they speak English?"

***

Ezabel lies in bed, the sheets pulled up to her neck. She stares in the mirror on the door at the black eagle on the right cheek. In her mind she sees and traces the eagle on her father's arm. With her fingers she traces the eagle on her face. They are the same. Tears roll down her face as her father enters the room.

"The doctors tell me you refused to let them operate on you," Jonas says as he sits on the edge of her bed and runs his right hand across her long black hair, then brushes away the tears before they can reach the brand on her face. "It's okay, no need to cry. The doctor will fix you; they guarantee there will be no scar, no mark left on you. Don't be afraid my little baby."

"I'm not afraid, I am mad," her voice doesn't carry the venom in her heart very well. She is lightheaded and weak from the drugs the doctor has been giving her. "How could you do it, daddy? How could you kill that girl's mother? You lied to me all my life. She told me everything."

"Did she now?" he says with a soothing tone. He knows the tranquilizers he ordered the doctors to give her keep the rage buried within them both. "She lied to you. I did not kill her mother. She was the nanny, and had I known the affection she held for her, I would have acted differently. But I was under orders, legal orders, from the government."

"You had orders to kidnap and torture a little girl and her mother?"

"No. Orders that gave me the authority to hold her, I did not kidnap them. And I told you the woman was not her mother. She was a Russian operative who killed two of my men. The girl's father was a very dangerous criminal, the leader of an international organized crime syndicate. Growing up with someone like that, who knows what twisted lies he fed her?"

She turns her head away from him. "Is your name really Jonas Williams? Or are you, John Warren?"

"I am Sergeant John Warren, military intelligence and special operations, retired," he says, patting his left prosthetic arm.

She can't see it, but she can hear him doing it.

"And I am Jonas Williams. When you work for the government, sometimes you need two names. Whatever she told you I did to her, or her nanny, was probably a lie."

She rips the covers from her body, exposing the black raised eagles perched on a sword that scar her body. "Would she do this to me if it was all a lie?"

He recognizes the markings instantly and quickly tries to cover her up.

She fights his good hand and stumbles out of bed.

He stands facing the wall, "Please get back in bed, before you fall and hurt yourself. I told you she's a very disturbed person. I don't know how she found you, but it won't happen again."

Ezabel climbs back under the sheet. "Is that why I'm in this prison you call a hospital?"

"This is not a prison," he says, "it is the best private medical facility for plastic surgery. And yes, you will be safe here until I find this woman and put an end to this."

"Why don't you just let her be? You caused her enough pain already."

"Sweetie, I didn't go after her, she came after you. What I did, was ten years ago. It cost me my arm and face, but I have moved on. It seems she cannot. I will not let her threaten you again. I am going to do everything I can to kill the bitch. I promise you that."

"I don't want your promises, I don't want your revenge, and I don't want your operations." Ezabel tells him. "You have been in and out of my life for as long as I can remember. You were gone more than you were there. Always on some kind of business trip that you could never talk about. You may have lost your eagle but now I have something to remember you by. And I don't want to ever see you again."

Warren leaves the room. He orders the doctor to begin her treatment in the morning.

The head surgeon says, "without her consent, that is illegal. She is eighteen and could sue us for doing that."

"I pay for this facility and everyone in it," Warren says softly so as not to be overheard by his daughter. "You will perform the operations immediately."

"Sir, let me suggest that we bring in her mother to see her. Wait a day or two, she will come around."

"No! I don't want her mother to see her like this."

"Sergeant, I understand," the doctor consoles, "but sometimes a mother's touch is more forceful than an officer's command. I am sure her mother will make her see reason and isn't that what we really want?"

"I'll have her mother moved here," he agrees, "she's not far away in Sioux Falls. But whatever happens, I want the procedure started before the end of the week. The longer you wait the harder it will be to reverse what happened."

WARREN SITS IN HIS OFFICE, at a lake house on Lake Oahe, a few miles from the secret medical facility in Mobridge. The hospital appears to be a small office building on the outskirt of town and there is a single road leading away from it and into the dense woodland surrounding his building. He is only minutes away by helicopter, which he keeps ready in a separate cottage on the private estate.

It is a peaceful area, with virtually no neighbors for miles. The perfect place to run his various operations from. His phone rings. "Hello, Sabastian, I was wondering when you were going to call."

"You know, it happened so fast," he begins apologizing immediately. "I did everything I could to stop her. But they were well organized... prepared."

"Of course, they were." Warren doesn't need this headache

now. He's still concentrating on his daughter, and how Maria has undone years of a carefully constructed dual identity. "Tell our clients not to worry, I will make good on their losses."

"Um, Mr. Warren, sir… that is why I am here."

"Here? You are in South Dakota?"

"Correct." He's sure he can hear the anger in Warren's voice and knows it will only get more intense as the conversation continues. But he's hoping that breaking the bad news before he arrives, gives his boss a chance to calm down before facing him. "She gave me a package she wants delivered to you. She has all of your product in her procession and—"

"What! How did this happen?"

Sabastian is sure he made the right decision in calling ahead. "Like I said, she was very well organized. She had the government on her side. If I may ask, sir, how did she find me?"

Warren curses under his breath, "maybe you should have asked her. Where are you, exactly?"

"Five miles away. I will be in the compound in a few minutes."

"Ok. I will meet you in the fishbowl when you arrive." Warren hangs up the phone then presses the intercom, "when Sabastian gets here, give him a full body cavity search, tox screen and all."

Warren goes to the trophy case where a couple of largemouth bass, a walleye, and a pike are stuffed and on display. He cranks the handle on one of the fishing reels three times, then turns another in the opposite direction twice, he pulls a third fishing rod out from the clips holding them in place. The rod moves an inch and the case slides across the floor, revealing elevator doors. He punches in his code and the doors open. He steps in and begins his descent.

As he goes down, he has time to think. How did this girl find Sabastian and his daughter? He runs through everything they have in common. It flashes in his head as the elevator doors open two hundred feet underground, the banker. *And she only could have found him through Gavril Avakian. The Javelin missile deal was a setup from the beginning. If Gavril is still alive, he won't be for much longer.* He rides the electric car through the tunnel under the lake until he reaches a door. He enters another personal code to open it.

THE FISHBOWL CONNECTS a series of four submarines that sit on the bottom of Lake Oahe. This is a steel dome that anchors and acts as the hub for the nuclear-powered subs. Each has a specialized purpose and was sent into the lake in the mid-seventies as part of the country's nuclear defenses. The main one is a ballistic missile launcher with ten MIRVs missiles.

After his last encounter with Morris, he felt a couple of hundred feet of water was safer than concrete and steel. Plus, there is a steel anti-depth charge net covering the whole facility, which can be rolled back to launch the missiles. Warren is sure no one in the government would sell him out this time, and risk losing a nuclear launch site. Plus, the devastation it would cause would be too great for even Morris to attack. No place is completely secure, but this is as close as one can get and still be on the planet.

The fishbowl has three different entrances; the one on the eastern side of the lake connects to his office. Another on the western side is mainly a warehouse and serves to bring in supplies. Then there is a water treatment plant further south, where one of the tubes runs to the bottom of the lake; one has to swim from there.

Sabastian is coming from the west.

Warren thinks about making him swim but doesn't have a wetsuit that would fit his fat ass, and he probably would die of a heart attack shortly afterwards. Pity, he does need to know what Maria has in mind.

SABASTIAN HAS a rough time getting into the fishbowl. He's met by armed guards inside the warehouse, then is thrown to the ground and has his clothes ripped from his body. He would not have objected so loudly to his five hundred-dollar Armani suit being torn to shreds looking for tracking devices if he knew where they intended to look next. Two men better than six feet tall and much more muscular than he, grabbed his arms and dragged him across the concrete floor. They throw him halfway onto a steel table and each man holds an arm and places their other hand heavily on his neck.

Sabastian can barely breathe from the weight crushing down on him. From the corner of his watery eyes, he sees three other men approaching. They are just as big, and one has black rubber gloves on up to his elbows. In his hand he holds something that looks like an elongated pair of pliers. He feels hands grab his legs then his buttocks spreading apart. He hears flesh rip and an excruciating pain fills his backside.

Flame and water run down his legs as they try to buckle. The water he knows is his blood, the flame can only be irreparable damage to his muscles. His legs are held fast and stiff by the guards as a new and very unpleasant sensation takes over. Something hard and multi-pronged begins routing around inside him.

Then he hears, "He's clean."

Extreme agony follows as the hand retracts from his anal cavity. The guards' hands disappear from his body, and he collapses onto the floor. The worst is over, or so he thinks. At least he's made out better than his men, they were shot to death in the car as soon as the doors opened. "There is a package on the back seat," he says weakly, lying on the floor.

"We already have it," says one of his inquisitors.

The first two men grab his wrists again and drag him into the next room. This time he can't walk even if he wanted to. They drop him next to a floor drain and he quickly shuts his eyes. A second later high-pressure water pummels his body, rolling the three-hundred-pound man over. The water has a foul disinfectant smell and tastes of toxic chemicals. Although he doesn't know it, the man sprays him for a full five minutes. His body is red and bruised by the water. Now, his entire body feels as though it is on fire.

The same man who informed him about the package points to a table. "There is a towel and a red biocontainment jumpsuit. Get dressed." When he doesn't move fast enough, the man kicks him in the ribs. "NOW!"

It's the least violent action taken against him since he arrived. After donning the jumpsuit, which has attached boots, hood, and face mask, Sabastian asks, "Was all this really necessary? I just came to bring him a radio and a message."

"You could be carrying a pathogen," the man pushes him down into a chair, jabs a needle in the side of his neck, and extracts a full vial of blood. "But don't worry, we will find out." He then pulls the hood and mask over Sabastian's head and face, zipping the hood all the way around to the back.

Sabastian hears a click and knows he won't be able to take the suit off. Panic sets in as the air inside the suit heats up rapidly. He can smell his own breath mixed with the pungent chemical odor of the sterilizing bath he just had.

The man holds up a small shoebox-size device with a black hose dangling from it. He moves it to-and-fro in Sabastian's face, as if offering him the air supply, then taking it back. Finally, as his eyes turn a bright crimson, the man snaps the black plastic connector to the circle in the facemask. Cool fresh air immediately fills the hood. The speakers beside his ears come to life.

"The boss will see you now."

SABASTIAN IS USHERED into a small elevator car and it starts descending. He holds onto the handle of the small suitcase-like air filter. Its motor hums, a green light flashes on top, keeping time with the numeric display, cool air blowing softly in his face. He is still in pain and walks gingerly from the car when the doors finally open. Two more armed guards are waiting. At least he is safe from them inside his suit.

They help him into a golf cart and drive down a metal tunnel. It opens into a huge circular room with several airlock-type doors. He looks up at the black ceiling, wondering if the lake is on the other side. The golf cart stops in front of door C6. The airlock hisses, the door opens, and there stands Sgt. Warren.

He is thinner than Sabastian recalls, but that was before the accident. His face looks almost normal, small lines here and there, but his skin is hard and waxy on one side. He isn't wearing his left arm.

"Come in, I know the guys treated you a little rough," he greets Sabastian with false humility as he points to the monitors behind him. "But it was necessary, we don't know what that girl is capable of. You could have been carrying a transmitter, a nuclear device, been sprayed with weaponized chemicals, or given a biological agent. That's why the suit. I just can't take any chances. You understand."

"Yes. Yes, of course," he responds honestly, even though he knows it was more forceful than necessary. "But my men—"

"They may have been subjected to the same subterfuge as you. But they are not necessary to our discussion, are they?"

"No, but they have families…"

"We all have families we are trying to protect. Are we not?" he asks and ends the conversation by turning back into his office. Once he reaches his desk he straps on the arm. He has to lift his chest and visibly straighten his body to support its weight. "Sit down and tell me the message she sent with you."

Sabastian sits across the desk and thinks for a second. "She sent a radio phone tuned to the frequency she can be reached at; said you probably would not be reachable at the number she had. She said, and I must repeat this part verbatim, 'I want to meet you alone and kill you with my own hands. It should be a fair fight, I am a woman and you half a man.'" He leans back, hoping he is out of reach of his boss.

The Sergeant laughs heartily. "Ah, a bit of poetry to disguise her plan. So, she wants to have a fair fight. I show up somewhere and she blows up a few miles to get me." He gets up and stands behind Sabastian, resting his heavy prosthetic arm on his shoulder, weighting him down. "And do you think I would show up alone? Hell no, not after what she's done. I will kill her, but it will be on my terms."

"Are you going to call her?" Sabastian asks sheepishly, "she says she will destroy all of your cocaine if you don't."

"I will call her, but not on her equipment. I have the frequency, thank you."

"No, don't thank me," Sabastian says as he feels the weight lift from his shoulder, "I only wish I could have stopped her. Killed her—" He doesn't finish his sentence. He can't once Stg. Warren raised his iron arm and dropped the solid steel fist on his skull. His head cracks like an egg and spews blood inside the hooded suit. He falls forward and drops the small suitcase on the floor.

Stg. Warren reaches down and switches off the air.

Two MEN COME in and put Sabastian in a large cart. As they wheel the dead man out of the office Warren orders, "Tell the team to send up the bubble. And let me know when they have the bitch on the radio."

"Yes, sir." They wheel the cart out and head for door A1 which leads to the submarine that houses radio equipment and incinerators. The bubble is a buoy that raises an antenna towards the surface. The wire spins out to a hundred and fifty feet. Close enough to the surface to get a signal but keep the base hidden from all eyes. The fishbowl receives information from several connections throughout the other access points, but it only transmits from the sub's radio.

The radio operator repeatedly broadcasts, "MD 159753" over and over. He broadcast on the frequency the radio phone was set to but gets no reply. After an hour, he reports back to Stg. Warren, "she's not there. There is no answer to our calls."

"It's ok, she's waiting for me to make the call," he tells his operator. "Patch me through, I will talk to her from here."

A few second later, she responds. "It's about time you called. I didn't go through all this trouble to speak to some lackey. How's Sabastian? Still alive I hope."

"Sabastian won't be joining us," Warren grumbles.

"Oh, dear," she says lightheartedly, "are you going to call his family, or should I?"

"I don't give a damn about his family, kill them all if you want. Let's cut the bullshit, shall we? What do you want from me?"

"Simply put, your fucking head on a plate," she answers, all frivolity gone from her voice. "I never wanted to kill anybody but you."

"Well, that's not going to happen," he states sternly.

"I guess I'll have to settle for your daughter's head then," she waits for a reaction. When he doesn't respond, continues, "I know you think I can't get to her again, but come on, you didn't even bring her into that secret underwater base of yours. You leave her in some half-ass clinic in Mobridge. It's like you want me to kill her. I don't, you know. I don't want to kill her, unless she dies in your arms, like Akilina died in mine."

Warren leans back in his chair, "you may know where she is, but I dare you to try and get her again. You want my head? I am going to cut yours off personally, for what you did to her."

"Ah, now we're getting somewhere," Maria wheedles, "you have your guys looking for me, I have a man with a rocket launcher targeting your daughter. By the way, he is just waiting for you to show up again. I don't know how you escaped the first time, but I doubt if that hospital is as fortified."

"Like you said," Warren counters, "we both have spies in this business. You think Granny is safe on the island?"

"Is that the best you can do? You think I care about what happens to her? I don't even know the woman. As a matter of fact, I thought she was one of yours, and now, I'm sure she is. Kill her if you want, it makes no difference to me." Maria knows the way to keep Christina safe is to feign disinterest in her wellbeing.

"No, she's your grandmother, my people confirmed it. I have had people on you for years. I could have killed you anytime I wanted to. But it was never about that for me. Your father got your little wet nurse killed. And you… I warned you to behave. So now, here we are. But no more daddy to protect you, just me and you."

Maria stays quiet while she gathers her thoughts. She doesn't want to seem too anxious, and must play him right, let him think he is in control. "I'll meet you anywhere you like. You come alone, I'll come alone. We can have one of those old western gunfights."

Warren laughs, "like you would actually show up. I am two hundred feet under water because I am sure if you had half a chance, you'd drop another bomb on me. But you can't this time, not without risking setting off one of the nukes. The U.S. won't forgive a move like that. Not like they did before. I think I will stay right here, and let my men hunt you down."

"I guess a scumbag like you must have some government backing," Maria jabs, "maybe the CIA likes the way you do business. You must have deep, dark, secrets about someone. I mean, to give you such a fancy hideout. I'm sure they don't care that much about your wellbeing."

"There are more government agencies than there are letters in the alphabet to make up acronyms. It's not what I know about people, it's what I can do for them that makes me invaluable. Your father, your so-called Uncle Nicky, you... you don't have a clue as to what you are up against. In our last encounter, some people grossly miscalculated your father's worth. That won't happen again, you are not worth as much as you think to your friends in D.C."

Maria starts clucking like a chicken then laughs, "I know you won't show up alone either, but I'm not worried. I'll take on all your men and still kill you. But I guess you are too chicken shit. Sooo, I guess it is back to your little princess. You know, she is none too happy with you. We had a little girl talk, I filled her in on all the things you did, and threw in a few of the heinous things I did too, which I wouldn't have done if it wasn't for you. Hope you don't mind... I wonder how she will feel about you after I have a couple of guys gangbang her. You know, like you did to my wet nurse. You made me watch and I can still see every second. It is what kept me going, she let me know you were still alive. Let me know when I was getting close to you. But unlike what you did to Akilina, I'm going to leave her alive. So, she can relive the experience night after night and know she has you to thank for it."

"OK, you are so eager to die?" Warren yells into the phone, "we will settle this now. I am sure you are still in Colombia with my cocaine, so I'll send my pilot. He will fly you to a meeting place on your plane. This way you have nothing to fear, and I can be sure you will come alone. It will be just you and me. None of your dirty little tricks."

"Okay," Maria hides her enthusiasm, "but I am going to bring one person with me, my second. You'll have the pilot, in case it is a trap. If my guy dies or fails to make the 'all clear' call, your cocaine goes up in smoke. And Princess will enjoy hours of man pleasures compliments of me. Having been gang raped, I can tell you, there is nothing quite like it."

"Enough of this bullshit," he says angrily, "tomorrow, my pilot will be in Barranquilla at the airport. You will have no trouble spotting him."

The phoneline goes dead. Warren doesn't like the setup but at least he will control the meeting place. With only one day to prepare and no location, she will not be able to mount an effective counter strike. He gets on the intercom, "Go get my daughter out of the hospital. Bring her here."

13

NOT MY DOG

Maria sees a husky man who just arrived at Ernesto Cortissoz International Airport carrying a hatbox.

Karl approaches him and asks, "I am sure your wife will love the hat."

"I am sure," he replies, "it was sent especially for her."

Karl escorts the man to a private lounge in the airport where two others take the hatbox. The two men sit, and drinks are brought to their table. The man objects to having a drink as he must soon fly, but Karl insists that he does not drink alone.

"What's your name?"

"John Smith," replies the man, as he drinks the iced whiskey.

"Hey, no need for the spy-type stuff," Karl shows his disbelief, "this isn't our fight. We are just along for the ride."

"Honestly, my name is John Smith," the man slicks back his blonde hair and reaches for his wallet in his jacket pocket. He flips it open and displays his pilot's license. "See. You know someone has to be named John Smith."

"Sorry…"

"Don't worry about it, I get that all the time. You should see

198

the trouble I have trying to meet girls in the bar. Telling them I'm a pilot and John Smith, not really a winning combination."

THE TWO MEN with the hatbox are taking their time in a seldom used men's room opening the package. They put a blast blanket over it before scanning the box with a metal detector. The heavy sand-filled Kevlar quilt would absorb the blast and any shrapnel should the hatbox turn out to contain a bomb.

Getting a bomb through airport security on the way out is difficult but bringing one in through arrivals is easy, even if it does have to go through customs. Sgt. Warren has enough pull in Colombia so the hatbox would not be opened.

Maria has enough sense not to trust Warren wouldn't try something, and it would be like him to try even the score by sending her an explosive device. The two men carefully lift the lid a fraction of an inch in the bathroom with the sign out front, "out of order." One holds the lid up while the other passes a dentist's mirror around the rim. He drops the mirror in the box and quickly looks away.

"What is it?" asks Maria from the stall furthest from the man. She saw his reaction in the mirror and needs to know what is in the box.

"Better come have a look for yourself," Fumu replies.

Intrigue quickens her steps as she approaches, saying, "Go ahead. Open it!"

Fumu pulls the top off and Maria peers inside.

She smiles at the smashed-in skull of Sabastian's severed head. Jagged bone fragments stick out of the mostly jellified brain tissue. "Warren did not like my message at all," she jokes.

"You should call off this plan," cautions Russell. "It is too dangerous."

"Nonsense, what did you think he was going to do to poor ol' Sabastian here? We have him just where we want him."

"Then let me and Fumu go in your place. The pilot won't be able to stop us."

"Won't he though?" Maria conjectures, "you don't know where he's supposed to fly to. He can just head out to sea and fly until the plane runs out of fuel. Then what?" Maria puts a hand on his shoulder. "We stick to the plan; he will never see it coming. I'm going to board the plane with Karl, you two are going to follow just out of radar range. We shorten the radar on the plane, so he won't know he's being tailed."

"What is to stop him from flying the plane into the sea once you are onboard?" asks Russell.

"Warren," states Maria. "Look at that head, he wants me. After what I did to his daughter, he's full of rage and aching for revenge. He is going to have his pilot deliver me alright, so he can see me die. I bet he wants to kill me with his own hand." She laughs at the thought of him beating Sabastian in the head with one good hand.

"Ok, you take off right after we give the pilot a thorough physical," Fumu agrees.

"Just make sure he is able to fly afterward," she cautions.

"We are just going to pass him through an x-ray machine. Just to make sure he is not sitting on a hand grenade," adds Russell.

"That would be dedication," Maria jokes. "Send Sabastian to his wife. She should know what happened to her husband. I don't know, maybe she'll want to give him a proper burial."

⌐ ╲┬┌

MARIA GREETS the pilot after he has been through the x-ray machine. She sits across from him, and the three men sit behind her. She looks into his crystal-blue eyes. "From Germany, I'm guessing."

"My parents are," John answers, "I was born in Bolivia… So, go ahead and get out all the Nazi jokes now. We have a long flight ahead of us."

"About that," Maria queries, "how far are we going?"

John smiles, "he said you were clever, and he was right. You have a Learjet 60; it will take us as far as we need to go. And don't worry, although they are new, I have flown a couple in the last two years. I will give the tower a false flight plan; I am sure you presumed I would."

"I wouldn't expect anything less from you or Warren," Maria says cordially, "shall we get this party up? And if you need any help in the air, both Karl and I have flown this jet many times."

John remains seated as the four of them get up. "There is just one more thing I need from you, Ms. Delitanni. I was told there is a package in locker 123. The combination is 1234."

Maria nods her approval and Karl goes and retrieves the package. He opens it in the same sealed off bathroom that Sabastian's head is in. He then brings the items to the table.

"What the hell is this supposed to be for?" Maria takes the two items from him and looks over the first one, a taser. "Well, we know what this does. But what is this second device?"

"It's a multiband oscillating transponder," Russell informs her, "I suppose he wants to find your tracking chip and put it out of commission."

"Oh, I get it, find it and shock it. Well, we won't need this thing." She tosses the transponder onto the table. "We know where the tracker is, it's just below my left shoulder."

"Maria, we are not going to shock you. We are not disabling your tracker. If we do, he can take you anywhere, and not necessarily to Warren. We won't have any way of knowing—"

"Isn't that the whole point of this mission? It will be okay, but first, let's make sure this thing works as advertised." She walks over to John, who is still sitting patiently, shoves the taser into his neck and pulls the trigger. A loud buzzing sound like someone has released a swarm of bees followed by a snap is heard across the airport terminal. A few heads turn in their direction but don't perceive anything that warrants their attention.

John slumps over in the chair. Russell grabs his face and shakes him. Fumu brings a glass of water from the bar and throws it in his face. He is groggy and disoriented.

"What… What happened?"

"Well, the stun gun works," Maria laughs. "I had to make sure it wasn't going to kill me. Can't take any chances, you know. Not that I don't trust him, but it's the type of dick move I would try. I'll go in the bathroom and zap myself; I don't want to piss myself in public, like you just did."

He looks down at his pants, which are wet from the water used to revive him. "No. I haves to witnesses…" he slurs, still not over the effect of the powerful electric shock. "Thems we tess with meter."

"Ok. I guess I do it right here," she agrees.

"No. Don't do it," Karl objects vehemently.

"I was told to tell you, if you don't do it, I don't fly you anywhere and your grandmother's life is over."

"Did your boss tell you that we will beat his location out of you, and dump your body in the ocean?" Karl threatens.

"Yes, he did," John says forcefully, having fully recovered from the taser. "Which is why I don't know where he is or the destination. I am to fly to a certain location, call in on the radio, and I'll be asked some questions. I answered over a hundred questions before coming here, so I don't know which ones they will ask. If they are satisfied, then they will give me the coordinates. I guess he didn't trust you either. Beating the location out of me would have been a dick move, probably one he thought of too."

The five of them sit staring at one another, each working out their own versions of good and bad scenarios. For John, it's hours of torture and finally death. Maria is considering whether Warren really wants to see her die, or will he be satisfied just knowing she is gone. The other three are wondering if they will ever see their boss again.

"Ok," Maria hands the taser to Russell, "go ahead and shock me."

"No. Wait!" John grabs the transponder from the table. "First, I have to make sure the tracker is actually working." He waves the black oblong baton in front of her body. It makes a series of beeps and high-pitched whistles. A green light comes on as it goes past her left shoulder. He puts the wand in his lap. "OK. Now."

Russell touches the taser's flat black face to her back a few inches below her shoulder blade. He looks at John, "this is almost over her heart. If it kills her, you have no idea the pain you're in for."

"Don't hold the trigger," John warns, "a quick pull and let it go."

Maria grips the arms of the lounge chair and arches her back. Russell's finger jerks and he fires off a jolt. A loud snap is produced, and Maria is thrown forward. Fumu, Karl, and John reach out and catch her. They gently put her back in the chair. Her eyes are closed and fluttering.

"Get her some water!" yells Russell.

John turns towards the bar, but Karl throws him back into his chair and sprints to the bar. This time the activity does draw the attention of multiple people, but none stop to watch for too long. The dangerous looks from the men surrounding the passed out young woman in the chair is something nobody wants to get involved with. Airport security turns and walks in the opposite direction.

Russell pours a little water in his hand and wipes the cool

liquid around Maria's forehead. He does it a second time, going around the back of her neck.

She mumbles, "do it already. I'm ready."

"It's already been done," says Russell.

They all laugh.

John picks the wand up from the floor and waves it in front of her then stops over her left shoulder. The wand stays silent. "Ok, now we go."

THE LEARJET IS CRUISING at ten thousand feet. Maria feels the plane change course a few times since leaving Colombia. First, they headed south, after about thirty minutes they turned east, now, John is changing direction again, heading northeast. The sun changes side each time the pilot makes a maneuver.

Maria sits in the overstuffed lounge chair, and Karl is across from her. She swivels to face him. "Now, we are heading for the Caribbean Islands. Not really a big secret that's where this show-down would take place."

"I just hope he doesn't burn up too much fuel trying to shake whatever tail he thinks we have on him."

"Yeah. Don't worry though, he won't be able to shake them anyway," Maria says and watches his reaction.

"What? I was kidding. How are you able to tail us?" he asks in amazement.

"Oh, yeah, I couldn't tell you that part of the plan," Maria confesses, "after all, you are working for Warren."

"What? No! You've known me for years. You brought me into the organization. How can you say that?"

"Trust me," Maria's eyes fill with tears, "it hurts me to say it. But your boss gave you away when he said he would kill my grandmother on the island."

"Hey, there were four of us who went with you to drop your

grandmother off," he protests. "Fumu, Diego, and Palmer, it could be one of them. Or somebody else, not even in our organization. Barry Thomas, for example, I never trusted that guy."

"Yeah, me either. But he didn't know about my stopover with my grandma," Maria pours two drinks from the bar in front of her and passes one to Karl. "Drink up. But it wasn't just my grandmother's location. I killed one of the mobsters who attacked the safe house. When I found his friends, they said it was the Russian who told them to look for me in the Bronx. Funny though, you didn't tell them about the girl."

"I didn't know about the girl," he says glumly.

"I know you didn't. Only Russell did. You weren't surprised when we visited Sabastian's place, but he was, and looked like he knew you. Like you were going to help him out. That was the clincher. Want another drink?"

Karl looks at his glass suspiciously.

"Oh, come on, I'm not gonna poison you. Where's the fun in that?" She jokes. "Besides, you are going to tell me what his plans are. Time for you to get back on the winning team."

"Ok, but I didn't want to betray—"

"Save it," she snaps, placing her hand in front of his face. "I heard all the excuses before. He threatened my family. He paid me a shit-load of money. You're a crazy bitch, and gonna get us all killed. I don't care why you did it, I just want to know what's his plan. Were you supposed to kill me on the plane?"

"No. Never. I couldn't do that," he says honestly. "He has a force of a dozen guys, ready to ambush you when you land. I will just radio back the all-clear signal. Then I'll report back that you died in a fair fight."

Maria's gaze turns cold. "Well, I have just one question left."

He has seen her like this before, very still, like a viper before it strikes.

"Where is this meeting supposed to take place?"

"That, I don't know. Because he wouldn't tell me," Karl's

fear is evident. "He was afraid I'd be discovered and talk. Like the pilot, no one knows where he is waiting for you."

"Pity," Maria states, "that's why I have my own team following us, and well out of radar range of this plane. But don't you worry, I have no intention of walking into Warren's trap."

The pilot's voice comes over the intercom, "buckle up, we are coming in for a landing."

Maria looks out the window and replies over the intercom, "where are we, Monserrat?"

"No, that's Sint Maarten. We will be landing at a little airstrip along the Dutch French border, and it may not be as smooth as you would like. I have to dive in and stop hard to avoid detection. It will be a lot like landing on an aircraft carrier. But I have ample experience doing that."

"Sint Maarten is kind of a populated place to hold a gunfight. Don't you think?"

"I don't get paid to think about my orders," John comments, "I just fly to where they tell me. But if you want my opinion, I think it would be very hard for you to send a missile strike here."

"Can't be any harder than D.C." Maria gets up and heads to the back of the plane.

Karl is strapping in and asks, "where are you going?"

"I am going to freshen up, want to look good at my assassination."

WARREN IS on the mountaintop watching a silver streak diving out of the sky. He adjusts the range on his binoculars to get a sharper view of the jet. It is nosed down at nearly ninety degrees.

John's voice comes in clear in his headphones, "we are ten miles out and making our final approach."

Warren smiles, the ex-fighter pilot is doing exactly as he wants. The plane will disappear off the radar screens as it passes from one controller to another. Sint Maarten's air controllers will never know they are missing the plane. He takes the microphone that is clipped to his jacket's collar, "were you followed?"

"No. I jinxed a few times and doubled back twice. We are flying in unescorted. Leveling out at five hundred feet."

"Will see you on the ground," Warren ends the communication. He adjusts the binoculars' range. He scans the horizon from one side to the other. No other planes are in the air. He refocuses on the Learjet and radios his team, "Give me a reading on the radar."

"Just the Lear, sir. Five miles out."

The plane is becoming clearer in his view and he adjusts the binoculars again. He sees a flash and a cloud of white smoke. He concentrates on the expanding cloud, red sparks and sliver streaks rain down from it. A fiery wing and part of the tail spirals into the sea. He drops his binoculars and the strap tangles with the microphone wire as he tries to get the mike to his mouth.

He yells, "what the fuck just happened?"

"Don't know, sir," responds the same voice, "the Learjet is gone from radar."

"Gone! It exploded." Warren grabs up his binoculars and searches the area as the cloud dissipates slowly. He sees parts of the white and silver jet floating on the ocean. He makes out a side of the fuselage floating in the debris field. He keeps scanning, looking for any sign of survivors. He grabs his mike again, "get a team down to the beach. I want some people in the water as soon as possible."

"The local authorities are on it too, sir. I am monitoring their traffic; they will have a coastguard boat from both sides on site in a few minutes. Myles and Clyde are on their way."

Warren continues watching the debris bobbing in the waves and thinks, *she must have had a bomb onboard, and was planning to drop on my position. Perhaps, it had an altitude detonator that went off prematurely.*

Well, it saved him from having to kill her and her man. But now, how will he recover his cocaine?

It's a good thing they don't know how far we were taking her.

It gives him a couple of hours to send in his strike team down in Colombia. Karl informed him the warehouse is in the middle of an industrial park. He believes a couple of the other warehouses harbor Maria's men and provide cover for the drug storage facility, but Karl didn't have any particulars on the size of their team or manner in which they were guarding his product.

Karl also told Warren Maria had compartmentalized the operation. He was on the initial assault team and overheard her giving orders to the transportation team as to where the holding facilities were. But ever since the hit on her, she clamped down tighter on sharing information. One team didn't know the members of another. Only the knowledge and use of code words could get someone through. Which, he cannot provide.

Warren knows he has to send his team in soon, as Maria's men are expecting a call from Karl on a prearranged number with a coded message within eight hours of her leaving Colombia, or they will know something has gone wrong. Either on her side or his, but they will destroy his billion-dollar product. He had John zig-zag his way to the island to kill time as well as to shake any tails. With four hours gone, he must execute a hastily put-together plan.

Damn her and her bombs. Neither her father nor she could ever stick to the rules.

MARIA GOES into the bedroom and locks the door. She pulls a lever under the right side of the bed then walks around and unlocks the left side. She pulls the bed forward from the rear wall—it rolls on tracks hidden in the floor—then flips it up against the door. She pushes the levers back in and locks the bed in place. In the wall is a hidden chair which she straps herself into. Next, she slides the thick blast door from inside the back wall around her, encasing herself in an escape capsule. She straps on the fighter pilot helmet and oxygen mask.

"Testing one two… Testing one two… Russell, are you reading me?"

"Loud and clear," Russell's voice fills the helmet. "Are you sure you want to do this?"

"No choice," she replies. "Karl has confirmed Warren is waiting to ambush me when we land. So, we go with plan B, the escape capsule. Are you tracking us?"

"Yes, the avionics are tied into our plane. Looks like he is on final approach to Sint Maarten. You are flying low, below radar. I pulled up a satellite picture of the area, and it looks like he's heading for a mountaintop landing strip north of South Reward. Maria, you are too low and going too fast, the escape pod might break up on impact. You could be killed if you do this."

"I will definitely be killed if he lands this plane," she reasons. "Morris designed this thing to withstand a head-on crash with a freight train. I was there when he tested it. It is based on the same principles as a fighter pilot ejection seat, I think it will survive an ejection."

"Please reconsider, we are less than an hour behind you," Russell pleads, "now that Karl knows you are onto him, he will help you fight. Tell him we all know what he has done…"

"What? Put my life in the hands of a man who has already betrayed me? That's crazy," she argues, "I'll put my trust in my father. When it came to shit like this, he was a genius. He designed this plane for me. And came up with this system after the Challenger explosion. He was working with NASA, can't get better people than that. I'll see you on the island, or in Hell."

"I see there is no changing your mind," Russell concedes, "we are going to swing around and approach the island from the other side, so it will take a few more minutes to reach you. See you soon or see you in Hell." He hates the mantra that has become their trademark of dangerous ideas. Now more than ever he hates saying it to her.

Maria takes a deep breath and pulls the pin in the ceiling. A red handle on a chain drops in front of her face.

Positive thoughts in negative situations are the way plans succeed. Morris' voice fills her head. His so-called power of positive thinking approach.

Well, Dad, there is no more negative situation than the one I'm in now. She counts to sixty Mississippis. *Here goes everything.* She takes another deep breath and yanks the handle. There is a rumble, and the pod shakes her from side to side. Then, silence, and she becomes weightless.

KARL TIGHTENS THE SEATBELT. The g-force of the plane pulling out of its dive pins him to the chair. He yells, "Maria, get in here and strap yourself in."

There is no answer from the back.

The plane races above the ocean and the island grows larger in the cockpit window, which he can see through the open door. Green, brown, black, and a patchwork of other colors that are signs of civilization are replaced by a sea of red, orange, and yellow that fill the cabin. He and his seat are thrown forward, then he's swallowed up by the intense heat.

Unwillingly, he takes in a deep breath of the scorching gas. Instantly his breath is caught within him as the gases cauterize his lungs, preventing him from exhaling. For a brief few tormenting seconds, he feels himself burning inside and out.

JOHN'S HANDS grip tight on the yoke of the plane, straining to pull it into his lap. He has done this maneuver many times for the air force, it's the basic bombing run, every pilot must perform it. Although this is not the F-14 he is used to, he's satisfied this plane has handled it well. Coming out of the dive, the plane is travelling well beyond its stated top speed. They are so low and fast civilian radar will not be able to track them, and the military radars are in a poor position to pick them up too. He will have to climb soon to get to the mountain top.

The instrument panel goes dead. All the needles drop to zero. He feels himself becoming weightless as he is pitched forward and down. The cockpit fills with fire, and in the second before it blows apart, he knows something has gone terribly wrong.

THE LEARJET 60 travelling at five hundred miles an hour explodes, ripping in two aft of the main compartment. The front section nosedives again and the wings snap off. The tail section pulls backward and down. The powerful booster rocket on the bottom of the escape pod fires for one second. It is long enough and powerful enough to send the pod hundreds of feet above the disintegrating plane.

The expanding cloud of burning jet fuel obfuscates the escaping capsule from view. It tumbles three times before a dozen winglets pop open around its body. They are slightly angled on three bands, one at the bottom, the middle, and the top of the six-foot escape pod. The bands on the capsule twirl as it falls through the sky. The spinning slowing its descent.

Maria doesn't feel anything inside the capsule but hears the high-pitched whine of the outer body as it spins. She watches the altimeter slowing down as the numbers go from a thousand feet back past five hundred, where it was when she pulled the red handle. She braces herself as it goes into double digits.

At fifty feet she hears the hissing of air valves opening and releasing their pent-up contents. Morris told her there would be no parachute on the escape pod as it would give away its position. Instead, air rockets like those used on the lunar lander would cushion the fall. "If you deploy it over water, it will sink to about twenty feet. You have enough air to remain in the escape pod for twenty-four hours, but if you can't wait that long, or rescue isn't coming, there is scuba gear in the stowaway," he had said.

Maria dresses quickly. She knows Warren is watching the plane's approach and isn't sure if he's seen the escape pod launch. Even if he hasn't, he will surely send men to investigate what happened. She isn't waiting around for Russell or him to find her. She is an excellent scuba diver and included with the gear are two small electric propellers that she attaches to her arms. *Some real James Bond equipment*, she thinks.

She turns the handle on the door and the pod starts filling with water. When it's half full, the floor falls away and the top pops open. The cylinder drops to the bottom of the sea leaving her in the open ocean. She kicks the fins, flattening them out then presses the buttons on the swimming aid controllers in her hands and gently glides away.

She passes Karl's charred body suspended in the water. "Traitor," she says.

"Maria, are you alright?" Russell asks.

"Yes. Good to know the radio pack works. I am swimming to the island."

"We will be landing in fifteen. Don't do anything, we will come and find you."

Maria hears the motors of approaching boats. She angles away from them and plunges a little deeper. "Hurry up. I can't go walking up on the beach like nothing happened. And by the time you get here there will be police."

"Keep heading straight and you should come to Dawn Beach.

You can ditch the equipment in the water and swim ashore like an ordinary tourist. I hope you are wearing underwear that can pass for a bathing suit."

"A very risqué one." She glides along with an extra pair of air tanks and a duffle bag of weapons hanging from her waist. With the four air tanks, the two on her back and the two spares, she can stay down for six hours if she controls her breathing. The duffle bag has two Uzis, two Mac-10s, a Browning 12 Gauge shotgun, and a M16. Also included in the assault package are a dozen hand grenades, two high explosives with remote detonators, magazines for all the guns, all individually shrink-wrapped in plastic. When she comes ashore, she will be ready.

14

GHOST

Maria sees more boats passing overhead. She is a hundred yards off the beach, sitting on the bottom in the shadow of a coral reef outcrop, making it hard to spot her in the black-skin diver's suit. It's part of her emergency escape package. Since the plane went down, dozens of boats have crossed her. Mostly small private ones, but at least two large coastguard ships have come to look for survivors.

Once she is a safe distance from the site she slows down and scans the radio channels looking for information on Warren. Her underwater radio has an automatic scanning function that locks in on any frequency with chatter. She hears a lot of official talk about the plane developing engine failure. Others are speculating that a fire onboard must be the cause of the crash. Many people saw the plane nosediving out of the sky moments before exploding in a spectacular fireball. Lucky for her, no one reports seeing the escape pod leaving the aircraft or entering the water.

She doesn't think they would have seen it. The pod is relatively small, and they were still way out from the island when the plane blew up. After sitting on the ocean floor for two hours she hears the message she was hoping for. It's a simple one that even she almost misses. "No sign of the pilot or the two passengers."

It's the number of passengers that catches her attention. No one knew, asked, or had given details as to how many people they should be searching for. How could they?

Then came the reply that seals it for her. "I don't care about the others, any sign of the girl?" It's his voice. He knows she was on the plane and is looking for confirmation she is dead.

The next message means they won't be looking for much longer. "The water here is very deep. Recovery efforts are probably not forthcoming from official channels. We will need more equipment if you want to be absolutely sure."

"Mark the site and return. We will see what washes ashore over the next few days."

MARIA SPENDS another hour on the bottom before the radio squawks again.

This time it's Russell. "Are you ready to dry off?"

"I was beginning to think you boys forgot about me."

"Not at all," Russell replies, "had to wait for the traffic topside to clear. Never can tell who is watching. I hope you were able to grab the package before your departure."

"I have a few toys you might like." Maria starts slowly to the surface. It's nighttime, perfect for her to rejoin the living.

They take the dive boat into the marina at Turtle Cove, a place mainly local fishermen and tour guides populate.

Maria changes into a black commando outfit. "Ok, what's the plan?"

"He is still at the church on the other side of the mountain," Russell opens the curtains and shows her their objective. "There are multiple roads up but only one that crosses the summit, it leads right to the church."

"Which means, he will see us coming," Maria is eating a bowl of French onion soup. "God, I am so hungry. Any chance of bringing helicopters from Nevis?"

"No, he has a small radar installation, and we scouted the area. It is covered with ground sensors. The only good news is, he wasn't expecting a big fight. We counted a dozen men, including him."

"He must be superstitious," Maria says, finishing off her bowl.

"Why do you say that?"

"Because he only picked eleven apostles. Look at what happened to Jesus, He was the thirteenth man. How close do you think you can get without tripping the sensors?"

"We can get near the summit from this side," Russell tells her, "about a mile away. After that it is all bad news."

"You wouldn't by any chance have brought a Javelin or two with you?" Maria smiles, she knows the missiles have the range of a mile and a half.

"Girl, I like the way you think. There are a couple stashed away on the plane, I'll radio Fumu to bring them over."

"How many men did you bring?"

"Nine," he replies, "three of us here. There are three guys watching the main roads off the mountain, in case Warren decides to bugout. And Fumu is with two others at the plane."

Maria goes quiet for a few minutes and her smile disappears. The three men watch her intently as she devises a plan. Then the corners of her mouth twist up. She looks like the innocent little girl they all watched grow up. They also know, she has something devilish in mind.

WARREN ORDERS four of his snipers into their ghillie suits to take their positions for the night. One covering each direction to the church gives him a semblance of peace. He sits by the radio console; the deadline for Karl to have radioed in has long passed.

There has been no word of any explosions in Colombia so he imagines Maria's people must know whatever plans they had blew up before she got here. With her gone, they might decide to divvy up the cocaine.

This is the perfect time to make his move there, and he already has three teams ready to roll. Two fast attack Humvees two blocks away and a bulldozer digging up a street one block over.

His helicopter pilot radios in, "there is no movement inside the main target. Infrared reveals the warehouse is full of large drums but no persons. Other warehouses show minimal activities. The north corner and the east on the main road are the most likely targets."

"Roger that," Warren responds, "Alpha team, you have the north. Bravo, take the main road in. Light'em, boys!"

The two Humvees roll down the street, picking up speed as they approach their targets. Both smash through the warehouse doors while the topside gunners pop out and open fire. The trucks go in a wide circle as gunners fire the 50-caliber machine guns from the tops, sides, and backs of the vehicles. They methodically spray the inside of the warehouses with bullets, killing everyone and destroying everything inside.

The bulldozer lifts its loader and crashes through the side of the warehouse. The cinderblock wall caves in as the huge vehicle climbs over the rubble with ease. Two men with Uzis jump from the back of the earthmover and fan out in the dark warehouse. They quickly confirm the place is deserted.

The Humvees take up positions on the main roads and one of the men inside the warehouse cautiously opens a drum. He looks inside and radios to the sergeant eight hundred miles away, "This drum is filled with water."

"Water? Are you sure, Manuel?"

"Sarge, I'm shinning my light in it. There's nothing in here but water. Santiago is confirming another drum has the same. I believe the intel you received was bogus."

"Check the drums in the middle," commands Warren. "Open them all, I want to be sure."

"Yes, of course." Manuel yells across to Santiago, "get some of the guys in here. We are going to be here a while."

WARREN SLAMS the mike on the desk. "That damn bitch knew about Karl the whole time. The coke was never in that warehouse. She never planned to blow it up. She thought she'd come here, blow me up yet again, and sell my product for herself." He is ranting to himself as no one dares to agree or disagree. "Now, I wish she hadn't killed herself. I would like to have cut her from cunt to mouth. Fillet that bitch."

One man sitting across the church in the north Transept keeping watch, ventures an opinion. "What if she wasn't killed in the explosion, Sarge?"

"What did you say?"

"I'm just thinking… It was very convenient; her plane blowing up as it's heading to the island. Maybe she's setting a trap."

"Are you saying John double-crossed me?" his anger amplifies, but now he has someone to direct it at, "that piece of shit, Karl. Yeah, I wouldn't put it past him. But John's been with me for years. We flew missions together. Boy, you'd better have something more than just a hunch."

"I was just thinking…"

"No. No way," Warren leaves the radio console on the altar and is now in the young man's face, his black-gloved fist swinging like a pendulum at his side. "We had codes. If something was wrong, he would have given the abort answer and I would have directed him to a safe landing site."

"You're right," the man quickly agrees. "But the cocaine has to be somewhere in Colombia. We should involve more men in tracking it."

"Now, that's a good idea," Warren says gleefully.

The young man sighs with relief.

"We will close up shop here tomorrow. Put all our resources into finding my property. A billion dollars' worth of product is hard to hide."

SUNRISE FINDS Maria standing on the bow of the dive boat.

Russell comes out to join her, "Couldn't sleep?"

"What are you talking about? slept like a baby. I am just excited about ruining that old goat's day." Maria goes to the radio equipment and turns the dial to the frequency John was on in the plane. "Hey, Warren! Warren, sweetheart, are we still on for our date?"

Three of Warren's men hear the radio call. Two of them push the third, the same young man who doubted Maria's death, to go wake their boss.

He reluctantly calls him out of a deep sleep from a safe distance. "Sarge, it's her!"

"It's who?"

Before he can answer, the radio squeals loudly.

Maria's voice booms from the speaker in the empty church, "Hey, sleepy head, I know you're up there. Can one of you cowards tell that one-arm freak I'm back from the dead?"

Warren rushes to the mike, "So, it was a fucking trick. And my man, John, is he dead?"

"Com' on, you didn't fall for the big explosion," she laughs, "you went ooh and ahh like the locals. I thought you were smarter than that. Your boy, John, yeah, he's dead. But hey, me and you, we still on for our little dance."

"And my cocaine?"

"Really, is that all you care about? I heard about your little raid last night. You shot up a bunch of Russians, and my old friend Barry Thomas. He was working for the Russians anyway, trying to steal weapon technology from my company, so thanks for the intervention. Neither the CIA nor the Russians are happy with you. But hey, don't worry, where you are going you won't be sniffing coke. You're gonna be sucking the devil's dick for eternity." She laughs. "I know you still got a bunch of guys waiting for me, but I'm still driving up alone. You keep those hotshots indoors and I won't blow up your coke. This time, let's play this straight."

"Ok."

MARIA DRIVES a jeep up the mountain road. She has the MAC-10 on the seat next to her and Fumu in the back. Just before she reaches the summit he jumps out with a black and green Javelin missile launcher on his back.

"Don't drive too fast, don't be in a rush to get this over with. You have to give me time to get set up," he pats the tail of the jeep.

She nods and continues over the top. "Russell, Fumu has been deployed. Where are you?"

"I'm approaching from the French side, I got good tree cover, will be on target in five minutes."

"Roger that," she replies. The jeep's mike is locked open so she can talk without touching it. "Team leaders sound off."

"Sniper Team West, we are in position, with one snake in the grass in our crosshairs."

"Sniper Team South ditto, we are locked on and ready."

"Assault Team One, we are right behind, you will hold at position one."

"This is Air Assault Team Two, we are just north of Sandy Ground, say the word and no one there gets out alive."

"This is Fumu, I have the church lined up, proceed as planned."

"OK, I'm going in." Maria continues down the dirt road at twenty miles an hour, not wanting to obscure Fumu's vision by kicking up too much dust, although, a little dirt will not stop a missile. But she must also give Russell time to get in position with the second Javelin. At a half mile from the old, dilapidated church she slows to five miles an hour. She is already within sniper range.

She pulls out the knob for the wipers, but instead of sweeping across the windshield, a metal plate pops up. She repositions the rearview mirror so she can see through the opening in the metal plate. It is arranged so a shot through the slit will go over her head. "Come on, Warren, show yourself you piece of shit."

As commanded, Warren steps outside the church doors. He has an M16 on his hip with the barrel pointing up.

Maria slows then stops a hundred yards from the church. She grabs the Mac-10 and waits.

"On target," Russell radios in.

"Good, let's take this motherfucker," Maria says with venom. She yells out, "How do you want to do this? Back-to-back then ten paces, or we start running and gunning?"

Warren yells back, "Like I would ever turn my back on you. Come closer, I'll give you a chance to get out of your vehicle. You are already within sniper range."

"What's the matter," she yells back, "did your snipers tell you the priest hole is too high up? Come forward and I will do the same."

"Don't worry about them, I told them not to shoot. I want the pleasure of killing you myself." Warren starts up the dirt road. His eyes darting left and right, looking for his snipers without turning his head. The M16's strap is taunt against his chest. His black-gloved iron hand hangs loosely at his side.

"Maria, we got six in the church and four marked in the field," Russell radios, "with Warren on the move, that leaves one man missing."

"We will have to deal with him as the need arises," she informs the team, "on my mark… FIRE!"

FUMU HAS the laser trained on the church's front door. He brings the door into the frame of the targeting window, squeezes the trigger, and a gentle stream of smoke pushes the missile away from him. The main rocket engine kicks in and flares the missile on its way. In ten seconds, it streaks over Maria's head, passes Warren, then slams through the church oak door. The building evaporates in a cloud of fire and thunder.

Warren is thrown to the ground by the force of the explosion behind him and the ringing in his ears drowns out the world. Rocks the size of quarters rain down on him and he grabs a handful as he pulls himself to his feet. Disorientated, he stumbles around, looking for his weapon.

THE SNIPER TEAMS squeeze their triggers in unison at the sound of Maria's command. Years of training together has turned the men into a single fighting force and their bullets strike individual targets with deadly accuracy. None of Warren's men had a chance to react. Each bullet fired is a lethal projectile penetrating a man's head, neck, or shoulder, leaving them dead in their foxholes.

The snipers cover up as soon as the trigger is pulled, guarding against what's coming next. None see the missiles that strike the church but the roar from the impacts shakes the ground beneath them. They look up from their vantage points to see the black clouds streaming skyward.

RUSSELL FIRES his Javelin on command. It hisses out of the tube on his shoulder and flies forty feet, then flames arch it upwards into the sky. And just as quickly as it rises, it nosedives into the heart of the church, arriving at nearly the same instant as Fumu's Javelin missile. The blasts pulverize the old church, turning it into a cloud of dust, and all that was inside too.

THE SHOCKWAVE BLOWS past Maria like a gentle breeze. She stopped a quarter of a mile from the church, a safe distance. She gets out of the jeep, Mac-10 in hand, and walks deliberately towards Warren. He appears to be on fire as the dust puffs from his body, wandering aimless.

Probably suffering the effects of a concussion, she thinks.

No matter, he's about to die, but first, she has a few words for him. She stops ten feet from him as he reaches down to retrieve his M16. She fires a burst from the Mac-10 and it tears through the receiver, destroying the trigger, breach, bolt, and magazine. The gun is useless.

He stands to face her. "Your bombs were late," he yells, the ringing still affecting him.

"I wasn't trying to blow you up," she yells back, to make sure he hears her. "We tried that once and you got away. My father told me, the only way to be sure a man is dead is to look him in the eyes and put a bullet in his head."

"Is he truly dead," Warren backs away from the destroyed weapon, "I really had hope of killing him myself. He ruined my business back in South America."

"Well, he's waiting for you. He never forgets an enemy or forgives one. I am sure you are going to have a hell of a time in Hell."

"You think I was just a hired guy. An overpaid babysitter while others negotiated a deal with your dear ol' dad. You were both wrong. I am the major player in the South American plan," Warren's hearing has returned. He steps back again, inviting Maria to come closer.

He's stalling. But I'll pay along. He still has one man unaccounted for. "You are just a puppet on the strings of some corrupt politicians. I have seen the likes of you many times. But your masters have tossed you aside and now it is me you will answer to. I hold your wealth and the key to your power."

"You still believe this is about Cocaine." He laughs. "Your father knew. He figured it out. It is about controlling the lands and its people. And the best way to control them is by controlling the government's power. Namely, its armed forces. The real power, as your father would attest to, is in arms control. The one who holds the biggest gun controls the war. Those idiot congressmen had you kidnapped to get control of the best gun on the battlefield. I would have done it differently." He steps back another few feet and speaks softly, "but had I known how much you cared for your Akalina, I would have sampled her sweetness myself. Before letting my dogs ravish her."

Maria rushes forward a few feet then catches herself. *He is trying to distract me. Must stay focused on the task at hand. The battle has yet to be fought.*

"Well, what are you waiting for?" Warren's eyes dart around and finally fix on a spot to the right of her.

Maria swings the gun behind her, firing in a sweeping motion at the ground. She keeps her eyes on Warren as the cries of a man come from her right.

"Oh, that! You weren't talking to me, were you? Well, that's the last of your men, so I don't need this anymore." She drops the weapon and pulls out her two steel gauntlets from her ammo vest. Slowly, she puts them on and flexes her fingers. "Shooting you would have been my father's way of getting revenge. I think I will make it a little more personal. I know you have an iron fist, so, as they say in the movies, put up your dukes."

Warren obliges and takes a boxer's stance.

Maria moves in quickly and lands a painful blow to his right side below the ribs. The inch-long spikes dot him with blood. She dances away just as quick. He steps forward and throws a wide left hook with his iron fist. She ducks, comes up on his left, and jabs him on his left rib cage. More blood spurts out. She smiles.

He stumbles back but regains his balance even as the pain rushes up his side. He realizes this girl is faster even if not stronger than him, and the gloves compensate for the lack of power in her punches. Plus, his prosthetic hand is limited in its motions. Out-boxing her is out of the question, so he grabs his iron fist and gives it a twist, pulls it right off and drops it to the ground. "You should have listened to your daddy. Oh, wait, you did."

"You should have kept the hand. If you think I won't hit a one-handed cripple, you are so mistaken."

"He underestimated me too." Warren forcefully swings his left arm down and a shining two-foot sword snaps out of the end of the fake arm. It hangs down to his ankle.

"I guess that makes you officially a Bond villain," Maria laughs.

Russell raises his rifle and takes aim.

Fumu places a hand on the barrel and gently lowers the weapon. "She will be pissed if you interfered with her kill."

"She may be mad, but she won't be dead," Russell says and raises the M16 again.

"Hey, have you ever known her to be outmatched in a fight? We trained her well, that blade isn't going to help him."

"Ok, but if she gets in trouble, I'm blowing his head off. I will not bury another friend."

"Agreed," says Fumu.

Warren slashes upward and then across as Maria retreats. "I guess you didn't count on me having something up my sleeve."

"Hey, good one," Maria says, bouncing on her toes still prepared to box, "I love it when a man doesn't take his death too seriously."

"Oh, I may die here today, but not before I kill you." He steps forward, slashing and jabbing the blade at her. He spins and the double-edged sword slices dangerously above her head as she does a shoulder roll.

She pops up behind him and throws hooks into his lower back. The punches send him staggering forward. She clanks her metal fists together and waits for him to recover. "Know what your problem is? you fight like an old man."

"AARGGH!" He comes at her with an overhead swing.

The flash of sunlight blinds them both for a moment and a loud clank of steel-on-steel rings in the air.

Maria catches the sergeant's blade in her left outstretched hand then pulls him in and throws a cross punch, breaking bones in the face.

Warren drops to his knees, blood pouring from his nose and mouth, his sword still in her steel-gloved hand.

She hears sirens in the distance and notices the lights of emergency vehicles racing up the mountain. Looking up past Warren, she also sees the lights of a helicopter closing in fast. "Oh, my dear Sarge, I think it's time we end our little dance of death. My ride is almost here. But before you die, know this, I am going to kill your daughter."

Warren gurgles something unintelligible through the blood in his mouth. Maria repeatedly punches him in the face, crushing his skull. She rips his prosthetic arm off and stakes him to the ground through his heart.

Russell and Fumu run to her side as the helicopter hovers overhead. It drops a ladder and all three clip their vests to the rungs. The helicopter swings up and they are hoisted into the air as ambulances, fire engines, and police cars reach the summit from both the French and Dutch sides.

Ezabel sees the black detective cars parked at either end of the street. They have been there for a month. She wonders how much longer they will remain. Her kidnapping has been over for three months. Her father's funeral was two months ago. The police haven't had any more questions for her in the last month, and all those who have come to pay their respects have done so.

"Momma, I'm home," she announces, coming through the door. She walks into the kitchen and gets a glass of juice from the refrigerator then walks into the living room and yells, "Mom, are you here?"

"Your mother has gone to the store," Maria answers, sitting in a chair by the doorway leading to the hall.

Ezabel drops her glass and turns to run.

"Hold on! I'm not here to hurt you," Maria says kindly, "I just need to talk to you for a couple of minutes."

"I find that hard to believe," Ezabel says, nervously backing up towards the kitchen.

"Where are you going?" Maria asks. "You can't get out through the kitchen without going down the hall. And I'll beat you to the front door."

"Maybe so, but maybe I'll grab a knife on my way." Her voice rises sharply in pitch, and she is visibly shaking.

"Look, you are a bundle of nerves," Maria consoles, "why don't you just sit on the couch and listen to me for a minute? Then, if you still want to go for a knife, I can't stop you. I'm unarmed." She opens the white jacket of her skirt suit and crosses her legs.

Ezabel takes a seat across the room. "How did you get in here? There are cops at both corners."

"Those guys aren't cops, well they are, but they are my men. And that's what I'm here to talk to you about. I know the cops spoke to you in New York and you didn't tell them anything about me. After all, you couldn't. Not without exposing what your father did to me." Maria uncrosses her legs and leans forward.

Ezabel pushes back in her seat.

"I have it from good sources that you didn't tell the Miami police anything either. Why didn't you? Your father is dead. But I suppose you could be trying to protect his memory."

"After what you did to him, I would not dare say anything. We had a closed casket funeral; they wouldn't even let me see his body."

"Then how do you know what I did was so horrible?"

"They told me they couldn't reconstruct his face!" The anger in her voice surprises them both.

"Well, he put up a good fight," Maria says softly, trying to ease the girl's feelings. "Just not good enough. He got what was coming to him. But I'm not here because of him, I'm here because of you. You are what my father would call a loose end. If he had his way, you would be dead. But I'm not my father."

"Really, where is he? And should I be expecting a visit from him?" She's being combatant. Fear is fading, and the anger emboldening her in words and tone.

"I'm not here to talk about either of our fathers. I'm here to tell you, you don't have to carry your father's sins on your face anymore. I am sorry about that, but it was the only way to ensure he would meet me in person." Maria reaches into her pocket and takes out a little black book. She tosses it on the table in front of Ezabel. "Everybody must pay for their sins and one day I'll have to pay for mine. Open it."

"What is it?"

"It won't bite you, open it and see." Maria waits as the girl carefully reaches forward and takes it.

Ezabel's eyes widen as she opens it to the middle.

"It's a bank book, with the accounts and amounts set up in your name. I'm pretty sure you didn't know anything about it, and I don't think your father was building a college fund for you. My guess is, this is part of the money laundering that goes with some of his less than public affairs. I thought you should have it." She looks at Ezabel with the same cold stare she had when she burned the eagle into her face. "On one condition, you forget about me. Starting with fixing your face, and the other places. If you should pass me on the street someday, you don't even look twice. Can you do that?"

"So, you are trying to buy my silence. Pay me off!"

"No. The money is yours; I think you should have it. This is about tying up those loose ends. Give me your word and we both live our lives. If not, no matter how many hundreds of millions of dollars you have, I will kill you."

"Suppose I take all this money and use it to kill you!"

"The people you could pay to kill me with that money. I know them. I will know. See what I'm saying?"

"Ok. I told the police I was blindfolded the whole time anyway, so I will stick to that story." She feels there is honesty in what Maria is saying.

"Good. The two cars on your block will be gone when I leave." Maria gets up and turns.

Ezabel sees the bulge in the middle of her back, a gun hung neatly above the waist of her pencil skirt.

Maria adjusts her jacket and leaves, satisfied this business is settled.

MARIA TAKES her grandmother to the castle. Christina had only seen it from afar and Maria feels it's about time she got a proper tour and met the other women in Morris' life.

It's an awkward affair for all involved. Meeting women she had only seen from a distance leaves her at both an advantage and disadvantage. She knows who they are, each being famous or at least notable, and yet not knowing anything more than what is reported in the newspapers.

Gisella had been shocked at the funeral to learn Morris' mother was alive. She could only remember him telling her once she was dead, no details of how or why. She didn't know when the woman had supposedly died, but assumed it was in his childhood and too painful to talk about. She was totally confused as to why he would lie about something like that, especially since he was so honest about everything else.

Yana wasn't surprised at all to meet her. "So, the mysterious Woman of the Shadow is his mother."

"Who?"

"You, Christina. I have seen you many times before." Yana says, sitting in the family room on the second floor of the Keep. She has held the position as the elder of Morris' women, as she refers to them. Elizabeth knew him longer but was much younger than her. "The others are not as observant as I am. A gift and a curse," she says, smiling, "but I have seen you before. Not necessarily stalking but observing. I asked Morris on a couple of occasions, and he brushed it off. I chalked it up to extra security he didn't want to talk about. Or, being who I am, you know, a movie star, you were a fan. Now, I wish he would not have kept you a secret all these years."

"Thank you," Christina says humbly, "I wish I had the courage to come forward sooner. But he made it very clear the danger I posed to him and myself. I've waited for so long for an invitation to meet you all."

"Well, you are one of us now," Maria hands her a glass of wine, "be careful what you wish for."

They continue getting to know Christina, and although Maria had many conversations with her, she holds back on much of what she could have told her. Here, she feels free to open up as the other two women don't mind sharing their intimate thoughts with Christina.

After dinner, Christina is at the bar in the observatory.

Yana enters and pours herself a drink, "I thought I'd find you here. This was your son's favorite room. He spent hours in that chair over there staring out at the Aegean Sea. I never knew what he was looking at or thinking, I joked with myself that he was trying to forget about us all."

"That is a horrible thing to say."

"Morris had a way of… how should I put this," she begins with sadness in her voice, "of putting things and people behind him. You must see that now. When he left me in Miami, I waited for years, then gave up. I thought I'd never see him again."

"But he did come back," Christina says cheerfully, defending her son.

"Yeah, but I never knew why. Gisella brought him back from the dead twice, and he left her too."

"That was an amazing story," Christina is still having trouble believing it, "but didn't she tell him to go?"

"She did. And he did. Then he went and got her. No reason, he just did. With all that was said today, I came to find you because I know you have questions you want to ask. But not in front of everyone."

"What makes you think that?"

"Remember I told you I worked in a strip club?" Yana smiles, "I can see what's on people minds. Not just men. You want to know if I know what happened to your son."

"You seem to be the leader of the group. If anyone was to confess, you seem to be the most likely to hear them out."

"I am. And let me start by saying, do not blame Maria." Yana holds Christina's hands, as if afraid she'll run away. "None of us saw his body, Maria wanted it that way. Morris had a way of pushing people to be at their best while doing the worst thing imaginable. I don't know, maybe Morris wanted to die. He wasn't afraid of death. For as long as I've known him, he looked forward to it. Maybe he felt he'd come back one more time. Maybe he felt it was time to head out there," she points to the huge picture window and the starry night sky, "and find whatever it was he was looking for."

Maria sinks down in Morris' big comfy chair and smiles.

***

"UNCLE NICKY, have I got news for you," Maria says excitedly into the phone.

"I was wondering when you were going to call," he responds nonchalantly, "I understand your birthday is coming up. The big twenty-one if I remember correctly."

"Yes," she agrees, although, she is twenty-four and he knows it, "my mother is throwing me a party out on the island, just like in the old days. I hope you will attend."

"I wouldn't miss it," Nicky hangs up and prepares to go to the mansion on Long Island. He puts in a brief call to his Consigliere Joseph Castor.

THE THREE MEET in the garden room a few hours later.

"Thanks for coming," Maria greets them. "I don't recognize any of the men in the house now."

"We have made some changes since Nicky's trial."

"Nothing drastic," Nicky confirms, "people get too comfortable, need to move some new guys in and others out. But what's on your mind, as if I didn't already know?"

"Yes, I am sure you are aware of my success down south. I was wondering, how would you like to expand your distribution network?" Maria is proud of how well her plan worked out.

"You mean our business," Nicky corrects her, "you are a full partner in the shipping company."

"Yes, of course," Maria nods, "I have a billion and a half in storage. And this is where I really need you to step in, about a billion dollars in product in lockup. I have guys in Sanchez's organization. I was hoping you could liberate the rest and merge the operation."

"Joe, you know who to reach out to, get the ball rolling."

"Of course, Boss. Miss Delitanni, it is a pleasure to see you again."

IT IS COLD AND DARK, but the two wise guys stationed outside the Sons of Italy are not bothered, as they wear their tracksuits open to their chests, and carry two guns, one hanging under each armpit in plain sight. It's 10 P.M. but the bar is closed to all but the invited guests. The streets around the area are lined with Cadillacs.

All the tables have been lined up and bedecked with one long white tablecloth to create banquet seating. The center of the table is covered with the finest Italian cuisine.

Nicky sits at the head of the table and as the fifteen invitees finish their meal and wine is poured, he stands to address the group. "Welcome to my friends from Brooklyn, Queens, Harlem, Manhattan. And those who have come from farther still, Las Vegas, Chicago, Philly, and Miami. I called this sit down because these are dark times, and we need to right our ship if we are to survive."

"Right our ship," said an old ponderous man from Chicago, "you could have started by telling us this was not going to be a private meeting."

There is a chorus of agreement from the other Dons and Capos.

"I thought it was necessary to let everyone think this was a simple meeting. In light of recent events, if the Feds realized that so many were travelling today… well, we would be having a different kind of meeting. And let's face the facts here, if everyone knew that everyone else was invited, then no one would have come. But let's put aside any mistrust or differences we may have for the moment."

Head-nodding and quiet agreement allow him to continue.

"That Porco Giuda! Figlio di puttana! District Attorney, has done great damage to all our families. And in the aftermath of the old Dons going inside, we have returned to the old ways of doing business. The way of blood and bullets. I, myself… I must confess… was part of this business."

"It's good to hear you say that," says Frankie, a man about Nicky's age, aka Frankenstein because of the five scars criss-crossing his face, although nobody dares call him that to his face.

"You murdered my brother and my niece, and that was before the Commission Trial was done."

"That was settled long ago, you know I had nothing to do with Angela's death. And your brother was the victim of the war he started over it. I heard it was his own son who did the deed. And it is your refusal to accept those facts that got you the beauty marks you wear now." Nicky keeps his voice smooth and calm, but his eyes penetrate the man at the far end of the table. "But that is precisely why we need this sit down tonight. We need to establish a new order and a new way of handling our business. There has been too much fighting within the families and too much interference from our friends outside the city."

The room erupts in arguments and curses as the men launch insults and accusations across the table. Nicky stands quietly as several of the mafia heads threaten to remove body parts. Slowly, the room comes to order,

"Let me continue. The Feds are sitting back watching as we finish off the job they started. We cannot form another Commission as the RICO law would land those involved in prison too. I suggest another solution, we elect an Arbitrator, one person who we can all take our grievances to, who will settle the disputes, whose word would be law."

"And how is that different from the Commission?" asks Fishhooks Louie, who earned the title by leaving his victims hanging from their own fishing boats down in Florida as he built up a protection racket among the Deep-Sea Fishing Tours business.

"With the Commission, all the heads were involved, so if one man was guilty of a crime, then they were all held guilty of that crime. With an Arbitrator, only the persons involved in that discussion can be accused of racketeering. The rest of us would not have any culpability in the different actions."

"And how do we choose this Arbitrator?" asks a very young boss from Queens. He murdered two older capos as soon as his Don was sentenced and is known as Billy the Kid in his neighborhood because he is a quick draw gunman for his family. He had been the Don's personal bodyguard and was present for all the family's business. He was lucky not to be indicted because his name was never mentioned in any of the wire taps. "From what I understand, if we elect an Arbitrator, that instantly makes us part of a criminal conspiracy."

"I see law school taught you well," Nicky smiles then motions to his office door.

His capo walks over and opens it.

"Let me introduce you to the lady from Long Island. Many of you know her, she's the grandniece of our friend from the island; may he rest in peace. She will be our first Arbitrator. Not elected by any of us. And when she is ready to retire, she will name her successor. Since none of us have a say in her appointment, none of us can be charged with conspiracy."

"And the fact she's your Godchild played no part in her being here," yells Frankenstein from the other end of the table.

"And what about the fact that you, yourself, wanted her dead just weeks ago?" ventures the Don from Las Vegas. He's very tanned, almost as dark as Maria. He had dealings with Morris and met her on a few occasions.

"Well, as I said, I have engaged in some poor judgements of late. That is behind us now and the contract has been cancelled."

"Gentlemen," Maria stands by Nicky's side, "as a result of our falling out, I came to him with this offer. Many of you have had dealings with my father, God rest his soul, and me. You know me to be truthful and honest. My father often told me, in business there can be many heads but only one leader. In this business it is very easy for interests to conflict and parties to clash. If you continue the course you are on, you will annihilate each other."

"From where I sit," offers the old, tanned Don from Las Vegas, "I see no reason to get involved in the affairs of New

York. The Commission Trial affected your families, we may have lost a few minor players, but we will recover just fine."

"You do a lot of business with the men in this room," Maria counters, "you wash our laundry, and we supply you with several products for your clientele. Power struggles here have rippling effects across the country. Or else you wouldn't have come all this way to meet with your friends in the Bronx. You can no more afford to let this thing deteriorate any more than us. While our adversaries think we are down on the ropes, it is time to move in a new, bold, and forward-facing direction. I believe this business plan to be sound and advantageous to all."

There is more bickering and name-calling, but by the end of the wine they agree to give this venture a try. She is never to be contacted directly; each family will have their own intermediary to submit a request for a ruling. They set a term limit of five years when Maria will have to pick a successor from one of the families. She agrees, as five years is more than what she's prepared to sacrifice when Nicky came up with the plan. She, of course, will not take over his family until after she relinquishes her powers as Arbitrator.

Nicky is okay with heading the family for a few more years, although, he has decided to do it from the farm.

15

DON DELITANNI

nthony 'The Ace' Calvinetti, known as The Ace for the string of gambling houses he owns in the Bronx wakes up to the sound of beeping and hissing machines. His eyes focus on the white curtains surrounding him and finally settle on a dark skin, black-haired man in a white lab coat. "This can't be Heaven because you're in the wrong place, Haji."

"Mr. Calvinetti, I am Doctor Hamza Bukhari, a cardiologist from Pakistan, and you are in St. Luke Hospital in Ossining, New York. How are you feeling?"

"You're the Doctor, you tell me."

"Sir, it doesn't work that way."

"Relax, Hammy, I'm just fucking with you," Anthony smiles then frowns as he feels the restrain on his leg as he tries to sit up. "Hey, Doctor, how about removing the leg iron so I can get comfortable."

Dr. Bukhari, a large man, smiles and presses the button on the bed's remote that raises the top half of the bed. "Is that better? How about I listen to your heart for a moment?"

"How about you tell me what the fuck am I doing here? Did someone shiv me? Poison me? What?"

238

"What is the last thing you remember?"

Anthony is a large man and easy to anger. He grabs the bedside railings and shakes them hard. "Always with the questions. Just give me a straight answer."

"You appear to have had a heart attack. They rushed you here from Sing Sing Prison. What do you remember?"

"A heart attack," Anthony sinks down into the bed. "I was in the yard. Walking, I guess. That's it."

"Had you been exercising earlier…"

"Do I look like one of those muscle-bound boys? Hey, did you operate? Did I die on the table?" Anthony asks with glee.

Dr. Bukhari laughs, "We did not operate, and you did not die. Not even for one second. We gave you some medication and are monitoring your condition. We will keep you here for a couple of days to see what happens, and we'll run some test."

"OK. I guess," Anthony says disappointed, then adds cheerfully, "if I do die, don't bring me back right away. I am serving a life sentence, if I die for a couple of minutes, I'm a free man."

"I don't think that will happen," Dr. Bukhari says, "not the going free part, I am a doctor not a lawyer, but I don't think you are dying." He leaves the room with a smile on his face.

The side curtain is ripped forward and the metal rollers rattle, "I don't think dying for a couple of minutes will get you released for the Iron Bar Hotel."

"Nicky Nails, what the fuck are you doing here?" Anthony yells, "you sonofabitch, you poisoned me, didn't you?"

"Hey, keep your voice down. You are still a prisoner and there are guards on the other side of the door." Nicky is wearing bright green orderly scrubs. He peeks around the curtain and waits for a moment before continuing, "you sent a message you wanted to talk, so let's talk."

"You poisoned me."

"Not poison," Nicky admits, "I gave you a little Nifedipine to get your heart going. Basically, you could be running at Belmont right now, if not for the ankle bracelet. The Feds spent a lot to put you in prison, I knew they weren't going to let you check out the first chance you got. Now, what's so important that I have to come all the way to Ossining?"

"You didn't have to come," Anthony scoffs, "we could have gone through the lawyers. Like we always do. What's wrong with the old way of doing business?"

Nicky clamps his hand over his eyes. "Doing business the old way is why you are a permanent guest of the government. And besides, I don't trust lawyers."

"You don't trust my lawyer," Anthony voice jumps. "He's my freaking brother!"

"I don't trust any lawyers!"

"Look, Nicky, I respected your father. God rest his soul. He was a good friend," Anthony takes on a tone of a father giving advice to his son. He is sixty-seven, twenty-two years older than Nicky and one of the last old guards of the family. "He was the natural choice to take over for Angelo. And when he made you Don, well, I had my doubts. You were too young, and too… unpredictable. Too many friends outside the family. But you proved to be a good Godfather. You built this family back up. We are the strongest on the East Coast. But I'm hearing some disturbing things in the pipes. You are getting a lot of us old timers… how do you say… worked up."

"Let me guess," Nicky sits down on the other bed. "You heard I'm going to retire. Well, I've been at this thing my entire life. I made more money than I can ever spend. As you put it, I made this family number one, and I would say, not just on the East Coast. Which was my goal all my life! But, you got to know when to call it quits. Go out on top, before I wind up as your roomy, or worse."

"Hey, no one is saying you don't deserve to take a break," Anthony motions Nicky to come closer, "we are having problems with who you plan to be your successor, that got everyone's nuts all twisted."

"Choose your words carefully, old man. She's my Goddaughter, and the closest thing I have to a child of my own."

"Maria is a great girl," Anthony watches Nicky as he looms over him. "But here's the thing. The bosses weren't happy when you made that first girl a capo, and you see how that turned out. Then you give Maria her bones, and she ain't even full—"

"You remember why I made her," Nicky glares, "it was after the Pittsburgh fiasco. And she is Angelo's Grandniece. How much more blood does she need?"

"Hey, how she handled the Slovs was great. But some are saying fifty percent has never been enough. She needs to be full Italiano to run the family. You know that. I suggest TJ as a candidate."

"You're kidding! Tony Jr., the guy Maria had to save in Pittsburgh? Fuck you, Anthony!"

"That's not the way I heard it," Anthony smiles, "my son tells me it was her ass she had to save."

MARIA, TJ, and Rocky pull up to an abandoned warehouse in a dilapidated section in Pittsburgh. The four-story building takes up the entire block. More than half the windows are missing, all the ones on the first two floors are gone. It is 2:00 a.m. and bitterly cold.

Maria looks at TJ in disgust, "Are you sure you want to go through with this? It looks like the kind of place one goes to, to get murdered."

"I know these guys well," Tony assures them, "I have a good Molly deal with them. I supply them over a hundred thousand doses a year. They are not going to fuck that up. This is one of their places where they run their rave. If we are going to put a casino in the place we need to take a look at it."

"Agreed," Maria says, "but we could have come in the daytime and had a better look around."

"True that," Rocky chimes in from behind the steering wheel.

"Shut your face, Rocky! You're just here to drive the car." Tony has his hand on the door handle and turns to Maria, "I don't even know why you are tagging along. How old are you anyway, sixteen? Don't know why Nails sent you along." He gets out of the car and shuts the door, forcing Maria to exit the other side. "These Slovs don't do business with women. And they surely don't like people of the darker persuasion, if you know what I mean."

"Nicky sent me along to cover your back," Maria says, "but I will be glad to sit in the nice warm car, and you can go in there with Rocky."

"No way! I'm just here to drive the car. Remember?"

Maria leans in the driver's window, "Not to worry, I got this fool's back. Just keep the car running and your hand on that shotgun. And every now and then check the mirrors." She quickens her step to catch up to TJ who has headed toward a side door where two men are waiting. "By the way, I'm seventeen and killed a dozen men already. How about you?"

"Look, just don't say nothing. I'll do all the talking. We will take a quick look around and be out of there. Half hour tops."

The first man at the door pats down Tony. He was instructed to come unarmed. Then he feels up Maria, paying special attention to her intimate places. She looks him in the eye without any emotion. Then the next guy does the same to her and laughs as he tells them to go upstairs.

The second floor is wide open. There are three rows of fluorescent lights running half the length of the floor. Thick and heavy black curtains hang from the ceiling to the floor in front of the windows. There is a trashcan fire burning in the middle of the cavernous warehouse. Four men stand around it, warming their hands. Three of them have machineguns hanging from straps at their sides. The fourth is wearing two western revolvers on his hip.

Maria whispers, "You got to be kidding me."

"Not a fucking word," Tony cautions her and walks ahead of her. "Hendrick, dude, how you been? How was that last batch I sent you? Badass Moon Rocks, right," Tony throws his brand name out louder than necessary.

"TJ, buddy, what is this business you have to discuss?" says the man wearing the cowboy pistols and hat and boots to match.

The men are all at the campfire. Maria stands a couple of feet behind TJ, but close enough to hear what is being said. She watches as the four men eye her up and down. Two of them look like they spend their days in the gym, or just got out of prison. Hendrick isn't very big, and neither is his money man, the guy they call Bugs.

Maria notices Bugs isn't used to carrying a gun, as he keeps shifting it around his body. The other two have forgotten about their guns and are staring at her like hungry wolves. She listens intently to Tony's sales pitch.

"It's like I said before, Hendrick, you are letting money walk out the door. Your clients come here looking for excitement. But there is only so much pharms they can ingest. So much liquor they can guzzle. Then, these college boys take daddy's trust fund money and student loan cash and leave. But if you let us put in some tables and slot machines… Henny, my friend, these boys will be dropping wads of cash. There is no bigger excitement than winning at craps, and no stronger addiction than chasing a losing night."

"These boys come here to dance, drink, and fuck."

"That's because that is all you are offering them," TJ counters, "we bring in some girls to keep their interest up. You handle all the booze and pills, that's all you. We bankroll the gambling, you know, we're the house. And we give you a nice cut of the take. You know what they say, Vegas wasn't built by winners. And it draws the young and old alike."

"I will think about it," Hendrick says, walking up to Maria. He runs a hand down her arm and across her backside. "In the meanwhile, let's see what your girls can offer."

"Ha ha," Tony stammers, "ah, she's not here for that. She's with me. I mean, my Godfather sent her along as, um…"

"If she is not here for fucking," Hendrick grabs Maria's arm tight, "what is she here for, spying? You Italians think you will come in here and take over my operation."

"No. No. Henny, that is not what is going on here."

"I tell you what's going on here. Either she stays here and puts out for me and my boys," he pulls her face to face with him. "Or nobody is leaving here."

Maria has heard enough. "I'll tell you why I am here. I'm here because if this meeting goes sideways, as it appears to be, then I have to kill you and your boys, and make sure this guy gets back to New York."

Maria grabs the two .45 revolvers and as they are half way out of the holsters fires a shot in both of Hendrick's legs. He howls in pain and falls away from her. She spins the guns in her hands and fires another two shots. Each shot hits the machine-gun-toting bodyguards in their Kevlar vests. She drops one knee to the floor and fires twice more, hitting them in the head. She trains both six shooters on Bugs who quickly drops his weapon.

TJ quickly walks towards the entrance. "We are going to let you take care of those wounds. Think over my proposal and give me a call."

Maria grabs Tony's arm. She hears two shotgun blasts. "Ok, now we can go." She starts backing away from Hendrick and Bugs. "These are really nice. I'm going to keep them as souvenirs of my trip to Pittsburgh. Do you mind?"

"TONY, what is really going on with you? All this talk about her bloodline, her not being worthy of a capo position in the family," Nicky pleads with his old capo, "just give it to me straight."

"I don't trust her!" Anthony struggles to sit up with both ankles handcuffed to the bed rails. "She sided against me in that Brooklyn deal when she was the Arbitrator. She cost me a fortune and this family too."

"She did not go against you, she avoided a bloody war. She looked over your offer and then made a counteroffer that should have been accepted."

"I offered a generous six percent of gross," Anthony wags his finger at Nicky, "gross. That would have made their family millions over a roaming card game. A gambling house on the Brooklyn docks was worth a fortune and their family didn't have a big stake in the business."

Nicky has been hearing this story for two years. He shakes his head and speaks low and direct, "you wanted to set up shop on another family's territory and offered them what they were already making on their own. I had a look at the numbers when you rejected the offer Maria put forth. Against my better judgement, that I'd be pulled in as a coconspirator. She proposed only another five percent. Not doubling your offer but giving the Santories a good profit. Everyone would have saved face and made out."

"Yeah, then she goes and picks some douche from out west to be her replacement as Arbitrator. Another stab in the back for our family!"

"Hey, keep your voice down," Nicky warns. "That was the whole idea behind setting up the Arbitrator Program. That it is not tied to any one family. That the Arbitrator be free to act independently. She picked a guy from California who hadn't been in the family for too long and has a good background in law and finance."

"There is another reason," Anthony says, "she is too closely aligned with the gangs."

"Maria is not aligned with the gangs," Nicky laughs, "she is the head of the gangs. It is one of the reasons I picked her. She will give our family the extra muscle that Morris and I could not totally solidify."

"How can we trust that her gang life will not outweigh her Mafia family?"

"Because I trained her for half her life."

"It is the other half that worries us," Anthony says. "Word is she killed her father."

"Oh com'on! Who among us haven't had to do a little dirty work once in a while."

MARIA ARRIVES at the mansion an hour before the scheduled meeting with all the other capos. She only made her bones six months ago, weeks after she passed on the mantle of Arbitrator. To her surprise Nicky isn't there yet.

The other capos start arriving and she drinks and talks with them while they wait on Nicky. "He's probably coming from the farm," Maria offers.

"Yeah," Rocky agrees, he made capo at the same time as Maria, "he doesn't spend much time at Sons anymore. Interesting though, your father's drink is still upside down on the bar. Only a slight little bit has escaped. Nobody sits at that end of the bar anyway; they think it's haunted. The few people who did, turned up dead."

"Not really that spooky considering the business we are in."

Nicky walks in and heads straight to the office in the back. He takes a seat at the head of the table looking out at the garden as everyone else files into their places. The senior capos and their advisors sit closest to him on either side of the banquet table. Maria and Rocky, being newly promoted, sit alone at the other end across from each other. No one sits at the end, as is customary. Nicky looks at both of them in turn, "youse have not picked your consiglieres yet. What are you waiting for?"

Rocky starts to speak and Nicky waves him off. "I called this meeting today because I have troubling news." He waits a moment as his glance runs the length of the table. "It has been brought to my attention that there is a rat bastard among us here."

No one utters a sound, afraid his gaze will settle on him, or her.

"Let me bring in the accuser and the guilty party will have his chance to defend himself."

Maria sighs softly to herself. Rocky gives her a querying look. Two men open the door they entered through and in walks an eighty-year-old Salvatore Cigneralla supporting himself with a large, polished, black oak cane. He takes the seat at the other end of the table.

"Don Cigneralla, I thought you were away," exclaims Lorenzo Agosti.

"Did you now, Luckless Leo," Salvatore, the head of the Staten Island Mafia, says with venom. "Is that why you informed them of my double's grandniece? And told them to check her DNA against my hospital records?"

"Don Cigneralla, I did no such thing. Who told you this lie?"

"Your partner in this deed."

The two men at the door open it, bring in a body bag, and with a loud thud throw it on the table.

"Open it!"

"I… I don't… I don't know who could be in there." Luckless Leo sees all eyes trained on him, except Nicky.

Someone at the table grabs the zipper and quickly opens the

thick black bag. Gianni Esposito's head falls to the side and his dead eyes lock on Lorenzo. He tries to stand but the two big men, Don Cigneralla's men, shove him back down and hold him there.

"Gianni and Lorenzo, you were tired of taking orders. You two pezzi di merda senza valore! You were going to take over my family. Thanks to Don Rocci, who knew I was on vacation when the Commission Trials began, tipped me off to that figlio di puttana's plans. It didn't take long for him to finger you."

"Nicky, Don Rocci, I would never…"

Nicky Rocci swiftly pulls his thumb across his throat and one of Don Cigneralla's men pulls back Luckless Leo's head by his hair, while the other cuts his head clean off with a Kopis sword as long as his arm.

The capo to his right slides back to let the blood gushing from Luckless Leo drop to the floor. Covered in blood he stands and says, "Don Rocci, may I avail myself of the facilities?"

"Of course," Nicky says, "in fact, we are all done here, you can all leave."

The old Don stands gently with the aid of his cane, "do you want my boys to clean up and dispose of this mess?"

"That will not be necessary."

"Thank you, my friend." He and his men leave with the others.

"Maria, stay a moment," Nicky calls out.

Maria stops in her tracks and turns back to the gruesome scene. Rocky pats her shoulder and follows the old Don out the room. Maria waits until the room is empty and the door closes, "Uncle Nicky, what can I do for you? Hopefully, not mop up Leo's blood."

Nicky carefully steps over the blood spreading on the marble floor. He stands inches from her face. "Am I talking to Maria now? Can she hear me?"

"What do you mean?"

He looks hard at her.

She backs up. "Yes, I can hear you."

"What the hell were you thinking, sending a body double here. To this kind of meeting," Nicky is holding back his anger, trying not to do something unthinkable to the girl, whoever she is, in front of him. "If anyone other than me had caught on to your deception, this girl would be as dead as Leo here. And you'd be next. There would be nothing I could do to stop it."

"I didn't mean any harm. I had no idea this was going to be that kind of meeting. I was just giving her a final test."

"Well, she failed!"

"She got past everyone, except for you."

"I told you many times," Nicky leads her out of the room as others come in to clean it. "This business is built on trust. And there is a short supply of it these days." They enter his private office. "If one person finds a reason to doubt you, it means death. As you have seen here today. Did you see what happened?"

"No," the girl is wide-eyed and scared, "I didn't send her with a spy camera. Those things are easier to spot, not that easy, but easier than the audio implant. Which is virtually impossible to detect without an X-ray. Even then you really have to know what you're looking at to figure it out. Uncle Nicky, my father used a body double many times…"

"But never here. Never during family business. Never. Now get the hell out of here before I cut this beautiful head off too."

She hurries for the door, but Nicky shuts it, holds up a paper, and writes on it, "Is she gone?"

She nods assent.

He writes, "How can you tell?"

"There is a warm feeling behind my ear when the implant is active. I can't turn it on or off, it's a one-way thing."

"What's your name, girl?"

"Ahnri Shepherd, Mr. Rocci." She looks down, ashamed of what she has done.

"Hey, I'm not mad with you. I am pissed at Maria for making you do it."

"If I may ask, Mr. Rocci," she says sheepishly, "how did you know I wasn't her?"

Nicky looks deep into her eyes; *should I help them with their subterfuge? But if I don't, they could be killed next time.* "It's all in the eyes. There is a look when someone sees something for the first time."

"You mean when that man was killed?"

"No. When you first saw me walking in. I knew right then you weren't her."

"Then why didn't you call everything off, or kick me out of the meeting?"

"Because then I would have to give a reason," Nicky opens the office door, "and that reason would have gotten you killed. Goodbye now, and I never want to see you again."

Ahnri hurries to the car waiting in the driveway.

Rocky opens the door for her, "Hey, is everything ok?"

"Yeah, I just have to work on my facial expressions."

"Maria, what the hell is that supposed to mean?"

ANTHONY MOTIONS for Nicky to come closer. He looks him in the eye and holds a cold dead stare for a minute. "Nicky, it's not just me saying these things. It's all the bosses. They never liked you working with the darkies, commies, and the Irish, for God's sake. They didn't like it when you made women and made them capos. But this thing with your Goddaughter, it's going too far."

"Since when do we need the approval of any other family on how we run business? Prison made you weak or crazy to speak to me this way. Ti taglierei le palle e te le darei da mangiare, se non fosse per l'amicizia di mio padre con te. All you old men trying to hold onto power, living in the past, looking at things with old eyes, you're done. She is going to take us into the next century. She has the brains, the heart, and she has my backing. I run this family—"

"Nicky, she can't run the family if no one works with her," Anthony pleads his case, "they will freeze her out and the family will suffer. In the end, someone will take her out. You know this game, you've seen it before. Give TJ a chance. Everyone has already agreed he will be acceptable."

"Junior," Nicky let's his name roll slowly from his lips, "is not acceptable to me. The others want him because he's weak. They will pick his bones clean."

"Nicholas Rocci, I don't lift weights in the yard, but that does not mean I don't have the muscles."

"Anthony Cigneralla, put it in the pipeline, if they come after her, they come after me. And between the two of us, we will burn their world to ashes." Nicky walks defiantly to the door. He opens it and looks around; the police are at the end of the hall. He looks back at the old man chained to the hospital bed, "enjoy your couple of days of free air on me."

THE CAPOS FILE into the large meeting room off the garden at the Long Island mansion. There isn't a table, or room, fifty-four men and one woman have come from around the world. Nicky summons the entire family leadership three weeks after leaving the hospital. There is talk, some good, some bad, and Nicky knows he has to act quickly before sides can be drawn.

He watches the closed-circuit monitor in his desk drawer with Maria. "You must never let anyone know about this. Not even your consigliere can know of the cameras and microphones in these rooms. You make sure they are off before the place is swept."

"Yes, Uncle Nicky."

"See those three there?" he places a finger on the screen, "and those five by the window? they are your strongest allies. Those guys there in the corner, I'd get rid of, right away. And very publicly. I can put you on the throne. But you have to want it, fight for it, and kill to keep it. You ready for this?"

"Yes, Uncle Nicky," Maria states in an assertive tone. "But I don't think everyone is here yet."

"There are bound to be a few who will have some excuse. Got held up in customs, couldn't shake the tail, whatever. Whoever did not make it to this meeting is out, you got that? It's a sign of disrespect, and you can't tolerate it." Nicky's voice climbs as he speaks. "I don't care if they had to gun down an entire police force, they needed to get their asses here. And on time. Let's go."

Maria follows Nicky down the hall to the big meeting room.

As they enter a cheer goes up, "SALUT!"

Several men step up to kiss Nicky's ring, then shake Maria's hand. Carmela takes a long time kissing the ring and pulls Maria close, "give me the word and whoever you need to disappear is gone."

Maria kisses her cheek. The capos start filling the seats, there are seven rows of five seats on each side of the aisle she walks down. There are a few empty chairs in the back. *Ok, nearly a full house, I guess I won't have to kill too many this week.*

Nicky addresses the gathering, "I am pleased to see so many faces. This family has grown and flourished since I was a boy. I remember one such occasion… it wasn't for quite the same reason, but there were fewer than twenty people here that day. Do you remember that, Maria?" He pauses and as she starts to speak, he continues, "Of course she doesn't… She was born that day."

Everybody laughs.

"I knew then that one day I'd be standing here in front of all of you… well, not all of youse. I didn't know half the people in this room now. But I knew I'd be standing here in front of this gathering to pass this ring." Nicky pretends he can't get the ring off his finger. "This is harder than I thought."

Again laughter.

He pulls the ring off and holds it up. "This is the ring Angelo gave to my father Nicolas, and he gave it to me. I don't know how Angelo came to own it; I don't see any nine-finger mobsters out there."

More laughter.

"Maria, hold out your hand. Oh, before we go on, is there anybody here who would like to challenge these proceedings?"

Joseph Castor steps up to Nicky and whispers in his ear.

"Well, now," Nicky says with a wry smile, "there seems to be a bit of mystery afoot. Someone who could not be here sent a package. Before youse all start running for the door, we had the box swept for explosives."

Two men bring the small shoebox up to the front.

Nicky lifts the lid slowly, reaches in, and pulls out a severed hand. He turns it back and forth before the crowd. "No note, but I guess it's hard to write if you're not a lefty. If I'm not mistaken, this is Cigneralla's ring." He sniffs the hand. "And this is Junior's hand. Lavender soap. Well, this explains why he couldn't make the meeting." He drops the hand back in the shoebox. "Will someone see if you can't dig up the rest of him and give him back his ring? It is a family heirloom. Maria, take this ring as a sign of your power and leadership of this family. Swear to put the family first and above all other things. Then all here, swear your lives and immortal souls to your Don."

The procession takes hours as each person comes by and kisses the ring which now sits on Maria's finger. While one elderly man takes an exceedingly long time to make his way to her, she whispers to Nicky,

"I can resize this thing, right?"

"Sure," he whispers, "take the stone out and put it in another ring. It is a three-carat ruby so be careful who you get to do it. Jesus, someone should have put that guy in a wheelchair. By the way, nice job with Junior. I knew making you the Arbitrator would teach you how to handle these guys."

"Most of these guys are just spoiled little boys. But I didn't have anything to do with that. I assumed it was your last act as Boss of Bosses."

That night, Maria Delitanni became the most powerful person in the world.

James L Hill is a native New Yorker, born and raised in Fort Apache, the South Bronx's 41st precinct during the 60's, a time when you needed a gang to go to the store.

Raised on blues, soul, and rock & roll gave him the heart of a flower child, and educated by the turmoil of Vietnam, the Civil Rights Movement, and the Sexual Revolution produced a gladiator.

James has a successful forty-year career as a software engineer designing, developing, and maintaining systems for the government and the private sector.

He returned to his first love, as a prolific storyteller with a slant on the dark side of life. *Killer With A Heart, Killer With Three Heads,* and the latest release in the Killer Series, *Killer With Black Blood, a finalist for the Silver Falchion Award,* published July 2021, are adult urban crime fictions. The final novel in the series, *Killer With Ice Eyes,* is a finalist for the Killer Nashville's Claymore Award of 2022.

While *Pegasus: A Journey To New Eden* is a dystopian science fiction, and *The Emerald Lady* is the first book in the fantasy Gemstone Series.

The next step on his journey led to the business of publishing. He started RockHill Publishing LLC not only to publish his own work, but to give others access to the literary world. His computer background and experience in word-processing gave him insight into what it takes to create good books.

http://www.jlhill-books.com/

ALSO BY J L HILL

Killer Series

Book 1 - Killer With A Heart

Book 2 - Killer With Three Heads

Book 3 - Killer With Black Blood

Book 4 - Killer With Ice Eyes

***

Gemstone Series

Book 1 - The Emerald Lady

***

Pegasus: A Journey to New Eden

www.ingramcontent.com/pod-product-compliance
Lightning Source LLC
Chambersburg PA
CBHW071231210726

48293CB00002B/664